George Freedman

for Ze'ev Hed

— George Freedman

HILLIARD HARRIS
PUBLISHERS

Published by

HILLIARD  HARRIS
PUBLISHERS

P.O. Box 3358
Frederick, Maryland 21705-3358

This novel is a work of fiction. Names, characters, places and incidents either are the product of the author's imagination or are used fictitiously. Any resemblance to actual persons, living or dead, events, or locales is entirely coincidental.

ELDERNAPPED Copyright © 2001 by George Freedman

All right reserved. No part of this book may be reproduced or transmitted in any form or by any means, electronic or mechanical, including photocopying, recording, or by any information storage and retrieval system, without the written permission of the Publisher, except where permitted by law.

First Edition

ISBN 09704304-3-4

Designed by HILLIARD HARRIS

Manufactured/Printed in the United States of America

July 2001

To "my club", five and a half couples who socialize together, attend each other's family events, travel together, and go way back . . .

"I should live all I can, it's a mistake not to".

Lewis Leland Strether

From ***The Ambassadors*** by Henry James

ACKNOWLEDGMENTS

I gratefully acknowledge the patient aid provided by software/hardware wizards Norton Greenfeld and Herrmann Statz. They finally succeeded in establishing an uneasy but workable relationship between me and my computer, without which this book would have been impossible. Also, novelist Jean Gould in whose Fiction Writing Workshop at a local Borders Bookstore I enrolled. Had she not encouraged me, I might never have gone on. And Sue Clark, my agent and book doctor extraordinaire. She helped me turn an amateur work into something much better.

Prologue

You have to be over sixty to be eligible to sign up for a Senior Seminars program. But, in fact, there is a more lenient lower age limit if you are an accompanying spouse, or in recent years, companion, and it is not uncommon to see an unwrinkled young matron in her early fifties sharing "room with private bath accommodations" with a grizzled septuagenarian.

Private baths are in fact an issue. Dorm rooms with a communal bath down the hall were the norm in early Senior Seminars programs, but these are being phased out due to the frequent mid-night bladder emptyings required by most of the students.

On the other hand, there is no upper age limit, although the catalog reminds prospective enrollees for certain programs that there are 'for the physically fit and vigorous,' such as the two-weeker in Costa Rica. It goes on to caution that, 'there is considerable walking each day in such places the Carara mangrove swamp and along the rim of Arenal Volcano.'

Otherwise, age-wise, the sky, in a manner of speaking, is the limit. And while there are few participants in their nineties and the pertinent bell-shaped curve peaks at around sixty-seven, people in their eighties abound. Amongst them, there always seems to be

George Freedman

one special sort of wiry little old lady with a too large head and a too small body on each tour. This old lady always stands out from the others, even when nothing happens.

This is as it should be. In any such activity that is tailored for the elderly, most "happenings" are humdrum. They tend to consist of no more than the pleasures of experiencing intellectual stimulation, seeing previously unknown places and meeting previously unknown people.

But there can be the rare occasion when a miracle, or disaster, intrudes. In which case this lady in her eighties can be counted on to be its prime mover, if not its actual cause.

Eldernapped

Day One

"Arrival"

Sure enough, Harry noted, there was one. And she was acting in an odd manner, even for "one of those." Out of the corner of his eye he spied her, a knapsack on her back, they always wear knapsacks, flitting from post to post of the arcade that gave shadow to the "Arrivals" doorway of the airport. Now he saw her, now he didn't. Was she playing hide and seek and seek? He pointed her out to Naomi.

"Where?" She asked.

"Right there, back of the third, no, fourth post to the left."

"I don't see her. Who? Who should I see?"

"One of those ET women, but this one looks like she's gone nuts."

Still Naomi couldn't find her, and now Harry didn't either and began to think he had just imagined her. But then she flitted again to the next post. "Oh yes, there she is, I think..." Naomi said.

There had been such an unusual elderly woman in no less than four of their previous five Senior Seminars programs. Harry and Naomi always spotted them at once. Their swift movements, accompanied by metallic glints from flashing eyes, were a dead giveaway. As was their unceasing high energy, which always put their schoolmates to shame.

George Freedman

These little old ladies bound out of the bus ahead of all the rest on the sightseeing excursions. They then go into their characteristic drumbeat stride, beating everyone, even the tour guides, to that day's designated destination. It doesn't matter whether it is all the way up onto the rooftop battlements of castles in Spain or all the way down into the chasm bottoms of the Grand Canyon. And they never even breath hard doing it.

Nor does their advanced age cause any mental slowing down. As the lecturers launch the classes held every morning, it becomes clear that these extraordinary individuals are the only ones in the room who read every word of every book or pamphlet or article on the recommended reading lists. This is impressive, since at Senior Seminars, in order not to put anyone to excessive strain at their age, reading is "recommended," never required.

Harry had dubbed them "ET Women," because they seemed so unearthly and had those same bulgy eyes and long knobby fingers.

"If only we could breed them," Harry, always the jokester, would suggest to Naomi. "We would have a super race. But where would we find suitable men?"

"Harry, you idiot..." was Naomi's reaction to this suggestion.

"Anyway, forget it," he would end with a sigh. "They don't breed."

All of which indicated that this woman, like those who had preceded her, was sure to make some positive, if not negative, effect on the upcoming program. Which led Harry to promise himself to pay her careful attention in the next two weeks.

This of course assumed that she indeed existed, because after all, those could just have been narrow shadows flickering around the posts as the sun interacted with puffs of white clouds in the blue sky above. Anyway, this program promised to be the best they had ever attended, for they had just deplaned at the Venice Airport,

Eldernapped

which has a feature that no other airport in the world can match, an attached vaporetto pier. And a view. Through the haze across a few miles of lagoon, Harry and Naomi imagined they could see, rising from a small forest of lesser towers, the great campanile in St. Mark's Square.

But they weren't going to Venice. They had already been to Venice. Twice. And knew, well, many of its attractions. Instead, they were headed for Padua or *Padova*, as the natives say, twenty-five miles to the west. It is a far less visited city, but one boasting its own unique charms. It would be the site for *numero sei*.

Having concluded his reflections on wiry little old ladies and the pleasures Padua promised, Harry now found himself back to the reality of the present moment. "Let's get going," he said to Naomi.

"What are we waiting for?" She rejoined.

With that, the two of them started to roll their wheeled suitcases down the sidewalk. They proceeded at a deliberate speed for Harry knew all too well that his wife found it hard to match his long-legged pace because of her arthritic knee. Naomi had to walk with the help of a cane.

Yet, that did not detract from the favorable impression she made on people who chanced to look her way. She had a smooth broad brow, waves of soft white hair crowning an almost unlined face, wide set hazel eyes, pearls at her ears and neck, and she was wearing the tasteful, light blue pants suit that he liked so much.

It was about fifty yards to the large, sleek, black bus bearing the three-pronged, chrome Mercedes-Benz symbol at its helm. On the side of the bus was a sign, purple on yellow, bearing the words, SENIOR SEMINARS.

"That has to be our bus," Naomi said.

Others, about their age, were headed for it, too. Most of them had white hair, or no hair at all, and skin with brown spots, and wattles and paunches. And several had canes. A few already wore their nametags, which had come in the mail a month before.

George Freedman

Do you know where our name tags are?" Naomi asked.

"Sure, right in this envelope."

"So..." He dug out the tags and they pinned them on.

As Harry and Naomi approached the bus, an intense feeling, harking all the way back to kindergarten and first grade, overcame him. It was a combination of eager expectancy and distrustful wariness. Opening day at school always felt like that. And why not? Aren't Senior Seminars in fact boarding schools for the elderly? Or perhaps it is more accurate to compare them to theme camps like the ones for tennis, drama, crafts and computers the grandkids are sent to during summer vacation. Except that in this case, all the campers are well advanced in years, and it's always summer vacation.

As they came closer to the bus they saw a young woman standing in front of its open door. There was always a young woman, always attractive, energetic and bright, assigned to take care of the details of the travelers' comforts and needs. A nice system. The student body ended up loving these caretakers and never failed on the final day to leave a generous group tip, although the instructions in the envelope made it quite clear that this was forbidden.

This group leader looked to be about twenty-five, with a smooth, flawless complexion and a body to match. She wore brown slacks and a soft, beige blouse. She had slung a sweater of deeper beige over her shoulders. Her shoes were designed for running. She had thick, honey brown hair that brushed her shoulders, and her pierced ears bore small earrings of yellow ceramic that made up the sum total of her jewelry. As for the remainder of her vital data, Harry found himself recalling, more or less, an old song dating from his early childhood, which placed it at around the time of the Hoover Administration. "Five foot two/eyes of blue/boopy, boopy, boopy doo..." it went.

Eldernapped

"Are you going to be our mother?" He said as he started to get on the bus.

"Yes, but they call me the administrator."

"I like mother."

"Whatever. But call me Julie."

With this introduction concluded to the satisfaction of all concerned, they mounted the high bus steps. Naomi was a bit slow because of her gimpy left knee. Maybe those gimpy days are soon to be over, Harry reflected as he followed her on. She was to get a titanium and polyethylene prosthetic knee joint replacement two weeks after their return.

Harry and Naomi made their way down the aisle to a pair of empty seats. Two men followed them, obviously not Senior Seminarians. Not only were they altogether too young by about a quarter century, but also they were uncouth in their appearance and behavior, as they pushed their way into the bus. One man was large and pendulous, the other small and ratty, with a gold ring in his left ear. Both had wide black mustaches and wore wrinkled, sweat-stained suits, shirts and ties. Each bore, in addition, a scowl supplemented by a furrowed brow, indicating to Harry a combination of hostility with deep concentration.

The two brushed Julie aside, sending her staggering against the outside of the bus. The bus driver, of an age to match that of his passengers, remained in his driver's seat, his mouth agape with astonishment.

The pair of interlopers moved row by row farther into the bus, examining each person on both sides of the aisle as they went. An air of menace and danger moved up the aisle with them.

Since this was a foreign country, possibly even more dangerous than his own, Harry was sure they were about to be robbed of their valuables and passports. He caught a glimpse of a woman in a rear row; the two men hadn't got that far yet. She slipped off her necklace that seemed to be made of golden nuggets the size of macadamia nuts and let it drop into the cleft of her bosom. He hoped she would get away with it.

Meanwhile, there were small screams from some of the women and gruff profanities from some of the men. Yet, there was no panic, as there might have been had the busload been made up of irresponsible youngsters in their forties or fifties. Or violence. No sense bringing on an unnecessary fibrillation episode.

But the intruders didn't seem to be motivated to steal anything. Rather, it became clear they were looking for someone. They peered into each face as they went and, deciding that that person wasn't the one they wanted, moved on to peruse the next and the next. As they made their way up the length of the bus they kept saying to each other in what seemed to be Manhattanish English, "That's not the one."

"These guys are Americans," Harry whispered.

To which Naomi responded, "Thank God they don't want us." Which was true, because, after undergoing swift but deep scrutiny, the two of them failed the test and were rejected.

In a moment the whole invasion was over. "She's not on this bus," one of them said to the other.

"Must still be in the airport," he replied.

They ran off the bus and in an ungainly, synchronized trot, were seen to disappear into the baggage claim area.

"Everybody keep calm!" It was Julie, her face flushed and her voice high-pitched, anything but calm. "Enrico," she shouted to the driver. "Let's get the hell out of here!"

The bus lurched out of its parking slot and zoomed into the traffic outside the airport. As it did, Naomi hissed to Harry, "Stop kicking me."

"I'm not kicking you."

But someone was. Harry and Naomi became aware of an increase of pressure at their knees. They looked down at their feet and discovered a small, coiled,

Eldernapped

female body. Bulging, steel-gray eyes peered up at them and long, knobby fingers stretched upward to grasp one of the armrests. It was the very woman who had been flitting among the shadows around those arcade posts. She was eighty-five if she was a day, and so thin and small that her weight could not have exceeded her years.

After a whispered, "Excuse me." The little person who was, in a manner of speaking, sharing their seats, slithered away and dropped into another one that happened to be empty across the aisle and two rows back.

"Anyway...welcome, seminarians." Julie stood beside the driver at the front of the bus now with a microphone in one hand, tour director style. She pronounced the word with a soft "a" so that it came out as "sem-i-nah-rians." Harry could tell she was trying to act as though nothing unusual had happened, and indeed he noted that the quaver in her voice diminished as the vehicle gobbled up more and more miles away from the airport.

"This is your two-week course," Julie went on, "based in beautiful, medieval Padova on the art, music and history of the Italian region you are now in, known as the Veneto. And I am your administrator, Julie Foster, which means please call on me for anything you need at any time of the night or day. I have a room in the same hotel and this sheet I'm handing out has my room number on it, if you ever need to get in touch with me.

"And this," pointing to a young woman by her side, "is Graziella Parziale, the assistant administrator,"

Harry had not noticed Graziella before and wondered why he hadn't, for he found her to be quite striking with her large mass of dark brown hair. It had henna highlights and extended in all directions with a thousand individual curling, corkscrew strands.

"Graziella is a real treasure," Julie continued. She comes from a little town near Naples and she speaks Italian like a native, because she is a native, but I'm no slouch either, even though I grew up in New London,

George Freedman

Connecticut. I majored in Italian Art History at Bowdoin College in Maine which, you already know, is running this program, and I have been living over here for the last year and a half. I'll also be your lecturer on the great artist Giotto who used to hang around in these parts. Now, are there any questions?"

"They're both such pretty girls," Naomi whispered into Harry's ear. "Can you tell, does either one have an engagement ring or a wedding band?"

But before Harry could answer, there was a many-voiced response to Julie's request for questions. "Yes, I've got a question. Who were those two roughnecks who barged onto our bus just now?"

"I've no idea. Do you know who they could have been, Graziella?"

Graziella gave a shake of her head that must have generated a small breeze to indicate she had no idea either.

"But I'm certainly going to complain to the airport authorities...or somebody...when we get to the hotel. I suspect they just got on the wrong bus or something. Anyway, let's get back to business. She took a deep breath that was needed because long, breathless sentences seemed to be her style,

"Welcome again to what I think is the best Senior Seminar in Italy, although a few months ago I was the administrator at the one in Perugia, also run by Bowdoin College, and let me tell you if you can ever sign up for the Perugia program, do it, because it's wonderful."

"Now, let me give out your room numbers," Julie went on. "But, once again, does anyone have any other questions?"

"Yes, well not a question, actually," Harry piped up. He felt he had been silent long enough. "I hope you people remembered to give me the room I wrote for...you know, the one with the balcony overlooking the fountain?"

This caused some muttering. One voice said, "What balcony?" Another inquired, "What fountain?"

Eldernapped

Then, "Did you read anything in the catalog, Lois, about some of the rooms having balconies?"

Harry's comment seemed to upset Julie, too. "I...I...didn't get any such request. Anyway, none of these rooms has a balcony and there is no fountain..."

"Don't mind him, Julie dear," Naomi butted in, who must have felt she had to at this point. "He's only kidding. He'll be kidding on his deathbed."

"Just trying to relieve a little of the tension," Harry said.

To which Naomi gave a severe rejoinder. "Enough already, Harry. Look at the scenery, because after all we're in Italy, and we're paying for the scenery." Which was true, but at the moment it wasn't all that great, for it consisted of long regimental rows of oil storage tanks along the highway, interspersed with occasional oil refineries.

"I'm looking, I'm looking, but as far as I can see, I might as well be in Newark."

The scenery soon began to get better as the highway turned into a mere two-lane road, and now the road ran beside a quiet river of a width to match its own. Road and river proceeded together through a sequence of towns and small cities made up of gray stone buildings, none of wood, many with balconies, some, in fact, overlooking a fountain.

"This looks like a river but it's really more of a canal," Julie announced. "It's an extension of the Grand Canal in Venice and it connects Padua to Venice. In the seventeenth and eighteenth centuries, the leaders of these two communities took barge trips up or down this canal to get from one city to the other. And many of them built grand mansions long the banks to reside in during the hot summer months, some of them very palatial. See, we're passing one of them now."

Harry pointed it out to Naomi, who he realized kept looking with a puzzled expression in every other direction. He could see it was still palatial, with a many-bedded

George Freedman

formal garden coming down to the water edge and with pillars and patios in strong evidence. Not only had this impressive building survived to this day, it looked lived in, in all likelihood still by leading citizens of the area.

"Notice that adjoining building...a little smaller, but just as handsome...just behind," Julie said, her tour guide role gathering momentum now. "Anyone want to guess what it is?"

"Servants quarters."

"Guest house."

"Mother-in-law apartment."

"Maybe, nowadays," Julie said. "But they were all stables to begin with. They held horses and carriages. Of course now, they're mostly used as garages.

"Oh yes, one other thing. It's too bad this isn't summer. In the summer they still run the barge trip, just like hundreds of years ago, and the summer students often take it as an alternate way to get to Venice on their free day during the second week."

"Oh, Harry, let's take it," Naomi said, ever impulsive.

"How can we? It's not summer yet," Harry pointed out with a patient smile.

An atmosphere of contentment now suffused the vehicle as it moved westward. Harry, looking around, could see that everyone's face, his own probably included, had taken on a pleasant, expectant look. This Senior Seminar, in spite of the recent unpleasant episode, promised well.

♦♦♦♦

Once settled into their room, Harry and Naomi took a short nap to sleep off their just concluded transatlantic voyage and its associated jet lag. Then, that evening, after a pleasant Italian meal, what else should it be, thought Harry, served in the hotel dining room, the students gathered for the first time in the hotel's first floor

Eldernapped

conference room. It would be their classroom for the next two weeks. As had been the case the previous five seminars, this would be the "Get Acquainted" session.

Everyone was to be called on to deliver a short autobiographical statement. Harry and Naomi always enjoyed this first meeting because no matter how interesting the place and the program were; it was even more intriguing to hear about everyone else in the group. And what they had to say was further enhanced by the fact that they had gathered together in this European place from every far-flung region of the United States.

The first to speak up, because she happened to be sitting at the end of the first row of schoolroom chairs, was a rather large lady of fair complexion in a wide-skirted, floral print dress. She was, she said, Dorothy Hinckel. Everyone listened with polite attention as she told them that she had retired three years before as head librarian of the medical school library of the University of Oklahoma at Oklahoma City, but still kept busy with her garden and good works. Primary among these was her volunteer programs for setting up libraries on reservations among the Native Americans in her home state.

"I don't think that one was ever married," Naomi whispered.

To which Harry whispered back, "So what's new about that? Half the single women at these seminars were never married, and the other half are divorced or widows."

"...And this is my third Senior Seminar and I think I will enjoy it very much," Ms. Hinckel concluded with a glowing smile that lit up her broad pink face.

Harry looked around for the next person to speak and was surprised that no one was standing, until he felt a jab in his ribs. "Get up," Naomi said. "You're next."

"I'm Harry Levine from Boston," he started right off. "Not really from Boston," he went on, "Greater Boston. I'm actually from a suburb of Boston about fifteen miles west, just off the Mass Turnpike.

George Freedman

"I'm a retired engineer. Worked for over forty years for the same firm, always in new product development...although there was a two-year period in the middle when I left to start my own company. But it went belly up and instead of getting rich, which was the original idea, I got poor. So I came crawling back to them. Which meant that I worked for the same firm in two twenty-year segments.

"I'm trained as a metallurgist," he went on, "so if any of you have any welding or corrosion problems or need structural failure analysis, my office hours these days are...any old time. But the fact is I do work about half time. I've joined in with three other fellows ...just boys they are, in their forties and fifties...and we're partners in trying to develop interesting new products for the benefit of mankind."

There was a pause. He could tell he had everyone's attention. "You know, the usual things like a cure for AIDS, a hobbyist's brain surgeon kit, a universal bra...one size fits all. Stuff like that. Of course, in the process we hope to make a bundle, and in my case it'll be about time..."

"Okay, Harry, that's enough. Sit down," Naomi said.

He sat. He knew better than to challenge her judgment on such occasions, and as she rose to her feet, he smiled up at her with affection.

"You see what I've had to put up with all these years," she said with a sigh. "And now you all can share my burden for the next few weeks. As for me, I'm Naomi Levine, and I am married to him, God help me.

"I've never had a career...although for a few years I did some editing for a local newspaper. We have two lovely daughters, both in New York, near enough so we can see them fairly often. The older one has a child...my beautiful granddaughter Sarah, who is eleven, and for anyone who is interested...and even if you're not...I can show you pictures. No matter where I go I always bring pictures. And the other daughter is still unmarried, but she's engaged and there'll be a September wedding.

"I've done a lot of volunteer work," Naomi went on, "mostly as a lay social worker with disadvantaged children, and I am still doing it a couple of days a week. And this is our sixth Senior Seminar," with which she resumed her seat.

Next came the O'Learys, who stood up together as though on the count of three. They were the same height, had the same haircuts and wore identical blue sweat suits. He said, "We're the O'Learys from Reading, PA. I'm Paul and I'm a cardiologist and I'm still in practice, although I only go into the office three days a week now."

Naomi nodded in approval and poked Harry to get his attention. "Always good to have a doctor in the group," she said in a low voice. "Especially a cardiologist."

To which Harry responded, also in a low voice, "I would have preferred a urologist." Then he added, "Those two look so much alike, they're more of a pair than a couple."

"She's probably a catalog shopper. They tend to buy two of everything."

"... And this is my wife, Rose," Dr. O'Leary concluded, after which he remained standing.

"I'm Rose O'Leary," Mrs. O'Leary said. "I'm a nurse, a school nurse in fact, and I still work full time. We have three children and five grandchildren. This is our first Senior Seminar and we're sure looking forward to it. We've heard such nice things about Senior Seminars." With that, the O'Leary's sat in unison.

Next, a large, florid gentleman with close-cropped white hair rose to his feet. He gave an impression of being a naval officer since he wore a dark blue blazer with brass buttons. At his throat was a white silk ascot. Every female in the group focused on him. Since there was no woman with him, he had to be single. Single gentlemen at the Seminars are always outnumbered at least three to one by single ladies. He informed the group that he was

George Freedman

Pelham Caldwell, "But everyone has always called me Pete." He was, "a retired lawyer, corporate law to be specific, from Dallas, Texas."

Pete went on to describe the sorts of corporations he had represented in his long career. He even interspersed some detailed examples of particular client firms in the northern Texas area. With no Naomi to stop him, Harry reflected, how long would Pete go on? But Pete resumed his chair in short order and beamed at his new classmates. He seemed happy that his presentation might have given them great satisfaction.

His place was now taken by none other than the dear little old lady herself, the very one who had shared Harry's and Naomi's bus seat earlier that day. Harry noticed that she was wearing a narrow white cotton headband that made her look as though she had a forehead and a half. He remembered that all of these special old ladies seemed to wear similar headbands, and he wondered why. He had never seen one of them sweat.

"I am Emily Thorndike," she said in clipped tones of the sort one learned to use in elocution classes, popular between World Wars I and II. "...from Elmira, New York, but I've lived most recently in Boulder, Colorado. I'm a retired college teacher. Taught archaeology, mostly of the Middle East, but I've done Greek, too. And now that I'm retired, I like to go to Senior Seminars. I've been to quite a few already..."

Just then, there was a knock on the classroom door and one of the desk clerks appeared. He signaled to Julie with a hiss that Europeans always use in such circumstances. Julie moved over to the door and listened while the man gave her a confidential message behind his hand. She nodded assent and turned to the group, her face now as red as it had been on the bus. "The police are here," she gasped, "and they want one of you people. They're asking for Signora Lucille Adams. Will Lucille Adams please come up?"

Eldernapped

No one moved. "Wait a minute," she said, as she turned to her student list, her forefinger going down the vertical column. "We have no Lucille Adams registered," she said to the clerk, first in Italian and then, for the benefit of the assemblage, in English. "Tell the police that we have no Signora Lucille Adams."

The class breathed an audible sigh of relief. The clerk shrugged his shoulders and left, and all present turned their attention to the next autobiographers, the Hansons from Phoenix.

He, Fred, had been in contracting. "Built quite a few tracts of single homes and condos around Tempe and Sun City in the last twenty years," he recounted, but he'd given that up in nineteen ninety-two when he retired. He was now doing a lot of golfing except in the hot summer months. Fred explained that it could get up to a hundred and ten in the shade in Phoenix, although you don't mind it as much as you'd think because it is so dry.

"Maybe we should tell him about the golfing Seminar we went to in Arizona," Naomi said as she jabbed Harry.

"Uh huh." He rubbed his rib cage. Was it his imagination or was she jabbing harder these days?

And Mrs. Hanson, Carol, was a homemaker who did a lot of volunteer work with an arts center in Phoenix's inner city. They had a son and a daughter and a grandchild. "A darling little boy, Jason, just getting ready to graduate from play school to kindergarten." They had been to four Senior Seminars before. And yes, they sure expected to enjoy this one, because they had been to Italy many years before on their honeymoon.

As these two talked, no one seemed to notice that Emily Thorndike was no longer present. Except Harry. While everyone else listened to the Hanson saga, Harry caught sight of Emily at the far end of the room where there was an open window. Like a hopping bird, she climbed onto its sill, slung her legs over it and, in the blink of an eye, was gone.

George Freedman

Day Two

"Fortitude"

The next morning, ablutions completed, Harry and Naomi appraised their quarters. Considering that the hotel had been built in the late fifteen hundreds, a fact they learned the evening before from studying a bronze plaque in the lobby, they concluded that it had stood up rather well over the centuries.

The plaque stated that during its long history the Casa del Santo had accommodated numerous cardinals, dukes, contessas and prime ministers from many nations, all listed by name and date. Hoi polloi, too. Hordes of anonymous pilgrims had also stayed there, seeking connectedness with the bones of Padua's own St. Anthony in the Basilica just across the street.

Naomi and Harry agreed that, in spite of being ancient, the hotel was, in fact, modern enough to match two-star AAA standards. Except for the shower. It was of the size and shape of a narrow coffin tipped up on end. While it worked all right, it presented an unusual problem. The showerers, at least those of more generous American dimensions, didn't have room to reach the faucets. Harry wondered how Pete Caldwell, or Dorothy Hinckel for that matter, had managed that morning.

Going down for breakfast at eight A.M., Harry and Naomi looked in at the hotel dining room and found it to

Eldernapped

be thronged, mostly with families. "Something special must be going on in town," Naomi said.

Later, Julie informed them that this was the weekend of St. Anthony's seven hundred and ninety-ninth birthday. People from all over the Veneto were in for the occasion. "But if you think this is something," she said, "come next year when he hits eight hundred. All of Italy, plus a lot of Europe, will be here."

"I'll be here," Harry said.

"Also..." Julie's eyes brightened as she imparted yet another nugget of interesting information, "...you should really visit the Chapel of the Tongue in the Basilica. If you do, you can see St. Anthony's tongue on display in a glass cabinet. It's still lifelike, while the rest of his body has decomposed. The story is that his tongue lives on because he was such a great orator and the fact that it survived till now is supposed to be a miracle."

"Wouldn't miss it," Harry said.

But they didn't join the pilgrims in the dining room. For breakfast, they had been instructed to proceed to a small adjacent building at the rear of the hotel where a special Senior Seminars breakfast room had been set aside. Most of their fellow students, now looking alert and no longer travel-worn, had already arrived. They had distributed themselves at the four-seat tables where they were being served the typical continental breakfast that most of them would soon learn to abhor.

There was no complaint about the orange juice and caffe latte, but the experienced European travelers in the assemblage, like Harry and Naomi, knew that in two weeks, if not in two days, the hard rolls with jam and the packaged domino rectangles of cheese that made up the rest of the meal would get boring. Some, having foreseen this situation, had brought brown paper bags holding Fortified Wheaties and Honey Nut Cheerios. "Smart them," Naomi said. "We should do that next time."

They looked around for their friends with whom they had planned this adventure, Art and Irene Maglio.

Aha, there they were, waving for Naomi and Harry to join them.

Julie and Graziella, standing in front of the refills table that held more rolls and coffee, signaled for everyone's attention by tapping a spoon on a goblet

Julie was in a crisp, long sleeved pink blouse, form fitting faded blue jeans and high heeled cowboy boots, into the tops of which the jeans were tucked. Graziella wore a loose long skirt of thin, light gray material, which floated gracefully as she moved. Her blouse, the shoulders of which were grazed by her two-inch hoop earrings, was of white cotton, embroidered in red. They do make an attractive contrasting pair, Harry mused.

"First day of class, everyone," Julie announced, "which will go on for the next two weeks, including Sundays, because we treat Sundays like regular school days, but the Wednesday of the second week is an exception because it is always a free day. Any questions?"

Hearing none, she went on to remind them that, as listed on the schedule sheet, she herself will be their first instructor, starting in about twenty-five minutes in the classroom in the next building. "There will be four other lecturers," she said. "So don't panic. You won't have to listen to me all the time. The rest of the faculty will teach the courses on the Veneto's literature, history, architecture and music.

"Our subject today will be the great Giotto, who lived right here in Padua during the thirteenth century. His paintings and those of his school can be found all over town, but we will concentrate on his greatest work, the frescoes of the Scrovegni Chapel. The Chapel is about a mile north of here and we will walk there after lunch today.

"There will be a break after the first class hour, during which I advise you to look into the little bar just off the hotel lobby for a quick espresso or cappuccino with a croissant or something. Italians always call these places

Eldernapped

bars, and even though you can get an alcoholic drink there, they're really more like coffee shops.

"Tomorrow morning, before the music lecture, Graziella will give you her patented one-hour crash course on 'Survival Italian'...all you'll need to make yourself understood in Padova." With this, Graziella nodded and raised her right arm as though she had just won a prizefight, and all cheered.

"Did they ever find that woman," a voice came from one of the tables. "You know, the one the police were looking for?"

"Oh, Lucille Adams," Julie said. "If I can believe what they were telling me after we met yesterday, she's some sort of dangerous lunatic who escaped from a mental clinic in North Dakota or North Carolina, someplace like that, and is hiding out...would you believe...as a regular student in some Senior Seminars program here in Italy. But, not to worry, we have no Lucille Adams in this group."

"Unless she's here, hiding under an assumed name," suggested Bill Eckdahl, once a school superintendent from a suburb of Wichita, who later confessed to being a dedicated reader of novels of international intrigue.

This stimulated an exchange to which many in the room made thoughtful contributions, especially the Senior Seminar veterans. Harry did not yet count himself among these and he contented himself with just listening.

The most veteran of the veterans seemed to be Nate Kniznick, a retired pediatrician from the Astoria section of Queens, and his wife, Belle. These were not only among the most senior members of this assemblage of seniors, being in their early eighties, they also held the group record for most seminars attended. Sixteen.

They looked their age, thought Harry, both being small and wizened. But their eyes were young, even when viewed through the thick trifocals each wore. Nate spoke up from his breakfast chair to make the point that Senior

George Freedman

Seminars are a great place in which to hide from the rest of the world. "Remember that fellow in the Anchorage program, Belle? What was his name?"

"Who can remember names?" She replied. "Sometimes I forget your name. But he was the one who was running away from his wife."

"He claimed he wasn't running," Nate said. "Just taking a break from her nagging. And you know, sometimes I think he had something there..."

"A break!" Belle cried. He was already into his second month of seminars, one after the other. His poor wife must have been frantic, with him nowhere to be found, vanished from the face of the earth."

"Norton Evans. That was his name." Nate remembered. "I never saw an old guy enjoy himself so much."

"You mean the way he made up to every widow and unmarried woman in the program? Don't you get any ideas like that, Nate, my boy? I'd find you."

"Don't be so sure. I never thought Norton Evans was his real name anyway, and I never thought he was from Nebraska, as he claimed. With that accent, the farthest west he had ever been was West Virginia or West Tennessee. Anyone who wants to disappear can fake an identity and sign up in a Senior Seminar under an alias...and most people could get away with it."

"I went to a seminar in Santa Fe a few years ago...I think it was 1991," Sarah Townes offered, pausing as she allowed herself to remember. "Yes, it was 1991. And a lovely program it was. It went along with the opera season they have there every summer, which, by the way, I heartily recommend. During that whole seminar, no one could stop talking about a similar case that happened the week before our week."

The room became quiet as she spoke, since her voice was soft and refined to go with her appearance, slim and stylish, which in turn went with her profession. The group had learned the evening before that even though she was retired from her flourishing home decorating business, now the biggest of its sort in Spokane, she still kept her hand in by writing a weekly column for the magazine section of that city's leading Sunday newspaper.

"This fellow was not exactly on a vacation from his wife," Sarah went on. "He was just getting out of paying alimony." This last was uttered with a finality that indicated she knew something about the subject.

"Did anyone ever hear about the old gent who just lives in Senior Seminars? He has no other home, and he never goes back into the normal world," yet another breakfaster chimed in.

"Oh, like the hero of The Man without a Country, who stays on the same Navy ship for years," Dorothy said. "Even as the ship docks at port after port around the world," she explained, her eyes circling the room, "he can never get off because of some terrible thing he did, so no nation would ever accept him."

"'Charlie on the MTA' is another one just like that," Art broke in. "That's a song that was once popular where we live. Charlie gets on a train in the Boston subway system but can't get off because he doesn't have a dime to put in the turnstile slot at the exit. But his wife...or is it his girl friend...keeps meeting him at different stations with sandwiches."

"'He never returned / No, he never returned / and his fate is still unlearned / He will ride forever / 'Neath the streets Boston / The man who never returned...'" Irene sang, by way of providing supportive corroboration for her husband's tale.

Harry, who had been craning his head, saw that the earlier question, the one about the old gent, had been posed by one of the three ex-pilots who had flown together during the Korean War.

They had come together for a reunion in this Italian place, their wives, too. From different corners of the States, after more than forty years of not having seen each other. Last night, everyone learned that the three ex-pilots were now retired from their respective jobs with United, Delta and Continental. Two had made Captain and one had been a Navigator. And now, all had lifetime air travel passes.

"This person is someone who has no connection with the outside world other than in Senior Seminars, which means probably no relatives or friends either," continued Captain Tom Sayre as though there had been no interruptions.

Harry had noted that Tom was the most articulate of the trio of flyers. In addition, he was at least six foot three and with his handsome silver hair, erect bearing and crinkly humor wrinkles at the corners of his eyes, he looked, as Naomi had earlier pointed out to him, like a reincarnation of Cary Grant in his later years.

"He just has one suitcase," Tom went on. "And it holds everything he owns, no other possessions in the world. He arranges his programs so that as each one ends on a Saturday morning, he gets on a bus or train for his next one, which he makes sure is nearby, no more than just two or three hours away. When Kate and I met him last year in an Alabama program...a very nice one by the way, on the seabirds of the Gulf along with the history of Mobile...he was already checking the bus schedules for New Orleans where he was enrolled in a seminar on the history of jazz with an added segment on Cajun cooking."

"And he told us that he had just been in Tallahassee for a Senior Seminar on Southern writers the week before," Kate Sayre interjected who, Harry couldn't help noticing, looked every bit as handsome, in her own way, as her husband did in his.

"He had an accurate count of how many Senior Seminars he had been to. What was that number, Kate?" Tom said.

"I think he said that the one he was attending in Mobile with us was his hundred and thirty-seventh, probably a Senior Seminars record."

Eldernapped

"And except for the Christmas weeks, when the programs shut down," Tom went on, a look of wonderment pervading his face, "he went to all those seminars one after the other, without a break."

"We wondered where a person like that would go during the two Christmas weeks when there are no Senior Seminars," Kate said, "but we never had the nerve to ask him."

"Probably found a hole someplace," Tom said.

This discussion of elderly students to whom the institution of Senior Seminaring was a total way of life, if not a refuge, gave rise to cries of astonishment from the tables in the breakfast room. "How could anyone afford it?" Someone asked.

Millicent Carter offered an immediate response. She wore a dark gray business suit with a severe white silk blouse and sported a helmet of straight brown hair. She had informed the others during "Getting Acquainted" that she was from Muncie, Indiana and was still working part time for her old company as an accountant. "Not really out of the question," she said, whipping a hand calculator out of her purse.

"Let's see...Senior Seminars charge an average three hundred and ninety bucks a week, as we all know, and that covers food, lodging, tuition, tour bus trips...quite a bargain in fact...which in fifty weeks, assuming two weeks off during Christmas, comes to..." She paused as she punched buttons. "Nineteen thousand and five hundred dollars for a whole year. And all he has to pay, in addition, is those bus trips or train rides between cities. Any person with a reasonable pension, and with Social Security money coming in as well, can easily afford it."

"But with European charges about double...I assume he includes some European sessions too...and with airfares..." another voice made a point.

"He can still afford it, Millicent replied in a decisive voice. Her thin pale lips made a long straight line across her circular face as she spoke. She popped the calculator back into her pocketbook which she snapped shut with a loud click.

There followed a moment of silence while the class contemplated the implications of this fact. This led to a comment by Pete, delivered with much judicial gravity, that with more than a hundred thousand seniors signing up every year for more than five thousand programs in about eight hundred campuses and other sites around the world, you have to expect a few oddballs. "We may be old," he said "but otherwise, we can be just as nutty as anyone else."

"Nuttier," Millicent added, who looked as though she had someone specific in mind.

Then Rose O'Leary observed that this perpetual Senior Seminarian, whoever he was, was acquiring an astounding amount of knowledge. "Since each Senior Seminars program consists," she said, "on the average of three separate courses, each given by a college professor or equivalent, that multiplies out to..."

"Four hundred and eleven," Millicent said. For this simple calculation it was clear she didn't need her calculator.

"That's like a college degree."

"Like ten college degrees."

"But there's more to it than that," Art offered, no longer joking about Charlie and his tribulations on the MTA, but perhaps thinking of legal implications. Art was an attorney, and until his retirement six years ago, had been a prosecutor in the Suffolk County Courthouse in Boston, "Anyone who wants to apply just a little clever subterfuge," he went on, "has the best way I ever heard of...as Nate just pointed out...to disappear."

"Which is what we all had better do out of this room," Julie broke in. "It's Giotto time, everyone."

♦♦♦♦

Eldernapped

The Scrovegni Chapel, Cappella degli Scrovegni said its sign, reminded Harry of a similar building he and Naomi had visited some thirty years before, the Sistine Chapel. Could it have been so long ago? Yes, for their daughters Judy and Debby had been with them. In their early teens they were then, and the focus of all male eyes.

The Sistine, with its frescoes by Michelangelo, was more magnificent than the Scrovigni with its frescoes by Giotto. But what does that matter? To be in an edifice, covered top to bottom with a masterpiece, if only the second greatest of its kind in the world, was still a stupendous privilege. Harry and Naomi were open-mouthed, transfixed by what they saw.

So were all their comrades who milled around them. Emily said, "The first stone of this chapel was laid in 1302 and it was finished in less than a year after that, which meant that Giotto was already painting his first fresco in thirteen oh three. Pretty fast construction for a building this size in pre-Renaissance times, but the Scrovegni family had a lot of money and put hundreds of workers on the job."

Emily had a strong and resonant voice for such a tiny old person. Her tinyness was emphasized by the fact that she wore a tubular black coat that made her seem to disappear when she stood in any shadowy place. But some of her still showed, because her disembodied white face with its white headband, white hair, white shoes and white stockings seemed to Harry like so many spooky body parts in the middle of the air. "How does she know all this stuff?" he asked Naomi out of the corner of his mouth.

"Maybe she should be giving the course, not Julie," Naomi returned out of the corner of hers.

This short dialogue concluded, Harry was now able to turn his full attention to the building. It wasn't small. Half the length of a football field it must be and with a ceiling higher than most mall atria. It was just a single open space with only a partial wall at one end to interrupt it, the better to display its surfaces.

"Notice the lights," was Emily's next comment, jarring him out of his reverie. Harry turned this way and that and observed banks of what looked like small searchlights at each end of the building. Their beams made the glories of the great painter's lines and colors leap out at them.

"You know, no one then, not even Giotto himself," Emily went on, "could have seen these paintings as well as we can now. How could they? All they had were candles and torches and oil lamps, and there are almost no windows. But whoever's running this place has to watch these high intensity light beams. I hope they are not damaging the pigments. Can you see, Mr. Levine? Do they have ultraviolet filters?" She said to Harry. He was the right one to ask, since he was the only engineer in the student body.

"Can't make out whether they do or not." He replied, peering at them.

"You know, I think she likes us," Naomi whispered. "Everyplace we've gone this morning, she's stuck to us like a leech."

"What's not to like?" Was Harry's reasonable reply.

There were three rows of paintings of Biblical scenes. They were arranged, one row below the other, all proceeding in sequence around all four walls. "Like a great comic-strip," Naomi said.

Giotto's seven hundred-year-old representations of human beings on the walls around them were so alive that there wasn't a person in that building who was not enthralled. Time moved on without anyone noticing. More than forty minutes passed when a warning bell rang to signal that in five minutes everyone had to clear out to let the next group in.

"Now that you've seen the main frescoes, don't forget the small images that serve almost as pedestals to hold up the lowest row," Julie said as she gathered her

Eldernapped

charges preparatory to leaving. "They're actually not by Giotto, but by his disciples. Still, their greatness is to be respected almost as much."

"Think of them as a coda to what he has given us, for they represent all the major human qualities, good and bad. There are fourteen of them, each about four feet high, seven Virtues and seven Vices, all female figures. They are in marked contrast to the colorful figures above, because all are presented as statues in pale white marble, which, of course, they are not. They seem three-dimensional but they are just two-dimensional pictures. You can identify which each is by name and location. Any questions?"

Thirty-six pairs of hands started to unfold and examine their class notes from that morning. Yes, there they were. The seven Virtues: Hope, Charity, Faith, Justice, Temperance, Fortitude and Prudence. The seven Vices: Despair, Envy, Infidelity, Injustice, Wrath, Inconstancy, and Folly.

"What? No Lust?" Harry asked.

"I think that comes under Infidelity," Naomi replied, her lips pursed in thought.

"Well, maybe," Harry conceded.

"Or Inconstancy?" Emily volunteered, who was still within earshot.

"Also, maybe."

As the group started to examine the rows of Virtues and Vices, attempting to sort out which would be which without referring to the notes, a brusque voice rang out, shattering the reverent atmosphere in the chapel. "I see you, Lucille. Hold still, we want to talk with you."

At once, Harry recognized who was shouting. It was one of the thugs from the bus the day before, the bigger one. What a surprise to see him there. Harry would never have put him down as a lover of art. And with him was the other one, the smaller one.

What followed was a sudden crush of bodies, mostly of people who must have felt that they had seen enough of Giotto and his wonderful Scrovegni Chapel. Everyone surged toward the exit door.

"Here, take this!" It was Emily. She thrust her black coat and her knapsack into Harry's hands, and turned and ran off. Confusion mounted even more, as the lights went out.

The darkness wasn't complete. A dust-laden beam of daylight came in from a small window high up at one end of the building.

"Don't panic, don't panic." Julie's urgent voice rang out. "Just walk slowly this way, toward the window, where the door is. It's time to leave anyway."

"What a good girl," Naomi said.

"She sure knows how to keep her head," Harry said by way of agreement." They made their way with the others, all calm now, toward the doorway.

With the same abruptness as they had turned off, the lights came back on again. They revealed two strange men among the elderly students. The smaller one, Harry could see, was running up and down the length and breadth of the building, seeking the elusive Lucille. The man was trying to look behind or under things. But there was nothing in the room to look behind or under. In spite of the fact that that great space was swarming with hundreds of Giotto's people, it was, from another point of view, empty. Not a box or a chair or, except for those banks of searchlights, a thing of any sort at all. And certainly not a sign of the Lucille he was seeking, whoever she was. And by now, Harry thought he knew.

The other interloper took up a position at the door and subjected each face to careful examination as it exited. It was clear that he, too, would be frustrated. No one who passed by him turned out to be the Lucille he sought. Yet, he was the one who a moment before had cried out, "I see you, Lucille!"

For their part, the group did not walk by him without comments of their own. Dorothy said, "Why don't

Eldernapped

you be quiet? I know your type...just the sort I sometimes had to kick out of my library."

Pete chimed in with, "Do you know what you just did, yelling out like that in a crowded room? It was tantamount to crying fire in a movie house. I've half a mind to see someone in the Padua City Hall and clap a law suit on you."

Tom didn't have much to say. He was a man of few words. They were, "I don't like you, fella." He stopped for a few seconds to glare down at the man from his impressive height so that the significance of his remark would sink in.

But it was Millicent who made the group's feeling most clear. "Drop dead, buster," she said.

A half hour later and they had almost made it all the way back to their lodging at the Casa del Santo along Padua's arcaded and twisting streets. As would always be the case in the course of this two-week adventure, Harry and Naomi trailed the rest of the enrollees of Senior Seminars Session #6039 because her bad knee slowed them down. This was especially the case at curbs and street intersections.

As they walked, Harry became conscious of what sounded like small hoof beats behind them. Before he could turn, he heard a familiar voice. "May I have my coat and knapsack, please?"

It was Emily. Or was it?

"You're Lucille Adams, aren't you?" Harry said.

There was no answer.

"And you're trying to get away from those two guys, aren't you?" Naomi said.

Again, no answer.

"So how come they didn't get you?" Naomi chimed in.

There was a long pause, but at last, Emily replied with just a single word, "Fortitude."

Harry didn't get what she was driving at, but Naomi did. "You mean you became one of the statues?"

"Not just one of them...a particular one of them."

"One of the Virtues."

"Of course, I certainly didn't want to be a Vice. I picked Fortitude, which seemed to be the right one in the circumstances. There's a small ledge just off the floor and I got on it and took up the same pose and the same facial expression as Fortitude. I stood in front of it and hid it with my body...but that idiot detective couldn't tell the difference. Of course it helped that I was wearing this white running suit."

"Oh, he's a detective, is he?" Naomi said.

"And it was you who turned off the lights," Harry followed up.

"Well, yes. As things are going, I never go into any enclosed space without noting where all the salient features are...and in this case I made a mental record of the location of the light switch."

"So are you going to tell us what this is all about? Are you going to tell us what is going on?" Harry persisted.

"What do you mean, what's going on? Nothing's going on."

Eldernapped

Day Three

"Homicidal Maniac"

Belinda Adams, although she preferred to be called Linda, always liked wandering in and around the great *Palazzo della Ragione*, which was why she had suggested to her very special friend that it would be a good place for them to meet this afternoon. She liked the Palazzo because it had that weird roof that looked like the overturned hull of a great ship—as big as the Titanic, complete with a keel and portholes. Why did they build it seven hundred years ago with that single vast empty interior space? She could only think it must have been a convention hall.

But it differs from today's convention halls. None today have their interior walls covered with fourteenth century frescoes of hunting scenes. Nor is it likely that any are flanked, as this one is, with two produce markets. On one side there is the *Piazza Erbe*, for vegetables, and on the other the *Piazza Frutti*, for fruits.

Linda looked at her watch. It's time. She headed for one of the arched, tunnel-like passageways that penetrate the vast structure at ground level and which connect the two markets. As she walked through, she passed dark, inviting restaurants and bars.

In one of these, comfortably seated, she looked with affection into the face of Guiseppi Fabiano who had just taken a seat opposite her. She knew her expression must have manifested more than mere affection, for she could feel her brow knit. This is no trivial matter I must talk over with him, she told herself. In fact, it's damn serious.

Between them sat dishes of golf-ball size spheres of gelati. One was *nocciola*, hazelnut, another, *cioccolato*, chocolate, and the third, *vaniglia*. But they ignored them. "Joey," she said, for she had anglicized and shortened his name, "I just saw my Grammy at the Casa del Santo."

"Linda," he replied, also having shortened hers, but for his own reasons, for he had explained to her that Linda means neat and sweet in Italian, and the bel part of Belinda, signifying beautiful, is only there for unnecessary reinforcement. "It seems your plan has worked. You got her to come to Padua as you wanted her to. How nice for you and for her. So now everything should work out. I look forward to meeting her. I hope she likes me."

"She'll fall for you head over heels, Joey dear. Anyway, she'll have no choice. She knows I love you, so that means it's settled, she'll love you, too." A pause, "Of course, you don't have to love her back, because...you know...she is a little strange. She won't be like most old Italian ladies of your acquaintance. But I hope you do...love her back, I mean."

"I will love any human who has contributed genes to your gene pool."

This gave rise to a delighted trill of laughter from Linda and it culminated with her leaning across the table to implant a nocciola-flavored kiss on Joey's mouth. She reflected that this is what it will be like to spend the rest of her life with Joey. As a neurosurgeon-to-be, he couldn't resist making gene jokes. She could do worse, she told herself. He could have taken up Bruno Parelli's specialty. Bruno, his best buddy and a classmate at the famous U. of Padua med school, was learning proctology, and in the same way was devoted to sphincter jokes.

They spoke in English. Although Linda's residence in Florence on a Mt. Holyoke junior year exchange program had made her fluent in Joey's language, and she could shift to Italian without missing a beat when circumstances warranted—as when food, art or love made up the main topic.

As for Joey, except for his accent, which Linda found no less than adorable in any case, his English was impeccable.

"But my plan hasn't worked," she went on. "Somehow the family has learned she was, like, coming here. I can't imagine how they did it. Up to now the Senior Seminars people have been so good about protecting privacy and everything like that, so no one ever knew how to trace her. Maybe they hired someone to break into the main Senior Seminars office in Omaha in the middle of the night and examine the files. I wouldn't put anything past them.

"Maybe they planted a mole," Joey offered, a suggestion which didn't surprise Linda, who knew he regularly read le Carre as relief from his arduous medical studies.

"However they did it, the point is, Uncle Justin is here, right here in Padua. Grammy checked and he's at the Plaza. It was the first place she looked. Where else would he stay but at the most expensive hotel in town? What an old smarty-pants she is.

"He must have arrived a few days ago, maybe even before she got here, and she tells me he's got a pair of detectives with him. They're the ones who've been trying to nab her."

Linda then described the scary incident a few days before at the airport and the clever tactic Grammy used to elude them again the next afternoon at the Scrovegni Chapel.

"And, oh yes, they've got the Polizia on her trail, too. That first evening the Padua police came right to the hotel and asked for her by name. Of course, that's not the name she's using now. She wouldn't be that dumb. Anyway, she got away that time, too."

"The police," Joey said. "You didn't tell me she was a criminal."

"Not a criminal, worse than a criminal."

"What's worse?"

"A maniac. A homicidal maniac." In the silence that followed it became Joey's turn to show a knit brow. "She's not really a homicidal maniac, you idiot," she said. The family, the Wharton side to be exact...her first husband was a Wharton...they claim she's a maniac...and dangerous. That's how they managed to have her put away until she escaped about two years ago. But she's no maniac. She's just my sweet old Grammy Lucy, and I don't think she would ever murder anybody, not unless they made her, like, real mad, that is."

"You mean she's been in a mental institution?" Joey said. From the tremor in his voice, Linda could tell he was finding this newest nugget of information hard to pass over without taking notice.

"Well, maybe not a mental institution, a nursing home...a 'special' nursing home. And when you meet my Grammy Lucy you'll know she's not ready for a nursing home. They were keeping her there against her will, because they claim that if they let her out she won't be able to take care of herself...she being so old and all...and that she might even hurt somebody."

"Commit murder?"

"Of course not! But if you want to know who could do murder," Linda continued, her voice slower and quieter now, "it's that Wharton crowd. And if you want to know my opinion, certain ones of them must have done a few murders already, here and there and now and then. I've often wondered why Grammy Lucy ever married that Robert Wharton in the first place, but she said he was very handsome and very charming, and she was only a naive young girl just out of college."

"Like you," Joey said.

"Of course, she knew he was rich," Linda went on, ignoring Joey's comment. "But that wasn't important to

Eldernapped

her. It was only later, after the first two or three children that she learned how he really made his money."

"So her husband was doing illegal things. He was, as you say, a crook?"

"Not really, but he was a heartless business man. As she once told me, he ran a cutthroat business, and one by one he demolished most of his competition...heartlessly...till now the company he founded has become almost a monopoly back home in the States."

"But that doesn't make him a murderer."

"Grammy thought it did."

"And what kind of business is it?"

"Something quite ordinary, but something important, the sort of thing that is in every home. Plumbing fixtures. Have you ever heard of the Wharton Valve?"

"No."

"Well, you would have if you were an American. Go into any hardware store or plumbing supply house and you will see bins of Wharton valves. But probably not in this country. I think Mr. Wharton died before he did much expansion overseas.

"Anyway, that's the point. When he died, he left almost everything to her. The Wharton fortune. So she's a millionaire. No, more than a millionaire. Joey, what's more than a millionaire?"

"A billionaire."

"That's right. Grammy's a billionaire. And that's really why the Whartons are after her. They don't want to wait till she dies for their money because the way she's going, bless her, they think she'll live forever. Sometimes I think so, too. And to get it, they'll stop at nothing. Even murder, I bet. Because they are all heartless, just like old Mr. Wharton."

"And this Uncle Justin?"

"Mr. Justin Wharton, her oldest Wharton son. I only call him Uncle because Grammy always told me to.

He's not really my uncle in the full sense of the word...I don't think. Is the son of your grandmother's first marriage your uncle?

"But don't worry, dear Joey, I don't share any of those rotten Wharton genes. I'm, like from the Adams bloodline. From Grampy Adams. I can barely remember him, but he was a nice man. He was rich, too. But his family isn't bothering Grammy. Neither are the Rosenbergs or the Herreras, and she was Mrs. Rosenberg and Mrs. Herrera before she was Mrs. Adams. But Grampy Adams was the last one."

"Till now," Joey said.

"Oh, I think she's finally run out her string. I don't think she'll ever marry again at her age. But with my Grammy Lucy, you never know. Especially, since none of her husbands seemed to last very long."

"Maybe that's what is in the genes, short-lived husbands," Joey murmured. "Her genes, not theirs."

"But all her kids are still around. You can't imagine how many uncles and aunts of one sort or another I've got. Not to mention cousins and half-cousins..."

"And they're all after her money?"

"Only the Whartons. The others don't seem to care so much. Maybe it's because they're all rolling in the bucks, too. Not that the Whartons are poor. Even without Grammy's holdings, they've each got their separate millions."

Joey stared at her. "Let me get this straight. This means you're a rich girl, doesn't it?"

Linda could tell that this was a new concept to him and that it would take him some time getting used to. "How can I be rich, when I have to support myself by serving espresso and biscotti at the bar every day at the Casa del Santo?" She countered. "And let me tell you, I couldn't live from one day to the next if not for, like, the tips. The salary is to starve from."

"Aha! The Casa del Santo. That's why you took that job, so you could be near your grandmother."

Linda wondered whether a passerby could see the light bulb that was flashing in his brain as he said this. "No, that was just a coincidence. Wendy told me there was an opening there five or six months ago, before I ever thought to suggest to Grammy Lucy to sign up for the Casa's Senior Seminars program. And I really did need some way to support myself. I can't keep asking Mummy and Daddy to do it forever. So I've been working at the Santo bar all this time, as you know as well as anyone, because haven't you been picking me up there most afternoons?"

"Every afternoon, except when I have clinic."

"And you know Wendy, don't you?" She went on, "my cello teacher? Remember that wonderful concert she gave at the Santo? Well, in addition to playing for *I Solisti Padovi* and giving cello lessons to klutzes like me, she teaches the music course to the seniors at this very same Casa. Anyway, that's how I got to be working at its bar. I followed up on her suggestion because I needed the job.

"Later, it occurred to me, seeing those peppy old ladies and gentlemen come charging into the bar every lecture break for their espresso and biscotti fix, that Grammy Lucy could become one of them. And it would be no strain for her. She's been going to Senior Seminars for years, anyway."

"So as I said," Joey persisted, "that was your way of being near your grandmother."

"It's her only chance. I thought she'd be safe when she's far away from the States and with me. Joey, you will help, too, won't you?"

She was pleased to see his head nodding yes, but it did not escape her that at the same time his face had taken on a dazed look, which led to her to reiterate her argument. "Only then will she get out from under those clowns," she said. "No one else in the family is helping, that's for sure.

George Freedman

"So I got in touch with her. She once told me her secret postal box number in Colorado where someone collects her dividend checks and forwards them to her, so she has money to live on. And, as a result, here she is."

The look of concern remained on Joey's face as he struggled to follow Linda's tangled tale, and that look upset her. But she thought she knew what was bothering him. "You don't mind that I have money, do you?" She asked, "I never actually see it and I've never really felt rich. It's back home in Elmira, New York, in a bank or something, in a bunch of Treasury certificates and mutual funds and trusts. Anyway, you should be glad, because now you can marry me for my money. When you finish at the U and then get past your internship and your residency, I can set you up with an elegant office and with a beautiful receptionist.

"But let's get specific, Joey dear," Linda continued, all business now, "I'd like you to meet Grammy as soon as possible. Let's see, today's no good because I go right from here to my lesson with Wendy and after that she's set up a little concert exercise in which I will be the cello part of a Schubert trio. Tomorrow evening would have been good, except that Grammy told me she is going to a concert at the St. Sophia church, and that will run late. No, we'll have to arrange something for later in the week, maybe even next week. How about Monday?"

"How about the Caffe Pedrocchi late afternoon that day? I'm done with clinic after four," Joey said with a sigh. "She ought to like the Pedrocchi."

"Sounds good, lover, you're on."

Linda moved her chair closer to Joey's. Their heads came together, touched in fact, at which moment a pleasant thought ran through her head to the effect that it doesn't get any better than this.

Even though their earnest conversation continued, their words now became so soft, no more than murmurs in fact, as to be inaudible to anyone who might have been close by.

Eldernapped

At the next table, the small bony man with the wide handlebar mustache and the golden loop in his left ear threw down his ballpoint pen and paper pad. With the two slobbering over each other like that, he found it was no longer possible to take notes.

"Don't worry, Vinny," Big Sam said. "Just relax and finish your coffee." Taking a swig from his tiny espresso cup, Big Sam's face took on a thoughtful look. "From what we've just learned," he said, "we can tell Mr. Wharton that he was right. The old lady has been in touch with her granddaughter, this Belinda Adams. We did a damned good piece of work tracing her down so fast.

"But more important, we know now that the old broad is going to a concert tomorrow night at the St. Sophie's church. And she'll be getting out late. That might be the best time to grab her.

"By the way," he went on, "we are going to have to get that granddaughter out of the way...and her boyfriend too, it looks like."

"You mean get rid of them?"

"If we have to."

A silence followed as Vinny contemplated the implications of this statement.

"As for now," Big Sam said, turning his eyes from the loving couple at the adjacent table, who continued to nuzzle each other, "I think we've learned all we're going to from this pair. It's time to report in to the boss. We can tell him we got enough to know what to do next."

Vinny nodded in agreement. "I think so, too," he said, but he found that, as always, his partner seemed not to take particular notice of what he had to say, a fact which did not surprise him. He was used to Big Sam's giving little or no consideration to his opinions.

Big Sam now led the way out of the romantic darkness of the arched Palazzo della Ragione passageway and emerged into the Piazza Frutti. There, in bright sunlight, he threaded his unheeding way past long rows of fruit stands piled high with glowing pyramids of oranges and apples of every possible size, shape, and color. There were melons, green and yellow, and apricots, persimmons, pomegranates, grapefruits, all interspersed with more somber mounds of figs, dates and blackish-green plums.

Vinny lagged behind. He would have suggested that they pick up a small bag of something, figs maybe, he loved figs, and he had never seen any back home in the States that looked as good as these, but he knew better. He had no doubt Sam would scorn his suggestion. He always did things with greater determination than Vinny, with no allowance for pleasurable diversions such as stopping to buy figs.

Big Sam increased the length and rate of his strides, causing Vinny to break into a trot in order to keep up with him as they turned the next corner onto Corso Milano, which brought into view the Plaza Hotel that dominated the scene a few blocks away.

Eldernapped

Day Four

"Crimes Never Happen In Senior Seminars"

"This is Wednesday, campers, our fourth day," Julie said. "I hope everything is going to your satisfaction. If not please speak up. Are there any questions?"

"Well, actually, not entirely to my satisfaction," Sarah spoke up. "For two days in a row now, they've served eggplant for dinner, once as a side dish and once as the sauce on the spaghetti, or as they say, pasta." It was clear she did not like eggplant.

"If you want to know, I don't care much for eggplant, either," Harry whispered to Naomi.

"I know, I know," she answered. "Maybe that's why for the last fifty years I've never made it."

"No problem, Ms....Townes," said the indefatigable Julie, walking over a row and peering down to read her nametag. A few more days and she will be sure to have them all memorized, Harry figured. "I'll talk to the chef and he'll whip you up something else on eggplant days.

"Now, any other questions? If not, I would like to introduce your lecturer for today's all day session on the music of the Veneto...Wendy Gross. "Wendy is from Columbus, or is it Cleveland? From Ohio anyway."

"You're right on Ohio, but it's Cincinnati. I grew up in Cincinnati," Wendy said with a quiet smile. "Anyone here from Cincinnati?"

One. The petite and pretty Marguerite LoPresti shyly raised her hand with the result that she and Wendy exchanged a friendly nod of acknowledgment.

Wendy was somber in a black sweater, black ballet dancer tights and black canvas shoes that harmonized with her deeply brunette hair in which one could see isolated filaments of white. She projected an overall dark look, unrelieved by earrings, rings, necklace or other decoration.

"Excuse me, Wendy," Julie said, "All those 'C' cities in Ohio are confusing. One of these days I'll get it right."

Julie continued, "Wendy's been living over here for the last seven or eight years and she's an important part of musical life in Padova and this whole region, in fact, since she's been a cellist with I Solisti Padovi for much of that time. That's our home town chamber orchestra, which some people think is the finest chamber orchestra in all Italy."

"If not all Europe," Wendy added.

"She teaches the cello and she gives concerts all over...goes on tour, just came back from where was it? Norway?"

"Yes, Bergen and Oslo," Wendy said.

"And she makes recordings all the time. So you can see, we're very lucky to have Wendy Gross as our music instructor in this Senior Seminar. With that...Wendy, take over."

"Thank you, Julie. Let me welcome all of you to my beautiful city of Padova which I want to point is not only beautiful, it's one of the most musical cities in all Italy." Her voice was pleasant and cheerful and now it became clear to Harry that the dark somberness had a purpose, to set off an expressive and enthusiastic face, dominated by vivacious eyes.

"It is very easy to hear wonderful music here," Wendy went on. "There are concerts around town almost every evening, and for those of you who may be interested

Eldernapped

I've posted a list," pointing to the wall at the rear of the room, "of what will be going on during your stay.

"In fact there is a very good concert tonight at the Chiesa di Santa Sofia or, as we would say, St. Sophie's Church. It is one of our newer churches. That means it dates from about the early fifteenth century and it is walking distance from here. The performers are five string players, the Ensemble Camaristico Andrea Palladio who will play chamber music of Bach and Mozart. They're a very fine group...and I know they are, because the cellist has been one of my students."

"Fine looking young woman," Harry commented to Naomi.

"Looks, looks, all you care about are looks. As a matter of fact her looks are just average," Naomi whispered back. "But what she has is personality and pep. That's what I like about her. And she's not so young. She must be forty-five."

"To me that's young."

"We will start off," Wendy continued, "with a discussion of the great Guiseppi Tartini, whose dates are sixteen ninety-two to seventeen seventy. He spent almost his entire life right here in this city. In fact he composed most of his music just across the street in the Basilica of St. Anthony, which we call the Santo. He was music director there for over forty years. After lunch today, I'm going to take you over there and into the church archives, where I'll show you some of his original manuscripts. Now...who knows what Tartini's most famous piece of music is?"

"The Devil's Trill." This response came without an instant's hesitation from Irene, and all heads turned to look at her.

"Quite right," Wendy agreed, and smiled at Irene with high approval.

"Aha!" Harry exclaimed sotto voce, sitting next to Irene. "Already you're the teacher's pet."

George Freedman

Irene, having known Harry for many years, ignored him.

"We will introduce Tartini," Wendy continued, "by listening to a CD I have of a piece of Tartini's music. It is a concerto for violin, Opus D-96, played by the Solisti and conducted by its regular conductor, Paolo DeLillo. The soloist is Ugo Ughi, one of Italy's greatest living violinists. You will be interested to know that Paolo lives right here in town in a very nice house just behind the Santo, and Ugo is a frequent visitor. In fact," her voice dropped to a confidential tone, "it happens I'm a tenant in Paolo's house and..."

Harry, sitting four down from Belle, caught her in the act of looking with some intensity at her husband, Nate, as though she was wondering whether "tenant" was the right term, but all she uttered was that first name, "Paolo!" That was enough. Harry got her drift, and, as he could tell, so did Nate.

"Are you on this CD, dear?" Belle piped up from her seat.

"Oh yes, I am, and if you listen carefully you can even hear me. Tartini has what amounts to a dialogue between the first cello and the solo violin in the second movement, the adagio, and you can make me out pretty well since I'm at the first cello desk in this piece." She spoke the final phrase with eyelids lowered to express a suitable level of modesty.

"Now, before I play this CD," she went on, as she approached a formidable bank of stereo components that had been set up that morning for her purpose just to the left of the whiteboard, "let me caution those of you who are wearing hearing aids. Tartini often features high strings and if you happen to have the high frequency response on your aids set with too much amplification, I am told the effect can be painful."

Looking around, Harry saw a half dozen hands going up to a half dozen ears where they made mysterious

Eldernapped

adjustments. After which, the music, as well as the music lesson, began in earnest.

♦♦♦♦

There was a pleasant commotion in the bar of the Casa del Santo during the morning break as the students, as in college student unions anywhere, burst in and milled around. Some made a crowd at the counter to give their orders, while their special companions, if any, plopped down fast to secure the most desirable tables.

As Harry backed his way out of the crowd, a tiny espresso and a dish of crusty pastries in one hand and a foamy cinnamon-specked cappuccino in the other, he spotted Naomi at a table for six. He was pleased to ascertain that his tablemates would include Dorothy, soft and pink, and Pete, rotund but dashing in his blue blazer with its shiny brass buttons and his white ascot. Flinty little Emily was almost lost between the two of them.

There was also a new student he had not spoken to before but he had noticed her in passing. "Marguerite LoPresti" her nametag said. She was the one who had raised her hand an hour ago for "Cincinnati", in response to Wendy's question. She was neat and modest, in a light brown pants suit and soft cream blouse, accented with a carved ivory brooch at its throat. Slim, small boned, shapely, pleasant faced, graying, with a modest but attractive hairdo, she was graceful in all her movements— a living example of Harry's "Levine Principle of Enjoying the Opposite Sex." This was, "When all is said and done, give me a good looking sixty-five year old woman, any day."

Let's see, who is she, he wondered. Oh, yes, a widow in search of her Italian roots who, as he recalled from her statement on the evening of Day One, used to be a psychiatric social worker specializing in eating disorders, mostly in young women.

George Freedman

Getting through the crowd at last and pulling out the one remaining empty chair at the table, he could not resist making an admiring comment about the technical features of the espresso machine up at the bar. "Twenty seconds, and it brews two espressos at once into these itty-bitty cups. Talk about fresh brewed. And you know, it turns out to be quite an exact process, taking place as it does within very controlled, narrow ranges of both temperature and steam pressure. And that's why they call it espresso, which I just found out literally means pressed or squeezed. The steam pressure actually squeezes the coffee essence out of..."

"Harry! Enough already!" Naomi exploded. "No one is interested in how they make espresso. God, I must be a saint, the way I've patiently put up with your technical explanations of everything for the last fifty-one years."

"Oh, I think you are quite mistaken," Emily countered. "In my opinion, you are very lucky to be married to an engineer. Engineers make the best husbands. My third, Ben Herrera, was an engineer."

Pete, southern gentleman, bowed with a smile, first to Emily and then to Naomi, and said, "Lawyers make pretty good husbands, too."

"I wouldn't know," Emily, said, "I was never married to a lawyer."

"Enough of this subject," Naomi interjected, as she nodded in the direction of Marguerite. "I don't think you've met Marguerite LoPresti yet, Harry."

"No, I haven't. Glad to meet you, Marguerite." And they shook hands.

The conversation next turned to Wendy Gross. "I think she's marvelous. I never knew Tartini was so interesting," Marguerite offered, her voice precise but ladylike. "What a thrill it is to be right here, just across the street from where he actually used to work. And we are certainly lucky to have Wendy as our teacher...who

Eldernapped

seems to have such a close personal identification with a composer like Tartini."

"She's not just a teacher," Dorothy added. "She's a real performing artist, too, and that's much better than just a teacher."

Everyone agreed with enthusiasm, but following that there was a prolonged silence while everyone sipped coffee. Harry broke it. "See that barmaid," he pointed, "The tall blonde one...she's a real beauty. She doesn't look Italian to me. Yet, she took everyone's order in perfect Italian."

"We're less than a hundred miles south of the Austrian border," Dorothy said. "So she's probably got some Austrian ancestry. You see a lot of blondes in North Italy."

"Oh," Harry said, "an Italian Valkyrie."

"She's not Italian at all," Emily declared. "And I know, because she happens to be my granddaughter, Belinda, from Elmira, New York. She's over here studying cello. In fact, she's studying with our own Wendy. That is one reason I picked this particular Senior Seminars program. It gives me a chance to visit with her."

"What a pleasant looking girl," Naomi said, stretching to look. "I hope you will introduce her to us."

"Indeed. I'd be most happy to do that. Belinda, Belinda dear," Emily cried in a loud voice, quite out of proportion to her diminutive body—and the attention of everyone in the room focused on her while she waved her arms like a semaphore. "Come over here, Belinda dear, when you get a chance. I'd like you to meet some of my friends."

This, in fact, was an opportune time, for, since everyone had been served, there was no one waiting at the bar. The young lady made her way to their table. "This is my granddaughter, Belinda," Emily said, not without pride, for Belinda, as Harry had already pointed out, was a beauty indeed.

"Hi, everyone," Belinda said, a bright smile lighting up her face as she held up her right hand and wiggled its fingers by way of greeting. "But please call me Linda for short."

"I don't believe in short," Emily said. "You'll always be Belinda to me." Then, going around the table, she introduced, "Mr. and Mrs. Levine, Miss Hinckley, Mr. Caldwell and Mrs. LoPresti."

"I would have thought," Harry offered, "that the logical shortened form of Belinda would be Belly. Anyone ever call you Belly?"

This caused modest laughter, including some from the young lady herself, who said, "Never, but I'll suggest it to my friends." She then continued, a serious look on her face, "I hope you are all, like, looking after my darling Grammy?"

"From what I've seen I don't think she needs much looking after," Naomi said. "She seems perfectly capable of looking after herself."

"Well, still," Linda said, "please keep an eye on her. I do worry."

"You can depend on us." This came from courtly Pete. "We'll all watch her, make sure nothing bad happens to her. I especially will keep watch. You can depend on me, Belly...I mean Linda...no, I mean Belinda." And he patted Emily's arm in a protective manner.

"So how do you find living in Padua?" Naomi said, on the face of it, a perfectly innocent question. But Harry found himself suspecting otherwise.

"Oh, I love it. I love everything about it," Linda bubbled.

"That must be because you have such a wonderful cello teacher," Naomi continued, her brows narrowing, which only Harry noticed, and which meant to him that she was already in the act of boring in.

"Of course. Isn't Wendy great? You must all have met her by now, because she told me she would be giving her first lecture to you all this morning."

Eldernapped

"Not only a wonderful teacher but a fine performer," Dorothy said. "We heard her on a recording just before this break, and I want you to know, when her cello part came up, I was just thrilled.

"Of course you must have been thrilled," Linda agreed. "That's because Wendy's cello playing is world class. But she doesn't push herself enough. She's content just to stay on in Padua and teach and play with the Solisti and give an occasional out of town recital, and take care of her nine-year-old son."

"What, no husband?" Naomi asked.

Harry thought. Here it comes.

"Oh, she's been divorced for as long as I've known her."

"A boy friend then..."

"Possible."

"Just like you."

Linda laughed. "Also possible."

Bingo! Harry thought.

◆◆◆◆

Harry found the concert at the Chiesa di Santa Sofia, as Wendy had promised, to be thrilling indeed. But while the performances by the Ensemble Camaristico Andrea Palladio were excellent, the major impact came from hearing the music in that building as two-dozen generations of listeners had regularly heard similar music there before. Although St. Sophia's was one of the newer churches in the city, Harry figured it must already have been at least a half-century-old when Columbus set sail for India.

As long as two city blocks, the church's interior was. Harry searched for its ceiling among high black shadows. He guessed it must be just as high as it was long. Up at front, beside the altar on its left, was the massive pulpit. Its spiral staircase, rostrum and canopy all seemed to have been carved out of a single, giant piece of mahogany. Here, a priest would conduct services in a few days, as Sunday services had been conducted on that very spot for going on six hundred years.

"I felt insignificant, like one little ant deep in an ant's nest," Marguerite commented during intermission.

Perceptive woman, this one, Harry thought. "Ant" was not a bad way to express his feeling, too.

"Perhaps that is what the people who built this place had in mind when they designed it," was Emily's thoughtful contribution.

"And the effect is not only due to the building's great size," Dorothy added. "It's also because of how dramatically dark it is in here. Even now, when the lights are up for intermission, it's dark."

"They probably designed that on purpose, too," Harry said.

As they came out from the church into the midnight street, Italian concerts or theatre never start before nine and thus never end before midnight, as Harry recalled from previous trips, they became for the moment part of a home going, milling swarm. They hailed many of their comrades from the Casa and were hailed back in return.

"Nice concert,"
"Wasn't that Mozart duo heavenly?"
"Loved the lead violinist," were typical comments.

And then everyone headed down Via Santa Sofia for the trek back.

What struck Harry was how short a time it took for the vast crowd of concertgoers to evaporate. In what seemed to be only an instant, the street outside Santa Sofia's main entrance, with the exception of two dozen or so Senior Seminarians became empty. No other pedestrians were in evidence, or cars, either, and as they walked, their loud footsteps echoed from the rows of ancient buildings on each side.

Eldernapped

"You know," Harry commented, "if I didn't know we were out on the street, I would think we were still back in the church. Except in this case, the church seems to go on forever...the same long, high, stone walls confining us on both sides...the same rows of high small windows...the same dim lanterns...the same yellow and black shadows...the arches of the arcades looking from the side like entrances from the nave to chapels."

"I would take," Naomi interrupted, ever pragmatic, less poetic, "...a taxi."

"No problem, except that I see no taxi," Harry responded. "Anyway, we know it's safe out here, and..." consulting his street map of the city under a lantern, "we've got less than a half-mile to walk."

Julie had assured them, when making announcements during the dessert course at dinner, a practice that was settling into a routine, that there was nothing to worry about at any hour, night or day, in the streets of Padua. "This is one of the safest cities in Italy, if not of all Europe," she told them. Crimes of violence or robbery are rare, and women are not even advised to be careful about how they carry their purses. "So there is no reason for anyone to bother with those ugly strapped-on pouches that look like a growth on your groin," she had added.

Yet, as Naomi pointed out to Harry and as he found himself agreeing, even though there was street lighting on every street, the deep, flickering, ocher shadow patterns they made were menacing.

The contingent from the Casa del Santo by now had coalesced and made a ragged but close packed group as they continued their walk home down a tunnel-like arcade. But the tightness of that assemblage soon loosened and stretched out, with a half dozen stragglers bringing up the rear.

No one was as far behind as the Levines. Yet, they were never so far back as to lose sight of the penultimate subgroup, there would always be one, that was only a little less slow than they. This evening it consisted of the same four who sat together at the concert and for that morning's coffee break, Pete, Emily, Dorothy and Marguerite.

Harry could tell, even from far back, that their deliberate pace was determined by Dorothy, and he so informed Naomi.

"Yes, Dorothy does walk with a slight limp," Naomi said.

"Early stages of arthritic knee with deteriorated cartilage like yours?" Harry asked.

"No, hip."

"How do you know?"

Before she could tell him how she knew, there was the roar of a car behind them. Loud as a sudden roll of thunder it was, since it was accelerating as it passed, and also because there was no competing sound from the silent city.

♦♦♦♦

"It was black," Harry and Naomi later testified "and big."

"What make?"

"How would we know? We don't know European cars," Harry said in response to a question from Lieutenant Cataldo, a detective of the Paduan police, who must have been given this assignment because he spoke passable English.

But it took no more than the turning of just a few pages of an auto catalog that had been thrust before him for Harry to signal for the page turning to stop. "That's it," Harry exclaimed.

Naomi confirmed his judgment by repeating his words. "Harry's right. That's it."

They had both pointed to a picture of a black Fiat, that company's largest model made this year, Cataldo informed them.

Eldernapped

What had happened, Harry and Naomi related, was that a large, late model, black car, a Fiat, had screeched to a stop alongside the four walkers. Its rear door sprang open and a pair of male arms reached out. In no more than one second, those arms grabbed one of walkers, a female figure, right before their eyes. They pulled her and stuffed her, screaming and kicking, into the car, which then leaped forward and disappeared around the next corner into what was later identified to be Via Ospedale Civile.

Harry then realized that the group of four walkers up front of them had become only three.

The session with Lieutenant Cataldo took place not more than an hour and a half after the remaining five of the original six had burst into the Casa's lobby to blurt out their grim tale to the night desk clerk. Then, with the time getting on to two A.M., the room that was used every day for their classes became filled with some thirty of their fellow students.

It was more crowded than usual, since some members of the hotel staff were present as well, desk clerks, waiters, and the porter. And Julie and Graziella were there, too. Almost all wore nightclothes and bathrobes. In addition, there were four policemen, three in uniform, plus Cataldo who was in regular street clothes.

Pete's head was bandaged with a turban-like dressing which displayed, just over his right eye, a dime-sized spot of red-turning-brown blood. As the others told it, he had attempted to battle the man in the car but had been thrown to the street for his efforts. No one expected any less from Pete. "I'll be all right," he said.

"It's obvious," Julie said, "we've had a kidnapping in the Senior Seminar. I've never heard of any kidnapping in any Senior Seminar before."

"Or any crime," Graziella added. "Crimes never happen in Senior Seminars. The people are all so...good."

The assemblage exhaled a group sigh. They knew that what she really meant was that the people who frequent Senior Seminars are all so advanced in years, with their criminal days, if any, far behind them.

"What a bizarre thing this is," Irene said, thus no doubt summarizing the thoughts of all her classmates.

"But why should anyone want to kidnap Marguerite LoPresti?" Belle asked, carrying Irene's comment to its next logical level.

"They didn't want Marguerite," a sharp, penetrating voice stated. Harry recognized it right away, and he could see that her classmates did as well. "They didn't want Marguerite," Emily repeated. "They made a mistake, the stupid louts. Even though she's a small woman, she's much bigger than I am. They didn't want her," Emily went on, almost spitting out the words. "They wanted me."

Eldernapped

Day Five

"Mother?..."

Justin Wharton sat in a brocaded chair with golden frame and legs, and looked out his hotel window. It opened onto a tiny wrought iron balcony the curved black bars of which interfered little with the view. If anything, they enhanced it as through them, he contemplated the Italian scene below.

So this is Europe. Strange that it had taken him all this time to get here. Unlike others of his acquaintance, his equals in years, education and wealth, he had never felt the urge to travel. Nor, for that matter, had he ever married. Which led him to wonder, had he missed much? Maybe this would be his chance to find out, about the former at least.

It was not the first time these questions had occurred to him. They came up all the time, unbidden. He could not keep them from intruding on his consciousness. But he had an automatic and swift defense, which never failed. As though with the click of a neuron switch, he made his brain change the subject.

As for those others, his relatives, his friends, rebuffed every time they tried, they had long ago given up suggesting that he come with them on a little overseas jaunt for a few vacation weeks, or that he meet a certain rather attractive single lady of their circle, who matched him in age, background and interests.

George Freedman

Yet, in spite of his inherent reclusive spirit, he was not unwilling to discuss these matters on occasion, sometimes with indulgent humor. He would praise the advantages of Woonsocket, Rhode Island where he had been born and which, except for his four years at Harvard, he had never left, as he would quote his favorite author. "Thoreau said, 'I have traveled a good deal in Concord,' "leaving his listener to conclude that, so far as lifetimes are concerned, one New England town should be enough for any man of sensitivity.

"Thoreau never got married either," was often the response.

"Which proves that I have a lot in common with Henry David Thoreau," Justin would reply with a final snap of his jaw.

The telephone. He jumped in his seat before he realized what it was. Even this is different in this faraway place. It rings faster and with a different tonal pitch than he was used to. But the voice in the earphone was American enough. "Hello, Mr. Wharton?

"Yes."

"This is Sam Peterson, Mr. Wharton. Vinny and I got her, we picked up your mother last night."

"Oh, my God!"

Justin could tell this was not the response Sam expected from his employer. A period of prolonged silence elapsed before Sam asked, "You okay, Mr. Wharton?"

"Of course, of course." Justin, in his turn, thought he was detecting a note of uncertainty in Sam's voice, "Anything wrong on your end?" he said.

"Nothing's wrong. Except...well...are you sure this is all exactly kosher, Mr. Wharton...us grabbing her off the street late at night with her kicking and fighting back? She really didn't want to come, you know, even after I kept mentioning your name. She's a tough old bird, Mr. Wharton...if you don't mind me saying ...your old lady. And that brings up another thing, are you sure she's eighty-five? Seems younger to us."

Eldernapped

"We've been over this many times already with our lawyer, Sam. You know that," Justin responded, conscious that there was a quaver in his voice. "And he advises us that with a person of her age who is not entirely all there mentally...showing signs of the beginnings of senile dementia in fact...and is physically frail, her children have every right..."

"Well, she seemed mentally okay to us last night, and physically, too. You should see Vinny and me," Sam said. "We're all over scratches and bites. The woman's a tiger. And you know, we always worry about things like that in our business. The old lady doesn't have HIV or hepatitis B, does she? Anyway...we have her in the country house. When do you want to see her?"

This was the part Justin dreaded. Not the least because it was the role for which he felt he was the least qualified in the family. Yet, it had fallen to him. The whole thing was Roberta's idea. Thin-lipped Roberta with a profile like an arrowhead, well named for their robber baron father.

"We were that close to obtaining power of attorney over her," she had fumed during one of what she called their Mummy meetings, "when she got away from that nursing home in North Carolina. Of course, once we have her back to the States, we'll find a more secure one...or we'll make it secure even if we have to post twenty-four hour guards." Her face had rotated like a slow radar antenna, as it always does after she makes what she considers to be a seminal remark. It is one of her less lovable mannerisms, and Justin remembered this particular occasion with more clarity than most others, to fix on the face of each of the male figures in the room in turn. In this case there had been three.

Even while holding Sam on the other end of the line, Justin could not keep himself from reviewing that short list. There was her hapless husband, poor Ben Dillard. He had long ago ceased to disagree with his wife. All he wanted was to be left alone, which he usually was.

George Freedman

He had ground away the previous three and a half decades as Purchasing Manager for the family firm, a job at which, to the surprise of the rest of the family, he had turned out to be quite good.

And kid brother Gordie, no longer much of a kid, in fact, since he was pushing sixty. Whenever he was subjected to a Roberta confrontation, he was just as bad as Ben, if not worse. At least Ben was useful as PM for Wharton Valve. But Gordie's career path, starting high, since he was a son of the boss, had been marked by steady demotions over the years till his career came to rest on a job of minimal value to the firm but for which he was, in fact, well suited. Supervisor of Grounds was his title, and anyone walking up to the main entrance of the Wharton Valve Headquarters building in Woonsocket would see neat flower beds in spring and a well ploughed parking lot in winter, both the result of his personal handiwork. Gordie had found his niche.

That left Justin himself. Roberta's eyes had finished their rotational arc and come to rest on those of her older brother. "Oh no, not me," he had protested. "In the first place I can't leave the plant. Without its Chief Financial Officer, even for a week, the place could go into a tailspin."

"Alfred can handle those duties without you for as long as it takes, Justin. He can pick up all the CFO things you do...you know that...and hardly feel the strain," was her cold response. "And if you do your job right, with the help of the Meadowlands Detective Agency we've engaged, you should be back home in less than a week."

She was referring to Alfred Dillard, her son. Only thirty-two years old, and already president of this great company. Justin's boss, in fact. Justin had to admit, the boy was more than merely all right for the job. He was a ball of fire. In just two years under his leadership, Wharton Valve had undergone a major expansion and diversification, with its acquisition of one of its major suppliers, Anderson Washer and Gasket Corp. Just the

Eldernapped

sort of move his grandfather would have made. If Robert Wharton were looking down, or up, at him this moment, he would be proud.

To give himself the credit due, Justin viewed his nephew's achievements not with envy but with pride. Which had led him to his next, weak, sally at his sister. "You know, Roberta, I'm not going to be good at this. I've never been able to talk mother into anything. So why not send the star of the family instead of me? Surely, Alfred can carry out this task better than any of the rest of us."

"What an idiotic idea!" was her snorted response. Somehow, he had expected exactly those very words, accompanied by that very snort. "You know that mother hardly knows Alfred, and in the rare occasions when we talk about him, she always calls him Albert. Anyway," Roberta had gone on, leaning over and patting Justin's knee in a sisterly manner, "you really are the best one for taking on this job. You're so diplomatic. Just think of yourself as a diplomat when you talk to her. More of an ambassador actually, an ambassador from the family."

The country house Sam had taken on short-term lease was one of a number of riverside, canal side mansions on the ancient Venice-Padua waterway. As they drove up to its entrance, Justin's unease increased. He was going to have a meeting with his mother. He hadn't seen her or talked to her in more than two years. Furthermore, from what Sam had told him about last night's events, she was not going to be in a good mood.

As he approached the imposing, handsome house, he could see that it was somewhat chipped at the edges and a bit gone to seed as far as the landscaping was concerned. But why did it have to be so big? It was huge. Easily, as large as the Wharton mansion in Woonsocket that Robert, flaunting the Depression, had built during the nineteen thirties, still the biggest private residence in that old New England mill town, and now the home of Roberta and Ben.

And it was old. Probably hundreds of years old. They had to take it for a whole month, which was ridiculous because they would only need it for a few days. But the local real estate agent couldn't be swerved on this issue, the travel agent reported.

Nor was it cheap. When she heard about how much it would cost, Roberta, stingy Roberta, blew her top. But she settled down. After all, where her mummy was concerned, the best was none too good.

"Hang the cost," she said with uncharacteristic generosity. "But when you get over there, Justin, make sure you watch how those two guys spend our money. I don't trust them from here to the next room."

The rented black Fiat, large and grand, another extravagance, passed through the massive iron gate that breached the high stonewall surrounding the place. It proceeded down the driveway and pulled up at the columned front entrance pavilion, as a four-horse coach might have two centuries before. With reluctance, Justin stepped out of the car. He brushed past Sam, who was standing by the door to help, if needed, just like a coachman of old.

The coachman image was weakened by the fact that the left shoulder seam of Sam's suit jacket gaped open for a few inches, as though someone had torn it in anger. A scratch of similar length on his left cheek added a further negative impression. The wound was inflamed and moist. It caused Justin to avert his eyes from Sam, as he made his way toward the building's entrance. But not before he noticed that Sam's left hand, too, had not escaped trauma. It was wrapped in a wide, white bandage, which gave it the appearance of a boxer's hand before he puts on his glove. Sam's left brow completed the list of damaged body parts. A rich, green/brown discoloration highlighted it from eyebrow to cheek. Justin knew a black eye when he saw one.

The door at the bottom of the long dark stairway was locked. Sam pulled an outsized antique key from his

Eldernapped

pocket and unlocked it. A large basement room, lit by small ceiling level windows was revealed. It was set up like a one room apartment, a studio it would be called in the States, which must have been meant for a servant. It had a single bed, bearing evidence of having been slept in, although made up. There were also a couch and chairs and a dining room table. This was next to a kitchenette niche that was fitted out with a sink, a small refrigerator, electric burner spirals and a microwave oven. At the other end of the room, a half-open door showed enough to indicate that behind it was a bathroom.

The apartment was decorated Italian style, walls not wallpapered but painted yellowish white. Several watercolors and oil paintings, all originals hung on it. Justin noticed a Venice canal scene, lovers in Renaissance garb eyeing each other with passion and a Madonna and child, both with halos.

Justin braced himself. He adjusted his gray tie that he thought went well with his white shirt and dark gray business suit. That suit looked tasteful and conservative, he was sure, on his tall, unfleshy body, topped as it was by the long narrow face ordained by his Yankee genes. He took a deep breath and walked in to confront the small gray-haired woman who was sitting by the table with her back to him, sipping a cup of tea. She must have heard his and Sam's steps, but she did not turn to face her visitors. "Mother..." he called out in a plaintive voice.

She did not reply. Instead, she took another sip from her cup. At last, with a sigh, she turned to face him.

Justin gasped and repeated the word, "Mother!" shouting this time,

He turned. "Sam," he exploded, his face now beet red, "how can you have been so stupid? This is not my mother."

The stunned silence that followed was broken by the lady herself, who spoke in a tone of remarkable calm, considering her unpleasant situation. "I don't know what the penalty for kidnapping is in Italy," she said. "But, since the Lindbergh case, hasn't it been death in the electric chair in the States?"

"My dear lady," Justin sputtered, "there has been a terrible mistake. We thought you were my mother."

"Oh, you thought you were kidnapping your mother. And you think that excuses what you have done. Well, I don't think so...and I don't think that will change anything as far as the penalty goes. Kidnapping is kidnapping, mother or not. Anyway, how could I be your mother? From the looks of you, you're as old as I am, if not older."

"Just like I was trying to tell you on the phone, Mr. Wharton," Sam interjected, pale-faced, "I thought she looked too young to be eighty-five."

"A mistake, a mistake..." Justin kept mumbling.

Sam echoed, "Ya, a mistake. We were supposed to pick up the little, skinny old lady and that's what we did, but it was sort of dark and..." his voice trailing off.

"Emily Thorndike. You thought I was Emily Thorndike. She must have been on to you. I remember now, just before you grabbed me, how she skittered away from the rest of us and into a doorway." She paused for a moment and then sighed, "That poor woman."

"Lucille Adams." said Justin. "Her real name is Lucille Adams. Emily...whatever...Thorndike is a name she has assumed. She's had several others. She was Charlotte Bronte a few months ago. Isn't that fantastic? How could she think she would get away with that one? Shows how delusional she's become and how necessary it is for me, as her son, to..."

"So you're the one who put your mother on the run. What are you after...her money? That must be it. I've heard of sons like you. Thank God, my sons would never do a despicable thing like this," she said with conviction. "Of course I have no money. But even if I did..."

Eldernapped

That hit home. Justin writhed. He had no interest in his mother's wealth, and on the one occasion that he had summoned up enough courage to accuse his sister of having that motive, she silenced him with a withering look. Yet, he knew Roberta as no one else did and, deep down, he suspected the worst.

The lady was still talking. "Enough of this," she said. "Get me out of here. I want to get back to my Senior Seminar. Because of you, I've already missed a whole day. Today we were going on a bus trip to Ravenna to see the mosaics," looking at her watch, "and by now they must have left. And that means," her voice faltered and her eyes turned moist, "I'll never get to see them."

Sam signaled Justin by cocking his head toward the door. Justin, ever polite, mumbled to his unfortunate captive, "Please excuse us." The two of them slouched out of the room, closing the door behind them.

"She's right. We've got to get her back." With mounting panic in his voice, Justin could barely get the words out.

"And then what? Have her blow our cover so the Italian police pick us up as kidnappers, like she said?" In contrast to his own, Justin detected no panic in Sam's voice."

You mean we keep holding her here?"

"Until we think of something better to do with her...although, short of, you know, doing her in and burying her in the garden," Sam said, his brow knit with thought, "I can't think of anything."

"You mean you would...kill her?" Justin was horrified.

"No, of course not. I just said it to make sure you understand, Mr. Wharton. We're in deep trouble.

She's right, we could be up on a kidnapping charge."

"But it was a mistake...your mistake."

Justin could see defiance in Sam's eyes. "Don't try to weasel out of this one, Mr. Wharton," Sam said, putting particular emphasis on the word "Mister." "You're in this as deep as we are, probably deeper, because you hired us to do it."

Justin felt his face turning apoplectic red again. It must have alarmed Sam, since he led Justin to a chair and made him sit. You never know with older guys like Wharton when that inevitable heart attack will kick in Sam must have been thinking.

"But there is something you can do, Wharton," he said, now forgetting the "Mister" altogether. "I just thought of it."

"What?"

"Butter her up. Buy her off. You got lotsa money."

Justin moaned. He had never bargained for anything like this. This was hardly what Roberta meant when she said he would be going to Italy as a sort of "ambassador from the family." Criminal conspirator was more like it. And the thought of the never-yielding Roberta, made him despair all the more. She would never agree to pay out any of the family's money for anything like this. What could he do?

One way, of course, was that he could take care of this lady on his own, whoever she was. Sam was right. That must be his course of action. No matter the cost. And it wouldn't be cheap. This woman looked smart enough to know that a few tens of thousands of dollars would be a drop in the bucket compared to what she could sue him for. And if she herself weren't that savvy or mean, her sons, she had mentioned that she had sons, all of them probably lawyers, they would set her straight.

He could sell all of his assets. That ought to be enough. Everything he owned was in Wharton Valve stock. He had never thought of diversifying his estate. What better repository could there be than the firm's stock? No matter how the rest of the market went, Wharton Valve always went up. But then, without his Wharton securities. he would have to live as a poor man in his old age.

Eldernapped

Of course, there was the company pension, based, in his case, on more than forty years of devoted service. That would keep him out of the poorhouse. Do they still have poorhouses? As CFO, he had made sure that the company pension plan was what was always referred to as "lean." He knew, who knew better? That meant "none too generous." Now, without his Wharton stock and with his retirement date only a year away, that very plan could come back to haunt him for the rest of his days, assuming of course that they would be spent out of jail.

There was a clatter on the stairway. Justin saw Vinny Anzaldi, coming down, the other private investigator from the Meadowlands Detective Agency. Like Sam, he, too, showed signs of having recently participated in some sort of physical combat. In his case, there were no obvious wounds or bruises. The man appeared essentially undamaged, except for an unsettling impression he gave of lack of symmetry. Vinny was missing about half of his mustache. Only an irritated red patch of skin on the right part of his face indicated where it once had been.

Justin could also tell that Vinny, too, was undergoing some emotional turbulence at this moment. His face was ashen and he wasted no time in greetings. "I was just tuned into the English language radio from the U.S. Army Base in Vicenza," he said between deep breaths, "and there's an all points alert out for us. We're called brutal American kidnappers, and they had a good description of you and me, Sam, and the big black Fiat...and Mr. Wharton...and the old broad, too."

The other two took this news with stunned silence,

But Vinny had more bad news. "Hey...how did she get out?" he shouted. His eyes were directed upward to the landing. No question, there was their captive. Or, to be more accurate, their erstwhile captive.

How indeed? Making no sound, she must have opened the apartment door, which Sam and Justin had forgotten to lock. She then slipped by them unnoticed as they were engaged in their earnest discussion.. She made it to the top of the stairs, just as Vinny was delivering his unsettling news.

As the three men looked up, she found the door to the outside world at the head of the stairs. She opened it. But she did not rush through it to freedom. Rather, she turned around to face them. Standing there for a moment, she looked down at them with her large, luminous brown eyes.

Those eyes had the frightened look of a doe at bay. Yet, spunky, Justin figured, for who but she could have inflicted those many evidences of battle on Sam and Vinny? While she, neat, little elderly lady, showed no sign at all of having been through any episode of physical stress.

Why was she just standing there, when she could have rushed out and away? She had something to say. Her message was, "I find you...all three of you..." but as she said it, those eyes seemed to single out Justin himself, "beneath contempt."

For an instant more, the three were dumbfounded and unmoving. Then, each in accordance with his own style started up the stairs. There was no reason they couldn't retrieve her if they acted with dispatch.

Vinny took the steps two at a time. He was fast in his movements, as one would expect from such a slim, small man. He had almost reached her, when he was met by what seemed to be a large rolling torpedo. It came at him, not point first as torpedoes would, but on its side, rolling like a log. It sent him spinning and on his way down did the same to Sam and Justin. It caused all three to end up on the floor in a pyramid of twisting male bodies, with Justin under the other two.

Justin could see, even from his supine position, that this woman, whatever her name was, had been the launcher of this missile. It turned out to be the umbrella holder from alongside the entrance door. It was not like ordinary, skimpy, stateside umbrella holders. This one was at least a foot and a half in diameter and was made of a single carved piece of tropical wood that must once have been an entire tree trunk. It had to weigh more than a hundred pounds. Centuries ago, it could have had been something like a sword holder, only to be converted into an umbrella holder in more effete modern times.

How the hell did this little woman manage to tip it on its side and roll it over to the head of the stairs in order to launch it? She was a resourceful lady indeed. And strong.

Since he was still on his back with the weight of the other two bearing down on him and causing shooting pains in his kidneys, Justin was the only one who could look upward. He saw that the woman had opened the door that led outside and walked out through it, slamming it as she left with as much dramatic impact as if she were Ibsen's Nora.

Minutes later the three men, limping and clutching elbows, backs and heads, emerged from the house. They searched the length and breadth of the garden for the lady, without success. Until they heard her voice.

"*Aiuto! Aiuto*," Justin heard her shout. She was still on the grounds of the mansion, not having succeeded either in scaling its ten-foot high walls or in opening the heavy iron gate.

"That means, 'help!'" Vinny translated for the benefit of his comrades.

"We've got to find her and shut her up before the neighbors hear her," Sam cried.

Had Marguerite LoPresti, also of Italian descent, learned that useful word from her parents in the same way Vinny had? No. In fact, she had heard it for the first time only two days before. Graziella, in her crash course in "Survival Italian", well named, as it was turning out, had taught it to the class. "...So that you can call for help in case you fall out of a gondola during your day in Venice...or for any other reason," she had said. "But what other reason can there be, ha-ha?..." The class,

George Freedman

Marguerite now recalled with a pang of despair, had joined in with her hearty laughter.

"Aiuto!" she called again, louder this time, but at once regretted having done so, for she now realized that while it may be alerting the neighborhood to her plight, it was, at the same time, telling her prison guards where she was. She next heard the thuds of pounding feet. They were heading straight toward the tall hedge behind which she was hiding.

♦♦♦♦

Marguerite LoPresti was not the only one who missed the ninety-mile bus excursion to Ravenna that morning. Harry, with Naomi by his side, stood on the sidewalk at the entrance to their hotel, framed by an arcade arch as though on a small proscenium stage, to wave their departing fellow scholars on. Under an adjacent arch, Emily, Pete and Dorothy did the same. The bus passengers, a jolly crowd despite last night's upsetting experience, waved back through their windows for a few moments. Then, the vehicle lurched forward, proceeded into the morning traffic of Via Cesarotti, turned the corner at Via San Francesco, and disappeared.

Those left behind at the curb looked at each other and sighed. Even though there were five of them, they felt alone and abandoned, and shortchanged. Harry tried to cheer up Naomi by reminding her that they had already seen the lovely seaside city and its magnificent ancient mosaics on a previous trip two decades before, "Nineteen seventy-three or -four, wasn't it?" But he received only a grunt of acknowledgment from Naomi in return.

She was right to be upset, he felt. It was too bad to miss a chance to view once more, things are often better the second time, those eerie, looming portraits, each made of thousands of little ceramic bits. The portraits depicted leading personalities of both Testaments, all looking heavenward with rapt, black-rimmed eyes. Harry

Eldernapped

remembered well their tortured, ecstatic faces erupting like explosions out of the high darkness and he recalled the chill they had sent down his spine. They've been staring like that for fourteen centuries, he reflected, but today, not for us.

Emily, Dorothy and Pete were even more upset. They had never seen the Ravenna mosaics at all, and now, along with the missing Marguerite, never would. Under a cloud of gloom, all of them turned and reentered the Casa del Santo, making their way to the Senior Seminars classroom, as Julie had instructed them.

"Sorry you're going to have to miss the Ravenna tour," she told them. Since they had been the only witnesses to the senseless abduction of the unfortunate Marguerite, who was still missing, the Padua police had called early that morning to request a meeting with them. "Nothing we at Senior Seminars can do about it...police business, you know," were Julie's final words before she got on the bus. In fact, that meeting was due to begin in the next few minutes.

They straggled into the lecture hall to find it empty of its customary, lively pre- and post-lecture people-clusters and their sounds. There was none of the joshing or horsing around characteristic of students everywhere. Nor was there the buzz of a dozen simultaneous conversations on a dozen different subjects. Not even on the most popular subject of all, matters medical.

Was it not just yesterday during the break, Harry recalled, that Harriet Aptheker, once an editor in a Grand Rapids' publishing firm, had demonstrated her high tech pill-reminderer. with every capsule, tablet, cap tab and soft gel in its own designated compartment? It chirped electronically when it sensed that the next dose was about to be forgotten. At which point, Bill Ekdahl, hoping to one-up Harriet, had countered with his newly discovered high intensity, yet minimal-side-effect, anti-inflammatory medication for joint pains. He was trying it out this week for the first time, but he'd noticed no difference.

George Freedman

Harry felt as he had when he was a kid, and was sure that every one of the other four felt the same. Each of them must be able to call up a particular, unhappy childhood moment, when because of some ailment or breach of decorum they had been made to stay behind, while their siblings and pals, chattering and with bright faces flushed with expectant pleasure, had gone off to the beach or a ball game or a picnic in the country or a day in the city.

The five shuffled into their customary seats around the room, amazing, Harry noted, how swiftly seat patterns establish themselves. Each of them seemed to be at a loss for something to do, so some of them drummed their fingernails on their desktops and others looked at the walls and ceilings as though they had never seen them before. Except for Harry, who instead fixed his attention on each of them in turn.

He could see that Pete's wound of the night before was not so angry looking now, and required no more than a small rectangular strip of plaster to protect it from further harm. The man looked the same as he did the first day they all had met, dapper in his blue blazer with its military-looking brass buttons, highlighted by the aristocratic, silken white ascot at his throat. As always, he gave the impression that, were he not here, he would be on his way to yacht races at Newport.

Dorothy, a forced, half smile on her broad pink face, wore a loose, flowered, print dress. Nearly a week of Senior Seminars sessions had established that, with minor variations, this would be her daily costume.

Turning next to Emily, Harry saw that she was wearing a simple, dark ensemble of maroon pants with maroon turtleneck sweater and maroon flat shoes. Her white hair was coiled into a bun in back. A thin gold chain hung around her neck. She looked solemn and dignified as befitted her years, and tight-lipped and grim as befitted the occasion.

Eldernapped

Harry went so far as to include himself in his survey. He knew that in repose, with his wire glasses on his high, wide forehead, he was cerebral looking. Yet, he thought he gave an energetic, almost youthful impression as well, for just as his thinning hair had not gone all the way to gray, his body had not gone everywhere to fat. He was in chinos, a lumberjack shirt of checked green and heavy-soled walking shoes. On his lap rested his familiar, visored cap which bore his ship's name, "USS LST 1026" and a small medallion that said "Amphibious Fleet." He had picked it up last year at the reunion that marked the fiftieth anniversary of its launching. Only twenty-nine of the original crew of eighty-eight had made it to that reunion, all sailors grown old.

His eyes fell on Naomi. She was stylish as always, wearing a light blue silk blouse that set off her smooth face and thick wavy white hair, a gray vest sweater, neat gray slacks and gray walking shoes. A pin of blue/green turquoise carved in Hopi style, purchased during the Arizona Senior Seminar, was affixed to the sweater on its left side, where it provided a single, dramatic spot of color. With the aluminum cane leaning against her chair, she gave a harmonious impression of cool silvery tones. But she disrupted this air of serenity as she asked, in a voice full of annoyance and impatience, "Where is that detective already?"

The silent room switched in a flash to a new and energetic scene. The door at the back of the classroom swung open and in strode Lieutenant Detective, *Agente Investigativo*, Luigi Cataldo of the Padua Police Department. They had met him late the previous evening, which, in fact, was earlier this morning. He was forty-five-ish, of medium height, with pale skin, light brown hair and brown eyes behind brown-framed eyeglasses. He wore a plain, loose-fitting, dark suit with a white shirt and a narrow black tie. His face featured both horizontal and vertical lines that delineated a tight mouth and a furrowed brow. A serious man, was Harry's appraisal,

Trailing him was a new actor in this drama. He had not been with the other policemen at the early morning session. He was younger than Cataldo and taller, also in civilian clothes, but these, in contrast to the attire of his boss, were form-fitting and in the latest Continental style.

Extending the contrast, this young man was of smiling demeanor and of darker aspect, with black hair and eyes. Quite handsome, in fact, according to no less an expert than Naomi. At a propitious moment, she whispered this observation to her husband, who was not surprised to hear it from her. He was introduced as Cataldo's second-in-command, Sergeant, *Brigadiere*, Franco Repucci.

Walking in behind them and closing the door after herself, representing Senior Seminars Management and for that reason not accompanying Julie and the others to Ravenna, was the second-in-command of the Padua sessions, Signorina Graziella Parziale.

She wore a short-sleeved, pink blouse embroidered with black thread. It had a wide neckline that showed off the freckled, light tan skin of her throat and chest. Her red skirt was full and edged in flounces. Sandals, with thongs that wound around her calves completed her ensemble. With her large hair and dangling jewelry at her ears, neck and wrists, she could have doubled for Carmen Harry imagined. He suspected, however, that he would never learn if she could sing the part. Whether or not the Carmen metaphor was apt, the fact was she made a striking figure, which was not lost on Sergeant Repucci. From the moment she first appeared, he seemed to have difficulty taking his eyes off her.

Noting the young man's reaction, Harry recalled a remark Naomi had made a few days before. "Our lovely Graziella is the essence of Italian womanhood.".

"Then why is it that I've never seen another Italian woman who looks like her?" Harry replied.

Eldernapped

The two law officers seated themselves in a pair of classroom chairs. The others took seats around them. Before the business of the day began, there was a knock at the door.

"I ordered coffee," said Graziella. A wheeled cart laden with a coffee urn and cups and a tray of almond biscotti made its way into the classroom.

In his quite understandable English, Cataldo got right down to business with a directness that was indistinguishable, Harry thought, from the style of any detective in any large city in the United States, if not, indeed, from those in "Law and Order," "Homicide" or "NYPD Blue." He nodded to Graziella to acknowledge her helpful presence, then turned to the five Americans. He thanked them for their willingness to give up their regular school day in order to participate in this meeting.

"I don't know if you can help us find the poor, unfortunate Signora LoPresti and the criminals who abducted her," he said. "But if anyone can help, you are probably going to be the best ones. Signorina Julie Foster tells me that you probably know Signora LoPresti better than anyone else, and, of course, all of you were witnesses to the criminal act itself. Please indulge me as I ask questions, and when you have something to say, please speak up."

He turned to Emily. "From our discussion early this morning," Cataldo began, "you claim you were the target of this abduction, Signora Thorndike, and not Signora LoPresti. What can you tell us about all this?"

"Quite a lot," Emily said. But before I get started, I have to make a statement about my name. Thorndike is not my real name. But of all the names I've had in the last two years, I've liked this one the best. Even better than my real name, which is Lucille Adams as you must know or suspect by now. So since you already think of me as Emily Thorndike, Emily Thorndike I'll be. Therefore...please...call me Emily."

"No problem, Signora Thorndike...Emily," Cataldo said. Now he paused. Everyone could see that he had one more thing he wanted to say before turning the floor completely over to her. Harry was gratified that it turned out to be the classic, cautionary admonition to the effect that she should try to tell no more than the facts, ma'am, just the facts. He thus implied that if she did so, he would try to keep from interrupting.

"It's my daughter, Roberta," she began. "She's responsible for all this. From the time she was a little girl, Roberta always had to be in charge of everything. Everything always had to be just her way...and her way right now is that I have to be put away. Old folks, my age anyway, have to be in old folks' homes. That's what she thinks."

"A bitch...we know the type," Harry muttered, but in such a low voice that only Naomi could hear him.

To which Naomi replied through clenched lips, "Which shows that even nice parents can have rotten daughters."

"'Roberta,' I'd tell her." Emily went on, "'One day you'll be old, too. Then, would you want to be imprisoned in a living morgue with a bunch of zombies, with nothing to do but wait for death?' But she doesn't answer me. She's always sure she knows the right thing to do. And nothing can change her mind.

"'You know what you are, Roberta?' I always say to her, 'You're a damn, conceited smartass! And a mean one to boot.'" Emily broke into a mirthless laugh. "That always pisses her off," she added, a note of satisfaction in her voice.

This crude language from tiny, refined Emily took her listeners aback and even non-English-speaking Franco seemed to sense that something unusual had been said. He leaned over to his boss who, in a few words, must have imparted its gist to him. Then he looked as astonished as the rest.

Emily had more to say on this subject. "Roberta thinks that I can't take care of myself. Let me ask you," her eyes sweeping the faces around her, "can I take care of myself?"

All her classmates nodded in the affirmative.

"She's even accused me of being dangerous to others. Once she even called me homicidal. How can a little old crock like me be dangerous to others? Or homicidal?"

There were explosive and indignant responses from those gathered round.

"Ridiculous!"

"Unbelievable!"

"Have-you-ever-heard-the-like!"

Except from Harry, who made no comment.

"She made matters even worse than they might have been," Emily continued, a hint of emotional trembling in her voice now. "No retirement home for me, as Roberta saw it. Or even one of those assisted living places. And no ordinary nursing home either. She always got me into special mental nursing homes, where the senile dementias and the Alzheimers people are kept and where they have ways to make sure no one ever is free to walk out or escape...because the Alzheimers wander, you know.

"Do you want me to tell you how they can tell when someone has walked out? Electronics. High tech electronics. They lock a special bracelet on your wrist that rings a bell if you go through an outside door. But those bracelets were never any problem to me, ha-ha." Her laugh sounded bitter. "My wrists are so skinny that, with the help of a little butter or lotion, I can always slip out of them."

"I am sorry to interrupt, Emily," Cataldo said. "And I know I said I would not do this...but will you kindly more quickly get to how this relates to the abduction of Signora LoPresti?"

"Of course, of course, but I assure you, you have to know all that I am telling you. So may I continue?"

"Please, please, dear lady...continue."

"Even after slipping off the bracelets, that still wasn't enough. I still had to find a way to get out and get away. Each time I escaped from one of those geriatric zoos, I had to resort to a bit of physical action. There was no other way. And that's probably where Roberta gets off calling me dangerous and homicidal.

"Let's see, there were three of those awful homes that Roberta put me into...one after the other...claiming all the time that I was too senile and incompetent to take care of myself. Three. But I was able to skedaddle from all three of them.

"After the first one, Roberta hired private...what do you call them...eyes, to search me out and abduct me and put me right back into stir again."

"Stir, stir?" Cataldo asked.

"Confinement," Harry explained.

"Aha," Cataldo said, a look of comprehension replacing his former one of puzzlement. This led Harry to realize that although the man knew some essential American argot as it related to criminals, his vocabulary was limited. He suspected that Cataldo would have liked to ask for the meaning of skedaddle as well.

There was a flurry of activity near Franco, caused by Graziella's moving her chair next to his. It seemed she was taking it on herself to assist Cataldo by translating the gist of Emily's disquisition for his sergeant.

"First, there was Cliffwalk Mansion in Newport," Emily went on, bending back the forefinger of her left hand with that of her right in order to emphasize the firstness of Cliffwalk Mansion. "That one was a snap. All I had to do was tie Hazel Landry, the director, onto the toilet seat in her executive bathroom, which certainly did her no harm, because I later heard they found her the next morning and freed her."

Eldernapped

"Attagirl," Harry mouthed, his lips moving, but without accompanying sound.

"It was just after that, that I started to have unpleasant interactions with Roberta's private detectives. She kept hiring new ones every time I got away...and you'll have to excuse me, Lieutenant Cataldo, I don't think much of detectives. In my experience, I find them to be a pretty dumb lot. But I suppose you'll tell me private detectives are the rejects, the ones who flunk out of police school, who couldn't make it as regular cops, and that's why they're so dumb."

Not waiting for what might have been his views on this subject, she went on with her account. "I kept a step ahead of them for a couple of weeks, but in the end they caught up with me in a barbecue restaurant near Chattanooga. Dumb as they were, they did manage to find me.

"Anyway, after I got caught in Chattanooga, Roberta had me put into a nuthatch for the elderly near Austin, Texas, called Longhorn Ranch. That was a lot harder to break out of, but a combination of a bribe to one guard, and a slug on the head to another with a hammer I found in a garden shed, did it. And I was careful. I didn't hit him any harder than just enough to knock him out. At worst it might have caused a mild concussion, no more."

"She's something, isn't she?" Harry whispered to Naomi.

"You can say that again," Naomi whispered back.

"Then...damn...the same thing happened. Once again, they found me. This time Roberta had hired two entirely different private investigators. I was enjoying the drag show at the Crown and Anchor on Commercial St. in Provincetown, when this new pair caught up with me. Still, I was doing better. It took the first PIs only two weeks to catch up with me, but I had been on the road for three months before those second guys finally fingered me and took me away with them.

Cataldo sighed for the obvious reason that he did not understand what was meant by "fingered". But before he could ask, Franco, now the beneficiary of a blow-by-blow from Graziella and thus up to the instant on what was being disclosed, leaned over to impart the meaning of this term into his superior's ear.

Emily took a deep breath and went on to number three. "The most recent nursing home I escaped from," she said in a casual tone as though she did such a thing every day, "was Misty Vista on the Blue Ridge Highway just outside of Asheville. I'm proudest of that getaway because it was the cleverest." A devilish look suffused her narrow seamed face and with flicks of her tiny pink tongue she seemed, cat-like, to be licking her lean chops with admiration for her own imagination and resourcefulness.

"I didn't have to use any physical force at all in that one," Emily made clear. "What I did...I searched out their cache of sleeping pills for the other poor old inmates and ground up about two hundred of them with the V-8 juice that the guards and staff had for breakfast that day.

"The funny thing was, it didn't even put them to sleep," she chortled. "It just made them kind of dull and they sat there like robots and waved goodbye as I walked out and got into the taxi I'd called from the phone in the director's office. Now I ask you, were any of those things dangerous, as Roberta says? No. I tell you, in every thing I did, I was especially careful not to hurt anybody...not permanently anyway."

"Really, Signora Thorndike...Emily," Cataldo said, a note of exasperation in his voice, "can we get down to business? Remember, we want to find Signora LoPresti and the information about how you escaped three times hardly seems to bear on this case."

"After that last escape," Emily continued without pause, almost as though she had not heard Cataldo's admonition, "I knew I had to change my tactics. I realized that wherever I went, even dumb detectives would find me.

Eldernapped

Because, even though you wouldn't think so, a little old lady on the lam stands out like a...a..."

"Sore thumb?" Dorothy suggested.

"Thank you, Dorothy dear. Sore thumb. So it was then I thought of Senior Seminars. I knew that in a Senior Seminar I wouldn't stand out...not too much, anyway. So I've been Seminaring-it for the last two years or so. And Roberta never found me...till now. What do you think of that?"

A stunned silence followed as everyone in the room contemplated the extraordinary adventures their friend had been through. What will she tell us next, Harry wondered. He got his answer in short order, for she offered, "Oh, you're wondering where I got money to travel around on my own? Well, money has never been my problem. I have this secret bank account in Boulder, which I set up years ago when I taught at the university there...just in case I ever got short. I just dial in my special number and then, in another fake name I use for this purpose, a line of credit rings up in a local bank.

"Which brings me to this locality right here and right now. The stumblebums who did the job on Marguerite last night again were a wholly new pair," she went on. "Never saw them before I hit the Venice Airport a few days ago. They were also the same ones that stormed our bus and followed us into the Scrovegni Chapel the other day. No question...those where the very same guys. But they made a mistake, the numskulls. They nabbed poor Marguerite instead.

"I suppose she looks a little like me. Still, they should have known she wasn't me. You can't believe how incredibly imbecilic they are..."

"Nabbed?" Cataldo asked, a puzzled look once again on his face.

"Surprised you don't know that expression, Chief Investigator," attorney Pete offered, "It's a term commonly used by American police. Nabbing is what police do. It means intercepting while the quarry is in a condition of flight from authority. Or, at the same time, stated more succinctly, but just as comprehensively, apprehending."

Dorothy smiled at Pete with approval.

Cataldo's reaction was not so favorable. His English was good, but not that good. And the look of puzzlement on his face remained.

No-nonsense Naomi bailed him out. About time. She's never so quiet for so long, and Harry was wondering when she would speak out about something, anything. "Caught," she said, "when they nabbed her, they caught her."

"Aha." Cataldo said.

Franco had a point to make, which he did in Italian. It must have had significance, for it caused Cataldo's brows to lift and his head to nod in approval. *Buon idea*, Franco," he said.

"Sergeant Repucci and I would like to know, Emily," he said, turning back to her and speaking English once more, "whether you feel you can identify those detectives who you say abducted Signora LoPresti. I know you gave us a sketchy description of them earlier, when we first met in this room. But, after all, you only saw them for a few seconds under poor conditions when they abducted her, and also when you were running away from them in the airport and for a moment in the Scrovegni."

"But the rest of us saw them," Naomi pointed out. "I'm sure we can make a valid identification if Emily can't."

"'What do you mean, Naomi, 'if Emily can't,'" Emily cried, testiness in her voice. "I certainly can. I can even give you their names."

"Really? Very good. Will you please describe them and give us their names?" Cataldo said.

"I even talked to them. They spotted me in the Venice airport as I arrived and introduced themselves. But I knew what they were up to, and just as they were about to put their hands on me, I escaped into the ladies' room.

Eldernapped

"There's Big Sam. Vinny kept calling him Big Sam. Sam Peterson is his name, a big lug with a big belly, brown hair and a wide mustache. The other one is small, skinny, all bones he is...Vinny Anzaldi. He has a mustache, too, and awful skin, must have had bad acne when he was a kid. Both are around thirty-five or forty. A couple of cut-rate private eyes from Secaucus in Jersey. Look, they even gave me their card." Searching for a moment in her knapsack, she produced it and gave it to Cataldo.

"Meadowbrook Detective Agency," he read aloud, "Secaucus, New Jersey, Samuel Peterson, President, Vincent Anzaldi, Vice President."

"And here is where Roberta stops taking after her father," Emily said, her eyes narrowing. "Robert always went first class in everything he did. Even nasty things were done well. But she's stingy. In addition to being overbearing and bossy, she's always trying to save money.

"Anyway, getting back to those two bums, even as they had their hands on me, I managed to persuade them to let me go to the ladies' room."

"Did they follow you?"

"As a matter of fact, after I had been in there a few minutes, they did...and a couple of women there got a bit uncomfortable because men were in their toilet. But they were calmer than American women would have been. Americans have a bigger hang-up about toilets than Europeans."

"I suppose you found a way to get away from these men this time, too."

"I certainly did. I told them I had to pee, and they said okay, and that they would wait for me outside. What else could they say when a geriatric case asks to use the john? You want to know how I did it?"

Cataldo shrugged and asked with resignation. "All right, tell us how you did it."

"Well, first I looked over the ceilings above each stall and picked the one where the heating duct ended.

After I closed the stall door, I climbed up and removed the filter panel that closed it up. Then I squeezed in and put the filter back behind me. Five minutes later, Sam and Vinny got impatient and burst into all the stalls...only to find me missing. Of course, it never occurred to them to look in the heating duct."

Several people in the room smiled. Harry nudged Naomi, who glared back at him in response. He could see she thought he wasn't taking this matter seriously enough.

"I stayed in the duct for about an hour," Emily said. If I've learned anything about escaping from dumb cops, it is never to hurry. Then I left the ladies' room and the PIs were nowhere to be found. I made my way to the bus, hiding behind some posts along the way.

"Flitted," Harry offered.

"That's right. I flitted from post to post. What an apt descriptive word, Mr. Levine." She paused. "Is this okay, Detective Cataldo? Am I doing all right?"

"Very nice, Emily. Are you finished?"

The guy's hoping against hope that she is, Harry guessed, because, interesting though her tale has been, she's been rattling on non-stop for quite a while now.

"Well yes, that's about all I have to tell. Except for one more thing. I just want to say what a good idea I had...using Senior Seminars, I mean. I've loved my two years at so many different Senior Seminar programs."

"We all love Senior Seminars," Dorothy broke in. "In fact, that's why we're all here."

Cataldo nodded to Dorothy in a courtly European way by way of noting the value of her contribution and then turned his attention once more to Emily. "I do want to thank you for your very detailed statement, Emily. It will certainly be very helpful in our investigation of this case.

"Now, I would like to ask each of the rest of you a number of questions." Harry felt Cataldo's eyes singling him out, and thought, why not? Very perceptive of the

Eldernapped

lieutenant to realize that I can wind up this interview session for him sooner and better than any of the others. Which means that I'll be next on the dock. Well, that's okay with me. I'm ready for him.

Except that Emily seemed to be having second thoughts about giving up the floor. "Well, I do have a little more to add that might be useful to you, Lieutenant," she said. "As I just told you, I've been taking these seminar courses for quite a while...and in all that time no one knew where I was. Roberta must have been furious." This last comment was followed by an elderly giggle. "Or maybe she thought I was dead." Again, she giggled. "I must have been to a couple of dozen such programs, and not only did I learn so much about so many interesting things...just like being in college again...I have met the most wonderful people...like the ones in this room this minute. And let me make it clear, I do so love Senior Seminars, don't you?" she asked them.

She had repeated herself. Harry, as well as Pete, Dorothy and Naomi, were sympathetic to this condition, being prone to it themselves. So, as with one voice, they all summoned up words of agreement to the effect that indeed, they, too, loved all the Senior Seminars they had attended and all the nice people they had met.

"And every so often," Emily went on, now on a roll once more, "I would change my name just to help cover my tracks. Let's see, for the first dozen or so seminars, I was Alicia Hapgood. Ceci is short for Alicia, so I went by Ceci Hapgood, actually. Ceci and I were good friends as girls when we went to Miss Porter's School together, but she's been gone for the last thirty years or so. Anyway she was very nice, and I was sure she wouldn't mind my using her name for a while.

"After I was Ceci, I decided to become Norma Desmond, from 'Sunset Boulevard,' you know? I got a great kick out of being Norma, and as a lark, for the breakup party at one Senior Seminar, I actually bought a turban hat and a short dress like we used to wear when we were flappers in the twenties. They made a great hit.

"You'll never believe who I was next." A twinkle of deviltry filled her eyes. "Charlotte Bronte...and don't you think that caused some comment? Everyone bought my story that I was a descendant in a cousin line...because as you all know, poor Charlotte married late and died young, and thus never had any direct descendants of her own.

"But finally I got tired of being Charotte Bronte and I've been Emily Thorndike for at least the last six or eight programs. And in the end that didn't work either, because, as you can see, Roberta finally found me, even way out here, in out-of-the-way, boondock Padua.

"Oh, I'm sorry..." realizing that with this remark she might have hurt Cataldo's feelings. "Don't get me wrong, Lieutenant. I think Padua's really very nice."

Her embarrassment caused the gallant Cataldo to raise his hand to calm her. His eyes, which Harry observed had been glazing over, cleared, and he said, "Please, dear lady, do not give this a thought. Please go on...unless you are finished with your statement. Are you in fact..." he sighed, "finished?"

No such luck. Not quite. After a deep breath, a signal that for her next comments she would pursue a different train of thought, she did go on. "Of course," she said, "I knew that at least one of our children would have to take after their father...and it turned out to be Roberta. Every time I look at her I see Robert. Not only is she the spitting image of him, but the way she talks and thinks, too. Except for that stinginess of course, her resemblance to him is almost uncanny.

"And it had to be the girl. Why couldn't it have been one of the boys instead? Be like Robert, I mean. But they're both soft as Jell-O..., which means that Roberta can make my sons do anything she wants them to. So we mustn't judge poor Justin too harshly. Even though, of course, he's the one who's here with Big Sam and Vinny

Eldernapped

and is trying to kidnap me. He's only doing it because Roberta has put him up to it."

At last. This is what everyone had been waiting for with grim patience. "Justin. Who is Justin? Justin what?" Cataldo asked, "Please tell me, Emily, what is his surname?"

"Wharton, of course. Justin Wharton. My oldest child with my first husband Robert Wharton, who was also Roberta's father and Gordie's father. But, as I said, only Roberta takes after him. And, to tell the truth, I don't know whom Justin and Gordie take after. Certainly not me either.

"Of course, Roberta's son Albert or Arthur, whatever she named him...you know when you have as many grandchildren as I have, it's hard to keep track of all their names...and now that I am living as a vagabond, I don't have all my old Christmas lists, so I am actually in danger of losing some grandchildren altogether...anyway, that one seems to have some of the original Wharton spunk. Only in his early thirties, and he's already running Wharton Valve. Robert would have been proud of him."

Was that a sentimental tear that trembled in the corner of her eye? Unbelievable. It was, Harry realized. And she wiped it away with her handkerchief.

Cataldo took advantage of this pause to say, "Have you seen this Justin Wharton here in Padova, Emily? Is there any possibility that you know where he is? Of course, right now our priority is to find Signora LoPresti and it seems very likely that this Signor Wharton has had her abducted, thinking she was you. So we very much want to find him. Do you understand, Emily?"

"Of course I understand. Do you think I'm slow-witted just because I'm a bit on in years? If you wanted to know where Justin is, you only had to ask in the first place and not waste all this time. I want to find dear Marguerite just as much as you do. He's staying at the Plaza Hotel right here in this town."

That galvanized the policeman. Cataldo leaped to his feet and, fixing his eyes on Franco, spat out a few Italian words, among the recognizable was the phrase, "Plaza Hotel."

With the same degree of alacrity, Franco jumped up and stumbled over Graziella, whose chair somehow had taken up a position so close to his as to touch it. After asking her forgiveness for his clumsiness, which she gave with a gracious smile, he burst out of the room.

"Guess who's dashing over to the Plaza Hotel," Naomi said.

"We can guess," her four comrades responded.

♦ ♦ ♦ ♦

Hours had passed. It was now approaching lunchtime, and the five senior seminarians huddled around two small, pushed together tables in the hotel bar. Joining them, was a sixth person, Graziella. Hovering above and around the assemblage, was Linda. She took away empty espresso cups and replaced them with full ones. Linda was as much part of the group as though she were the seventh member.

"Quite a morning," Pete commented. "After he finished with Emily, that Lieutenant Cataldo put each of us through as thorough an investigation as I have ever seen in the United States." This was uttered with such an air of assurance that everyone knew that in his professional capacity as an attorney he had seen more than a few.

"At first it was almost as though we were suspects ourselves," Naomi offered. "But of course we're not. Rather, we're helpers, almost like assistant detectives. As Lieutenant Luigi said...he did say we could call him Luigi after I asked him if we could...when this case gets solved and we get Marguerite back, we...this little group right here in this very espresso bar...will probably have a lot to

Eldernapped

do with it. When he said that, I could tell he really meant it."

Hearing this from Naomi did not make Harry happy. He knew his wife, and he suspected the worst. "Careful, my love," he said, "I know Lieutenant Luigi...Luigi...hah...will appreciate any help you can give him...but don't go overboard...."

"I've never met a detective before," Naomi went on without pause, as though she had not even heard Harry's cautionary words. "Are they all so reasonable and intelligent? He surely looks as though he's a very nice, steady young man. In fact, he looks like a family man.

"Yes," Graziella confirmed. "He is a family man. But not really so young. He has three children, one in college already." All eyes turned to her as though to inquire how she knew, and she, sensing their question, added, "Franco told me."

"You know, now I'm glad we stayed this morning after all," Naomi said, "because what's more important, going on one more Senior Seminars bus ride or rescuing Marguerite?"

Harry did not share her glad feeling. "As I just told you, Naomi, don't get carried away. I've lived with you for over fifty years, and even though you've always been able to be and do a lot of different things...and I must admit, you've often surprised me...you've never come across as much of a detective, even an assistant detective. Remember what Cataldo told us. This is a very tough case, because as small as Padua is, there are over a quarter million people here.

"As he pointed out," Harry went on, "we don't even have a photograph of Marguerite to publicize...like in the newspapers or on flyers on lamp posts or on the news on TV...that say, 'Have you seen this woman?.' Here in Padua she's a needle in a haystack. And there are damned few clues."

"That's not really so," Emily reminded him. "I did give Justin's description and that of the two sleazy PI's to Lieutenant Cataldo. That ought to help."

"You're quite right, Emily," Pete agreed. "You gave invaluable information which we would otherwise never have obtained. And the fact that you figured out that they would be staying at the Plaza Hotel...talk about detective work...that was very clever of you, Emily."

"Just like I told my boyfriend, Joey," Linda piped up, who had taken up a position just back of Emily's chair, so as to be able to pat her right shoulder with grand daughterly affection, "my Grammy is sure a smarty."

"But they are no longer at the Plaza Hotel," Graziella pointed out. "You remember, only fifteen minutes after Franco left here he called back from the Plaza to tell the lieutenant that all three men had checked out early this morning. And they left no forwarding address."

"Damn!" Pete exploded. "Just as fast as we find them, we lose them."

"Do not be discouraged, Mr. Caldwell," Graziella continued. "You recall that Lieutenant Cataldo was going to...what, what did he call it...?"

"Put a trail on them," Naomi said, helping her out. "Or is it a bug?"

"Yes, put a trail," Graziella said. "Taxis, rental car agencies, airport departures, apartments for rent, things like that. And by now all that has already been started by Franco. He will find out where they are hiding out. He thinks they must be in some kind of hideaway someplace nearby."

"Hide-out," Naomi corrected.

"Hide-out," Graziella accepted. "Because according to the hotel people, they had no woman like Marguerite with them, so they must already have put her in that hide-out."

Graziella now drew a long, deep breath that allowed her to segue gracefully into another subject. "But

Eldernapped

in the meantime," she said, "Franco is coming back here very soon. He and I have an appointment for twelve o'clock so I can show him Mrs. LoPresti's file."

"Good for you," Naomi reacted with enthusiasm. Then, concerned that her words would be given an incorrect interpretation, went on to note that, "Of course, who else could do that? You're the one who has everyone's file, aren't you?"

"But what do you have in the file?" Harry said. "Not much. After having attended five Senior Seminars before this one, as I remember it, all that you administration people have on Naomi and me is our names and birth dates and social security numbers, as well as the fact that Naomi is allergic to penicillin. And, oh yes...plus a list of our major chronic conditions. That's all."

"Quite true," Pete said. " What is coming out of all this talk is how little we really know that's going to help us find Marguerite. Come to think about it," his eyes sweeping all the faces around him, "we know almost nothing about any of us. After all, we only met for the first time just four days ago."

"And yet we are already such good friends," Dorothy added with a smile.

"You are not quite right, lover," Naomi said, her mind still on what Harry had pointed out, "You haven't given us a complete rundown of what the Seminars people have on us. They also have Judy's and Debby's phone numbers to contact in the event of an emergency...our daughters," she explained to the others. "And didn't Marguerite say she had two sons?"

"One a lawyer and the other some sort of businessman, both in Cincinnati," Dorothy recalled.

"Yes, in fact I do have that information with Mrs. LoPresti's sons' phone numbers all ready for Sergeant Repucci in our business office," said Graziella, quite businesslike now, and she tossed her head in its direction in the main hotel building.

"So Lieutenant Luigi, or Sergeant Franco for that matter, once he gets their phone numbers from Graziella here," Naomi continued, "can call those sons and tell them of this terrible occurrence, and they can certainly provide pictures of their mother or anything else the police may need.

"In fact, maybe one of them should fly right out here to be a material witness or something. No question, if anything like this had happened to Harry or me, both my Judy and my Debby...not just one of them, but both...would be here by now. By the way, how does a material witness differ from an ordinary witness?"

Pete was about to clear up Naomi's confusion on the different kinds of witnesses, when Harry, sputtering a bit, butted in. "By God, she does sound like a detective," he said. "Where do you get your technique, Naomi dear? From which crime show on TV? Let's see, Monsieur Poirot, we never miss one of his episodes. Or Inspector Morse, he always gets the murderer. Oh, I know, 'Murder She Wrote.' You think you're the Jewish Jessica Fletcher."

"Careful, big boy," Naomi rejoined. "You may have to eat your words because I think I know how to get this investigatory procedure off the ground. In fact I think I know exactly how to find Justin Wharton and Marguerite along with him.

The room fell quiet as everyone contemplated the significance of her remark. But not Naomi, she was already off on a different tack. "Anyway, what's wrong about being like Jessica Fletcher, which is to say, like Angela Lansbury?" she asked. "Of course, you've never noticed, husband dear, but she wears very smart and tasteful clothes for a woman of her age...not so different from the way I dress, as a matter of fact."

"Bullseye!" Harry said. "As usual, I'm right on. I'll have to warn all our friends never to invite you again for dinner parties. Now that you've become Jessica Fletcher, one of the guests is sure to be murdered by the time we get to dessert. Although, clever old broad that you

Eldernapped

are...excuse me, Naomi, I mean that Jessica is... you'll have that murder solved before midnight...while some poor slow-witted detective watches you do it, as though you were a genius."

Harry had more to say on this matter but his attention was now diverted by Dorothy who was waving her hand before his face. He could do no less than to yield the floor to her. She had been quite reserved till now, having participated only a little in the discussion, but it was evident that she had an important point to make.

"Lieutenant Cataldo really seems very smart to me, Harry," she said, "not slow-witted at all, and very nice in the bargain. I think, taking it all in all, and considering that we're are in a foreign country and all, we...and Marguerite...and Emily...are in good hands."

There was no question, to Harry at least, if not to all the others, that Dorothy had a positive genius for stating the obvious. There was an awkward silence for a moment while everyone mulled over what she had said, but Pete, always the gentleman, remarked, "Good point, Dorothy." .

"Well, I think so too," Emily added, picking up the ball from Pete. "And we need to be in good hands, because the problem, if you'll excuse me, is even more complicated than just the fact that they have kidnapped Marguerite, horrible though that is. Remember, that was a mistake...they are still after me."

Harry's eyes were fixed on Naomi's through all this diversionary dialogue, and he now said, "What did you mean just now, Naomi, when you said, you know how to find Justin and Marguerite, as though you really know how?

"Never mind."

"C'mon. Stop with the never mind. Do you really have some ideas on how to do this or don't you?" Harry was getting impatient.

"They can't be any good. I only get my ideas from watching silly TV detective shows, as you are always telling me."

"I never... well, hardly ever...tell you anything of the kind. But now, Naomi, tell us. What ideas?"

"Oh, I don't think you'd be interested. After all, my ideas are no more than the sort of thoughts that would occur to a woman. You would never think of them and neither would our clever Lieutenant Luigi. And both of you are probably right. In matters like this, you men certainly know best."

"All right," Harry said. He knew when he was beaten, having been through many similar conversations with Naomi during the preceding half century. Since he had to know what was in her mind, he had no choice but to capitulate without further fight. "You win," he moaned."

"Well," Naomi said, after taking a long breath and putting down her tiny coffee cup on its tiny dish, thus drawing out the moment of her upper hand as long as she could. "Consider this. In the short time we have known Marguerite, what have we all noticed about her?"

"She's such a nice, sweet person," Pete suggested.

"True, but that's not what I'm thinking of."

"Bright, intelligent, good looking," Harry offered.

"Always with the good looking. No, that's not it either."

"Well informed?" Emily said.

Naomi shook her head, no.

Silence. Every Senior Seminarian had given an opinion except Dorothy. All eyes were on her, now in deep thought. Then, at last, she offered her considered comments for all to hear, "Neat, dainty, stylish, well groomed."

"Good girl, Dorothy," was Naomi's smiling reaction. "You've hit the nail on the head. Whoever has Marguerite locked up in some hide-out...by which of course I mean Emily's despicable son, Justin...excuse me, Emily, but I

Eldernapped

think he must be just as awful as your Roberta...must have had an earful by now about the fact that a whole day has gone by...and she has not had a chance to change into clean underwear."

"Or a fresh blouse," Dorothy added, who Harry could see was now operating on a new high level of self-assurance.

"And she's slept the night, but with no nightgown." was Emily's additional contribution.

"It occurs to me that they probably provided some clothes for you, Emily," Naomi said, "But none of your clothes could fit her."

"Certainly not," Emily agreed. "Next to me, Marguerite is a giant."

"And another thing about Marguerite," Pete added, now onto a different train of thought. "She's quite strong in her opinions. Even in the few conversations I've had with her, I was impressed with how she always stands up for what she believes in. So I agree. She's probably giving that Justin hell, right now."

"All right, we all admit Marguerite is a neat, clean woman who likes to change her underwear and sleep in a nightie," Harry said. "So what?"

"I'll tell you so what, Harry, my love. But first...I can't believe you've lived with me all these years and this hasn't occurred to you, my big smart engineer husband. Neat as Marguerite is, I, your wife, am just as neat, not to mention dainty, stylish and well groomed, too. And in all those years, do you ever remember me going more than one day without my changing my intimate apparel?"

"Sometimes twice a day," he muttered in a chastened voice.

"And how long do you think they will want to keep poor Marguerite captive?" she went on, drumming her fingers on the tabletop.

"Until they collect my Grammy and get safely out of Italy and back to Woonsocket, R-I...and that could be, like, a long time?" Linda said. "Unless this other lady...Marguerite?...if she got away from them earlier some way, like escaping or finding a telephone...can tell us where they are."

" 'Tip us off' is the expression in this sort of circumstance, dear. Say tip us off," Emily instructed.

"Tip us off," Linda said.

"This is what I think, for what it's worth," Naomi continued in triumph, her eyes drilling into Harry's. "No earlier than eleven or midnight tonight, when he assumes we've all gone to bed, one of Justin's private investigators is going to try to sneak into this hotel and into Marguerite's room. She hung on to her purse when she was snatched, as any woman would, and that means she has her key with her. So the thug will have no problem unlocking the door to her room. Then he will empty her bureau drawers and closet and take out her suitcase of clothes...because sure as shooting, he won't want to go into some ladies' store in downtown Padua to buy her a whole new wardrobe while they're holding her."

Dorothy and Linda said Naomi's idea was brilliant and stated so without reserve. Emily voiced approval in a tone that combined mild enthusiasm with skepticism. Pete declared concurrence, but perhaps only to be polite. Graziella, possibly because of her status as mere employee, smiled without making a commitment.

As for Harry, he just drew a deep breath and shrugged his shoulders, but he could not restrain a glimmer of reluctant admiration in the look he now gave Naomi.

She wasn't through yet. "And don't you think," Naomi went on, her steely gaze now firmly on Harry and Pete, "somebody...maybe one or two of us...should be waiting in her room tonight to grab him when he comes?

♦ ♦ ♦ ♦

Except for the fact that the large stone building had been created in the sixteenth century by the school of the great local architect Palladio, Lieutenant Luigi Cataldo's fourth

Eldernapped

floor office in the Santo-district PPD headquarters resembled most of its sort to be found in the Western World. All the rooms and alcoves on that floor were defined by thin wallboard partitions of which Palladio would never have approved, and were painted the same ugly shade of light green favored by law enforcers everywhere.

Cataldo knew this to be the case since all the lead-cops in cop dramas shown, Italian-dubbed, on Padua TV worked in offices identical to his. These included, but were not limited to, those of Oxford's Detective Morse, Chief Inspector Maigret of the Paris Surete and Lieutenant Fancy of NYPD Blue.

He had been able to confirm this fact for himself. Some five years ago, taking advantage of a not to be resisted, one-time special, low round-trip airfare, he and his wife took a vacation in the States. They visited a cousin of hers, also a police detective, who had taken him one day to his headquarters in Precinct 90 in the Williamsburg section of Brooklyn. As he walked around, he felt as though he had never left home.

Cataldo sat at his desk, the top of which was clear but for a half-finished cup of coffee, a neat pile of papers located center front and a framed family portrait at its farthermost right corner. It showed his attractive, slightly overweight wife, a handsome teenage son, a pretty teenage daughter and another son, plump and preteen. He signaled through the waist high glass pane that separated him from the desks of his underlings for Franco to come in. He did, seating himself in a straight wooden armchair in front of Cataldo's desk.

"Would you believe," Franco asked, "that Levine woman actually wanted us to station one of our men around the clock in Mrs. LoPresti's empty room in the Casa del Santo? She insisted one of the kidnappers would be sure to break in there tonight to pick up some clothes for her. Or if not tonight, tomorrow." He followed this with a short chuckle.

Cataldo, not one given to easy laughter, sighed. But his basic reaction was the same. While he felt that he had no choice but to treat this Mrs. Levine with courtesy, it had to be coupled with dismissal, for was this not the naïve suggestion of an overactive imagination? And from an elderly American female, at that? And did not this mean that he was fated, unless he took clever precautions, to have other, larger problems with Mrs. Levine, if this case went on for a few more days? Not only her. This nice, earnest, motherly person will be certain to enlist her circle of aged, well meaning friends to join her in cluttering the path of his progress in solving this case. Which they must not be allowed to do, especially when a crime as serious as a kidnapping is concerned. We mustn't forget that the unfortunate Mrs. LoPresti has already been missing for almost an entire day.

On the other hand, he could tell that his assistant had something to offer of a more positive nature. Franco wanted to praise the swiftness and thoroughness of the aid he had received only an hour before from the Executive Office of the Senior Seminars organization. "The assistant administrator of that Office dug up, from her records, the names and telephone numbers of LoPresti's two sons in America," he said. "Both live in the province of Ohio, and since the assistant administrator speaks such good English she volunteered to call them for us. In fact, I'll be going over there again as soon as we finish here."

Cataldo chose to show no reaction to Franco's statement. Rather, he asked, "If you were a rich American, with a couple of detectives in tow to help you abduct your old mother...and you wanted to get her back to the States, and you learned that the police were after you...where, after checking out of the Hotel Plaza, would you go next?"

"I've been asking myself the same question, boss," Franco replied.

Eldernapped

They followed this dialogue with a detailed discussion dealing with the matter of setting up roadblocks, already done, at crucial intersections, tollbooths and other checkpoints both in and around Padua and elsewhere in the country. These extended from Turin and Milan in the west and along the Bergamo, Brescia, Bologna line to Venice in the east. Similar actions had been taken in the northern salient from Como, where the Swiss Alps begin, across to Udine at the Austrian border. As for the region south of Padua, an east-west line going through Rome covered it.

What Cataldo had done, in effect, was to issue and implement an all-points alert, a dragnet. It included descriptions of each of the fugitives, as well as the large black late-model Fiat in which they would most likely be traveling, along with pertinent particulars about its rental history.

Franco had learned that morning where the Fiat had been rented. It was from the Hertz agency in downtown Padua's Plaza La Stanga, three days before. The customer was a Signor J. Wharton of Woonsocket on the island of Rhode in the United States, and Signor Samuel Peterson was listed as alternate driver. It had not been turned in as yet, but that was a matter of no concern to Hertz, since, according to their records, the renter had not specified a date of return, other than to indicate that it would be for no longer than six or seven days at most.

The alert detailed that this car would, in all likelihood, be carrying four English speaking passengers, three male, one female, two of the males in their forties and the other male and the female in their sixties, along with descriptions of their physical characteristics. And all should be carrying American passports.

A cautionary statement was added to the effect that while none of these people was expected to be armed, they would stop at nothing by way of bribery or trickery in order to attain their goal of getting out of the country. They will be inhibited by a ready cash problem at some point, and they will have no choice but to resort to the use of traveler's checks, personal checks, credit cards or ATM machines.

"I would bet that's how we'll get our first lead," Franco mused. But Cataldo, less ready to speculate, took no position either way.

Similar alerts had been posted at taxi stands, airports, railroad and bus stations, ferry ports and even vaparetto docks.

Cataldo and Franco then went on, their voices a quiet murmur, to a different tack—one which posited the premise that the kidnappers were still in the immediate neighborhood. "It's certainly a good idea to stake out all of Northern Italy as we have done, but I have a feeling that they've never left Padua or its vicinity," Cataldo said as he produced a large street map of the city and its suburbs. He unfolded the map and spread it out on his desk. With heads together, the two perused it, their attention focusing first on one locality, then another. This led to the formulation of a number of well-considered scenarios the fugitives might attempt by way of escaping the region.

Cataldo always liked to bounce ideas off others and to listen well to those they might offer him. He believed that no idea, no matter how outrageous, should be rejected without careful consideration, unless it's of the sort that had been offered by Naomi Levine, which had already been forgotten.

"Damn," Cataldo said, interrupting these quiet ruminations without warning. "I forgot to alert Passport Checking. "

Being a man of quick decisions, he picked up his phone and with a few terse words, corrected that oversight. He thus enlisted the aid of the province's efficient passport checking bureau. It would determine in short order whether passports for any of the Wharton party had been turned in on registering, as Italian law requires, at a hotel, motel, inn or pensione anywhere in northern Italy.

Eldernapped

"They're activating their network at once," he informed Franco with satisfaction as he returned the telephone to its cradle. Good boss that he was, he hoped Franco had paid close attention to what he just did and how he did it. The prompt, purposeful action he took was a good example for the young man, and it should benefit him as his career developed.

These deliberations went on for another hour, and would have lasted longer, except for the unannounced appearance of Chief Rudolfo Nutile. Nutile was head of the Padua Police Department and the boss of Cataldo's boss. He brought an air of urgency with him. He would not sit down, nor did he come all the way into the office. He just stood at the open door.

Chief Nutile was reassured to some small degree by the actions Cataldo had initiated, but a worried look remained on his face. "This case has international ramifications," he said, "I wouldn't be surprised to hear from the American Consulate before the day is over."

"Don't worry, Chief," Cataldo said. "We've got every aspect of this case covered. I expect to have the LoPresti woman back and those kidnappers locked up in very short order. There is no way they can get very far out of Padua or engage in any activity within the city without our intercepting them. But just in case they do manage it, we've got all of northern Italy covered."

Something in Cataldo's voice must not have resonated with as much confidence as his words indicated. "Very short order is not good enough," the Chief expostulated. "I want this case cleaned up by no later than this time tomorrow!" And with that, flashing a glaring look—first at Cataldo and then at Franco—he turned and left.

◆ ◆ ◆ ◆

It was getting on to ten in the evening and the Casa del Santo was settling into its routine of quiet after dinner inactivity. As Harry walked by the Casa's deserted dining room he could see that all chairs had been upended and cantilevered with their seats resting on their respective tabletops, leaving the floors clear for vacuuming and mopping to be done before breakfast the next morning. Most other guests were either in their rooms for early bedtime or in the television lounge watching familiar American sitcoms. Since all dialogue is dubbed in Italian, much of the action made no sense to them, but they watched anyway. This left a few stragglers who wandered about the lobby, reading bulletin board announcements of the next day's menus and Senior Seminars events.

Harry was not interested in those announcements. He would learn soon enough what tomorrow's program would bring. His purpose was to approach and address a multi-branched rubber tree that stood in front of the large plate glass window facing on the street. "See anything?" he said.

"Not a thing," the tree, or rather Pete's voice from behind it, replied. "This town is dead as a doornail. A few people walked by before about nine-thirty, but since then, no one. And hardly any cars either. Which is all to the good, don't you think, Harry?" Pete's disembodied reply went on. "Makes it easier to spot anyone who might show up," it communicated.

"If anyone ever does..." Harry muttered, keeping his voice low. It seemed to him that the desk clerk was giving him a peculiar look, and he didn't want to be observed in the act of talking to a tree.

♦♦♦♦

There was no traffic around the Basilica di San Antonio, except for a yellow, low-slung Lancia. It pulled into an empty parking spot beside a larger-than-life equestrian statue. Horse and rider stood alone in front of the looming, unlit church, casting a massive moon shadow into which the vehicle disappeared as it came to a stop. Like most sports cars of its type, it had only two seats,

Eldernapped

both of the bucket variety. There was just one occupant, the driver, who, with difficulty, managed to squirm out.

Vinny knew that his skinny body and workman's garb did not match the image his car projected, but it was night, the square was almost empty, and no one was looking. He locked the door and headed across and down the street to the Casa del Santo.

He walked at a slow pace, keeping close to the line of joined buildings at his left, lost in their darkness. As Vinny approached the Casa, he noticed what at first glance looked like a wide, metal, double door in the wall of the building. It had a pair of scowling bronze gargoyles cast into it, one on each bronze panel. A week in Padua had taught him that such ornaments on doors were not unusual in this city. He tried to push them open, but they were locked.

An ice cream shop adjoined the hotel a few feet farther on. It was closed for the evening, but its empty tables, tablecloths removed, and chairs remained in their normal array under the arcade that roofed the sidewalk. Vinny selected one from which he could look into the hotel lobby through the large plate glass window that made up part of its facade.

Vinny made no sound or movement as he sat in the nighttime shadows for half an hour, until at last, a car drove up and headed for the double doors. It tooted its horn and, after a moment, the doors divided, the two halves swinging inward to reveal a driveway.

As he had guessed, this was more than just a doorway, it was a gate. These same bronze doors must have worked like this for as long as the hotel had existed. They had been opened by human hands in pre-electronic times, and for horse-drawn carriages instead of cars.

The car moved down the driveway, took a turn and disappeared. The gate, again without visible human aid, and with no more sound than a click, swung shut once more.

George Freedman

Vinny looked up above the doors, left and right, and discovered just where the arcade roof met the wall, a foot-long black box. The axis of the box was angled to point its eye at the front license plate of any vehicle requesting entrance. A glance into the lobby, past a large rubber plant, which almost obscured his vision, informed him that the desk clerk, looking at a small television monitor by his side, had seen what the box had seen. It was his forefinger, still extended, that had just lifted from the button, which activated those bronze doors.

The time for action was near. Vinny got up, careful to keep within the shadows, and approached the gate. He sidled along the hotel wall, hugging it on the backside of the TV camera so as not to be observed. Then, deciding that there had been enough rehearsal, he returned in the same manner to his chair.

With the evening getting later, more hotel patrons were returning. Cars were now drawing up at the gate in rapid succession and going through the same electronic admission procedure. As the fifth or sixth vehicle prepared to enter, Vinny made his move. He did it in such a calculated way that anyone looking at the car would have missed a fast moving shadow behind its rear right window—the side that was just out of the sight line of the television camera. The shadow accompanied the car and both proceeded down the interior driveway, as the doors of the gate clicked shut behind them.

◆ ◆ ◆ ◆

The man, lying on his back on the floor, was writhing as though in intense pain. His eyes were half-shut and Harry, bending over him, could see that he was barely conscious. Harry was not the only one attempting to minister to the fellow. Many other faces were hovering over him and a number of hands fiddled with the man's clothes, trying to loosen them. People were talking in excited tones..

Eldernapped

"That's him. No question. It's one of the guys who stormed our bus that first day." This came from a male voice that Harry didn't bother to identify. Nor to challenge either, for that was also his opinion. Emily's, too, who said, "I know the little bastard. It's Vinny. Vinny Anzaldi."

"It's one of them all right," Tom confirmed with the assurance of a flight captain announcing a routine landing.

"But what happened to his mustache?" Kate said. She was standing next to Tom, bending over the recumbent figure. "Never saw a man with half a mustache before."

"The poor bugger is seriously injured and all you can think of, Kate, is that he has a funny mustache?" Tom said.

"Not so serious," a new voice interjected, this one with an Italian accent. It came from a young man kneeling at Vinny's side. "All that blood at his head is coming from his left earlobe. He must have lacerated it as he fell down these stairs. Earlobes bleed like hell."

"I think there's a lot more wrong with this guy than just a torn ear," another young man spoke up, his English also accented. "He seems to be hardly breathing."

"He'll live," the first fellow said, a note of authority in his voice. "Although to tell the truth, any person could be killed who had a fall like he just had. Lucky he's so thin. A heavier man would have landed with a harder impact."

"Thank you for your learned medical opinion, Doctor Fabiano," responded number two, the one who had just taken the more pessimistic view. His emphasis on the word Doctor introduced what Harry thought was a note of sarcasm.

"As far as I am concerned, I am not so sure he will live. I think he has serious internal injuries."

"Thanks for your learned medical opinion, Doctor Parelli," Dr. Fabiano countered. "But in this instance, as our American fellow students would say, I don't think you know your arse from your elbow...which I wouldn't have expected from a person majoring in proctology. In my opinion, it is very unlikely that he has internal injuries. I feel no swelling in his abdomen, nor do I detect any abnormal temperature."

Who the hell are these two guys, Harry asked himself. He would have confronted them with this question, except that Millicent beat him to it. "Who are you two young men?" Millicent asked. She was wearing a bright crimson chenille robe that made a bold blotch of color. She pushed herself into the crowd of observers and leaned over the injured person. "Are you doctors?"

"No, not yet, but soon to be," Linda explained, answering for them. "And they're both friends of mine. This one's Joey Fabiano and that's Bruno Parelli."

Linda. Emily's granddaughter, Harry thought. How come she's here? And how come she has two soon-to-be Italian doctors in tow?

" Oh...?" Millicent said, the look on her face showing that she also was not sure what to make of this explanation, in view of the fact that it was one-thirty in the morning, which seemed a little early for the bartender girl to be reporting for work. And why, if indeed she were reporting for work, did she require to be attended by two stalwart fellows who either were or were not doctors?

The presence of Linda Adams and her two friends was not Harry's only puzzle. The other one was how the devil did this guy happen to fall down this long stone stairway?

Harry turned his attention to the two young medical people. They seemed to know what they were doing, as they continued to examine the prone body before them. "I don't think that left forearm is broken...only a bad bruise," Joey said.

"But what about the right leg?" Bruno continued. "Could have a fractured fibula."

Eldernapped

"You could be right, but we won't know till we get him to X-ray." "Right, we have to get him to X-ray"

"I'll call an ambulance," was Julie's instant reaction.

"And I'll call Franco," was Graziella's.

Lifting his eyes from the poor man on the floor, Harry discovered, to his surprise, that the place was mobbed. Was everyone there? The entire Senior Seminars class and their mentors? It seemed that way, for the second floor landing at the base of the stairway was packed. They were all clad in a wide variety of nightclothes and bathrobes. Those who had not found room on the landing spilled onto the staircase itself. It was clear that the pandemonium outside their third floor rooms, a few moments before, must have awakened them.

Harry's musings were interrupted by a familiar voice. "If you want to know why Linda and her friends are here," it said, "it's because I asked them to be. I thought we'd need some strong young folks to help us catch this bum...which, as you see, they just did." Naomi's voice, with its Boston accent, Linda became Linder and asked, ahsked, must have been as unmistakable to everyone present as it was to Harry. "I thought one of those thugs holding our poor Marguerite," Naomi went on, "would be coming back tonight to pick up some changes of clothes for her. Personal things, you know what I mean? And I was right. See that suitcase on the floor?"

Everyone looked. Sure enough, there was a suitcase of medium size lying on the floor next to Vinny. It had burst open during its flight down the stairs to reveal that its contents were made up of different items of female clothing. Fred Wexler, who happened to be standing next to it bent over to examine the tag that was hanging from its handle. "'Marguerite LoPresti,'" he read, "'53 Walnut Ave. Cincinnati, Ohio 45224.'"

"Mrs. Levine, y'know, predicted this man would break in here tonight...and that's exactly what he did," Linda offered, her voice rising so that everyone could hear.

"Isn't she brilliant? Not only that, she's actually the one who caught the beast. She stuck out her foot as he was running by her and trying to get away down the stairway with the suitcase and tripped him up.."

"Not with my foot, Linda dear, with my cane," Naomi corrected. "It was lucky I decided to come out of my room just then. I was nervous and couldn't sleep...and I thought I heard someone tiptoeing around the corridor. When I saw Vinny running toward the stairway, I knew what I had to do. I hate that cane, but sometimes it comes in handy."

Expressions of praise for the valiant and resourceful lady arose from the gathered crowd. "Wow!" they said and, "Quick thinking," and, "Good girl, Naomi."

Added to these was a special one from Harry. "When you're right, you're right, honey. I have to admit you hit it on the button this time." He walked over to her, bent down, and implanted an affectionate kiss on her brow.

"But how did he get in?" Pete said, mystified. "I was serving my watch in the lobby, as we agreed. Well, not myself alone. Dorothy here had offered to keep me company. And we were sitting behind that big rubber plant so anyone coming in wouldn't see us. I had just relieved Fred here. You did the four to eight watch, wasn't it, Fred?

Fred nodded yes.

"Anyway, Dorothy and I didn't see him come in. And you didn't see him come in either, did you Fred?

Fred nodded no.

Harry now felt that it was up to him to explain to the others what was going on. "It was another one of Naomi's ideas, that we should watch the entrance to spot anyone suspicious coming in this evening. So I arranged this watch system just like we used to have in WWII on my Navy ship.

Eldernapped

"After Fred and Pete and Dorothy stood their watches, Art Maglio did the midnight watch which he's right in the middle of this minute. I was going to take the oh-four hundred to oh-eight hundred segment. Looks like there's no need for me to lose any sleep over that assignment now, thank goodness."

"The desk clerks told us there was no other walk-in entrance to this place, except for the fire doors. When they open, an alarm sounds," Pete said, still puzzled.

"Joey and Bruno and I were in the maid's room where they keep the sheets and towels?" Linda piped up, by way of confirming Naomi's explanation of their presence. "And we had the lights out so no one would, like, know we were there?" As she spoke, she indulged in the endearing mannerism that Harry had noticed before, that of raising her voice at the ends of simple statements, thus turning them into questions. Which did nothing to lessen the tentative nature of certain other things she said, since she also had the habit of pointing out that nothing is what it is, rather, that it is like what it is.

"That's just a few doors down from Marguerite's room." Linda rattled on. "That was our station...and it was going to be our job to lurk there and leap out and catch this...person...if he ever, like, showed up? But we didn't hear or see him coming down the corridor, did we, fellows?" she concluded, a real question this time, although rhetorical.

But the fellows were occupied with their patient, who now seemed to be losing whatever symptoms of consciousness he had displayed. His eyes were now closed and his low moans were becoming fainter till they seemed to stop altogether.

"Where's Paul O'Leary?" someone on the stairway asked. "He's a doctor."

"And his wife Rose is a nurse," someone else added.

"Dr. O'Leary...Paul...we need you..." the call came up.

"Or Nate Kniznick, he's a doctor too."

Joey and Bruno must have heard these pleas for medical help, but they ignored them. They continued to work on Vinny, trying now to resuscitate him by maneuvers of chest pounding and mouth-to-mouth.

Dr. O'Leary did not respond. It was hard to believe, but he and Rose must have slept through all this commotion. Nor could Nate Kniznick and Belle be found, but their absence was explainable. No one wears hearing aids when they go to sleep. On the other hand, Harry could see, as he swept his eyes up and down the staircase and its landings, that every non-medical classmate, which was everyone else, appeared to be present.

There was a shuffling in the region of the upper steps. Someone was going to get one or the other of those two. Which seemed to be the prudent thing to do, even though the embryo physicians were doing the best they could.

Another good idea was to clear the space. "All right everybody," Julie said, clapping her hands, "let's give these people room to work. Let's all go back to bed. Come on." And like the good troupers they were, the crowd turned and, each following the one in front of him or her, marched back up the dozens of stone steps and left.

With the exception of Joey, Bruno, Linda and Naomi. And, since Naomi was staying, Harry felt he had to hang around as well. As did Emily.

She stood over Vinny's seemingly lifeless body. Her jaws were working and it appeared that she was getting ready to spit. She said through clenched teeth, "Good enough for you, Vinny, you sleazy little son of a bitch. We're going keep you alive so you can tell us where Justin...wait till I get my hands on that boy...and your pal, Big Sam, are keeping Marguerite. Then, if you have to kick off, it'll be okay with me." Such vituperation seemed out of place coming from the mouth of this fragile looking, little old lady, but so did almost anything she said at any time, on any subject, Harry noted.

Joey's eyes now met Bruno's, which signaled agreement that they had done all they could. They left Vinny's side and came over to join Linda, Harry and Naomi, who were sitting on the fourth and fifth stair treads. After one more look of disgust at the unfortunate Vinny, Emily came over as well. "Nothing more we can do right now," Joey said. "He's breathing all right now, so I don't think there's any real danger. And someone did call for an ambulance...am I right?" he said.

"Oh, yes, Joey," Linda assured him. "Julie said she was going to do it. I'm sure it will be here very soon now."

The sound of running footsteps could be heard on the upper landing. It was Paul, at last, rubbing his sleepy eyes. A few steps behind him came Rose. They were wearing identical, unisex, blue pajamas that showed through their identical gray bathrobes.

"That's Dr. O'Leary," Harry said for the benefit of Joey and Bruno.

The two rose to meet Paul midway up the staircase. A minute or so of agitated three-way discussion followed. They spoke in quiet tones, their words muffled, but even if the others could have overheard them, they would not have understood the medical terminology, Harry figured. As it concluded, Paul was heard to say, "As I told you boys, I'm in cardiology, not into physical trauma, but maybe we'll get lucky and the man will turn out to be having a heart attack. So, okay, let's examine him, shall we? Where is he...at the bottom of the stairs, you say?"

As everyone turned and started down the stairs, they stopped in mid-step. Not only was Vinny gone, so was the suitcase with Marguerite's clothes.

George Freedman

Day Six

"Help is on the Way"

Six hours after the turmoil on the stairway, Harry and the rest of the students began to file into the breakfast room. Not with their usual pep, however, for many showed the effects of lost sleep. Once they plopped into their seats, they looked long and hard at the coffee pitchers on each table before mustering enough energy to pour themselves their respective cups. Except for Emily, who, as on all mornings, had hit the ground running.

The bags under her eyes were no larger than usual, nor darker, Harry noted. Nor were her eyes more heavy-lidded or red. Nor was she silent. She announced, "I think we should all be very cheered up by what happened this morning. Even though that slime ball Vinny got away, he was rather badly hurt. Probably has a rupture or a fracture, something like that. I'm sure he won't be able to walk without limping for the next few weeks. Also, he's going to have to do something about that half-mustache, probably shave it all off and hope for the best when it grows back. Meanwhile, all we have to do if we want to find Marguerite is to look for a little weasel who limps and who has no mustache.

"But more important," she chattered on, "we now know that Justin and Marguerite are still in the neighborhood. They haven't left the Padua area. Must have rented some sort of pad nearby. It should be child's play for our Lieutenant Luigi to track them down."

Eldernapped

Pad, Harry mused, his brain beginning to emerge from its fuzzy state as his coffee took effect. How come the old girl uses a word like pad? But then he answered the question for himself. Emily has been hanging around a lot with granddaughter Linda/Belinda.

Julie, with Graziella following close behind, burst through the breakfast room door. The pair seemed to stumble as they made their way to their normal speaking station at the second's table. The room fell quiet and the quietness deepened. There was not even the tinkle of spoons in coffee cups. Despite their sleep-deprived state, everyone seemed to sense, from the demeanor of the two, that something was wrong. Normally, Julie would be making announcements of the day's lectures and activities, but not today.

The sounds that came from Julie's mouth were not uttered in her customary strong, confident voice. Rather, they were faint and halting, almost impossible to understand. From where Harry was sitting, only a table away, he could see tears on both of the women's faces. Then Julie managed to pull herself together enough to impart the terrible news that Marguerite LoPresti was dead.

That woke the crowd, Harry included. Gasps filled the room.

"No!"

"It can't be!"

The intensity of the sadness this news generated was extraordinary, thought Harry, now devastated, like everyone else. It was because of the fine person Marguerite was, far beyond the usual in possessing lovable qualities, a sweet woman.

"That's ridiculous," Harry sputtered in a loud voice. "Marguerite can't be dead. Emily was just pointing out that the fact that that little bum..."

"Vinny," Naomi filled in.

"Yes, Vinny, was stealing the suitcase of Marguerite's clothes last night, which has to mean she's all right and probably staying right here in Padua."

"Or vicinity," Naomi added.

"So there can't be anything to worry about." Harry patted his brow with his handkerchief. "Because why would they want her clothes if she was dead?"

"But that's not what Franco said," Julie sobbed through her tears, not persuaded by this line of reasoning. "Tell them, Graziella."

"Franco said..." Graziella said, picking up the thread as Julie had asked her to, "Franco said that in Italy, in almost every kidnapping, the victim is almost always killed on the second or third day."

"But that's when the kidnappers are Italians," Pete rushed to point out. "In those cases the victims are always either important Italian politicians or rich owners of big Italian companies...while our Marguerite is just an ordinary American lady. Anyway, our kidnappers are nothing more than good old American slobs...not Italians."

"Another thing," Nate spoke up, adding another cheery note, "Italian kidnappers always send a small body part like the left ear or one of the pinkie fingers before they actually carry out the execution. So if you follow my advice, you shouldn't get too upset, unless you get a funny little package in the mail...and that hasn't happened yet, has it, girls?"

Somehow, this did not provide any consolation. Quite the opposite, for now Julie and Graziella were wailing.

At last, Julie, her words interrupted by occasional pauses for deep breaths and blotting of eyes with a tissue, said, "I'm sorry...I should be able to handle this better...especially since the training program the Senior Seminars corporation puts all us administrators through instructs us on what to do in case of a...a...death. We do get them, you know. Deaths, I mean...since everyone is so..."

Eldernapped

"Old," Belle offered, supplying the word poor Julie was searching for.

"Yes, old. Most of the other administrators have had one or two deaths over the years. But this could be my first one..." With that she gave way to steady crying. Belle, who was sitting nearby, gathered her into her arms, speaking comforting words into her ear with the gentle self-assurance of one who has had occasion in the past to do the same thing with a daughter or granddaughter.

Belle's sympathetic action must have had a good effect because Julie managed to control her emotions enough to inform them that whatever Marguerite's fate turns out to be, her nearest relatives will be on the scene. "Graziella called Mrs. LoPresti's sons in Cincinnati yesterday and they will both be flying in today," she said.

"Of course. That's what good sons do," Naomi said.

At this point, Harry heard the soft, shuffling sound of outdoor slippers that had become familiar to him during the course of the week. Yes, it was Wendy Gross. Today's music class would be on the legendary Vivaldi, composer of five hundred concertos. She told them he was a contemporary of Tartini who had lived and produced his music just down the road in nearby Venice.

Would this lecture happen at all now, Harry wondered in view of the agitation that her students were experiencing? Not to mention Wendy's own distress on learning that the sadness in the breakfast room was caused by the kidnapping and possible demise of one of those students. When she was told that the poor victim was none other than Marguerite LoPresti, she asked, "Wasn't she the one who spoke up during the Tartini lecture to say she was from Cincinnati, like me?"

"Yes, that's right," someone said, at which Wendy turned pale and found a chair into which to sink.

Wendy's anguish must have been contagious, because without warning, Emily exploded with new distress of her own. "Justin couldn't have done this!" she said, her voice high-pitched and trembling. "And he would never have allowed those private investigators of his to do it either."

For the first time since Harry had met her, Emily looked helpless and distraught. The sad picture she presented reminded him and everyone else in the room that, in spite of her many remarkable qualities, she was no more than what she appeared to be, a helpless, little old lady, and a mother in the bargain. "He's always so considerate of everybody..." She wept. "So careful never to hurt anyone's feelings..."

Dorothy, who was standing near Emily, took her by both hands and led her to a far side of the room where she sat her down.

"Too much...Robert always said he was too much of a soft touch, and that would always hold him back. But that is what makes me love him so. He's my darling boy, my sweet darling boy, my Justin..."

"There, there," Dorothy said. "Of course he couldn't have...your Justin would never do a thing like that to anybody..."

She was interrupted by the appearance of Franco. From the look on his face he had some important new information to communicate. He said something to Graziella as he handed her what looked like a woman's blouse, a high quality one in fact, because even from where he was sitting, Harry could see that it was of silky, white material and elegantly designed.

"Franco tells me that this was found in the parking lot next to the Santo and it was turned in to his office less than an hour ago," Graziella said as she examined it. She looked long and hard at something on its bottom hem, which she then pointed out to Julie.

"Look," Julie said. "This has to be Marguerite's blouse. See, it has a laundry tag pinned to it with her name on it." She held it up so that those at the near tables could see the abbreviated word. Peering through the middle ones of his trifocal lenses, Harry spelled out

Eldernapped

LOPRES, inscribed in black with what must have been indelible ink.

"Yes, it must be Mrs. LoPresti's. That's what I figured, too," Graziella agreed. "So what does that mean? Does it say she is okay...or not?" a question she repeated in Italian to Franco, to which he made a quick reply.

"Now he thinks she must be alive after all," she announced with a sigh of relief, "and that the man who fell down the stairs...Vinny...must have lost it out of her suitcase in his hurry to get away. He thinks it was in the Santo parking lot because that must have been where Vinny had his getaway car."

"You know," Tom spoke up, "my two buddies and me," nodding to his flying companions from bygone days, "we ran out right after Vinny disappeared and made a pretty good search up and down the street...all the way up to the Santo in fact, but we didn't spot him. And we didn't notice a car getting away, either. Still, he must have been there, hiding in the shadows someplace. He's a real sneaky little guy, that Vinny."

Naomi, like the well-behaved schoolgirl she once was, raised her hand. Oh God, Harry thought, what is she going to say?

With a nod, Julie recognized her. As Harry expected, Naomi got out of her chair and, thumping along with her cane, joined the little group at the front of the room. "The time has come for us to get off our behinds," she proclaimed through clenched teeth. "That blouse clinches it. It's an insult to our dear friend Marguerite. Imagine having some guy invade your room and raid your clothes and then leave something like this lying around on the street...in a parking lot for heaven's sake...for anyone to pick up." Her angry eyes drilled into Franco's as she said this, and his reaction was to avert his and stare down at the floor as he shuffled his feet. That's Naomi for you, reflected Harry. World's best deliverer of guilt trips. It was clear to him that Franco had never encountered her like before.

"I'm sure the police will eventually find her," Naomi went on, "and when they do, she will probably be in good shape. Forget this dead business, Julie and Gaziella. But how long will it take them? The criminals who kidnapped her could have released her right away, as soon as they realized she wasn't Emily. But they didn't choose to do that. Now, it looks like they are going to just hold on to her. It could turn out to be for a very long time, and in the meantime our poor Marguerite will be going through hell.

"I think the police have to find Marguerite right away. Today. Or if not today, tomorrow. No later than tomorrow. And the way things are going I'm not sure that's going to happen...unless we pitch in and help..."

Cries of, "Right on."

"You betcha."

"Count me in."

"All of us in this room can make a real contribution to whatever the police are trying to do," Naomi continued. "I'm sure Lieutenant Luigi...and Sergeant Franco too..." nodding in his direction, "will appreciate any help we can give them. Now they can see that they should have listened to us when we told them that one of Justin's stumblebums was going to come to Marguerite's room last night for her clothes. We were right, weren't we? Graziella, tell Franco we were right. So, let's all get on it! What do you say, everybody?"

The response to Naomi's call for action did not match up to the resounding roar of approval that might have come from a football team being cajoled between halves to rescue a losing cause by an inspirational coach, but it was at least a subdued version of same, Harry thought. And he expected no less.

He could see that Graziella was translating Naomi's words to Franco, who didn't seem pleased to hear them. Nor, for that matter was Harry himself, who had caught Naomi's drift without needing a translation. He knew his Naomi well enough not to be taken in by any such broad,

Eldernapped

exhortatory statements she might make. They only served as cover for something very specific that Naomi had in mind and was keeping to herself for the moment.

♦♦♦♦

Gordie Wharton wondered why his sister needed so much luggage. There were six pieces, including two large suitcases on wheels, two matching garment bags and a pair of soft-sided , oversize designer satchels. To Gordie, these looked like fancy duffel bags. "For shoes and my traveling makeup box and other bulky sundries like my hair dryer," Roberta explained. "I'm sure I'm forgetting something...but we've had just a few hours to pack," she added by way of an apology for not having taken more.

He wondered whether six heavy bulky cargo items for a single passenger meant that she would have to pay an extra fare. He had no way of knowing, for he had flown only once or twice in his entire lifetime. He also never understood women and the strange actions they took. Roberta, less than any of them. Which must be one reason why, like his brother Justin, he had never married.

On the other hand, Alfred, Roberta's son, brought only one medium sized suitcase, somewhat travel worn at that. He also hand-carried an attaché case and his laptop. "But we don't call them laptops any more," Alfred pointed out. "That term became archaic about a year ago, Uncle Gordie. Now we say 'notebook.'"

Oh, notebook." Gordie repeated, trying to sound interested.

"Get a move on, Gordie," Roberta interrupted. She had been saying these very words to him for the last half-century at least, and he had never seen any reason to respond. Nor had he ever gotten a move on. In this instance, he could tell that Roberta felt there was a more than usual need for speed. The Wharton family was going through an emergency, and it was up to her to resolve it. She was making Alfred come with her, Gordie could tell, to assist her. Just like everyone else in the family, Alfred couldn't oppose his mother's wishes when her mind was made up. This whole trip had to do with something awful Justin had done, in Italy of all places, involving a woman.

"Involving a woman" didn't sound like Justin, Gordie mused. He's never been the sort of man who would lose sight of his obligations to our mother in order to, what? Have an affair? Yet, from what Roberta said, that must have happened. Which proves that there is a first time for everything.

Gordie heard that some men, when they approach their mid-sixties, were known to change where women were concerned. Is that what they call becoming "a dirty old man?" Hard to visualize Justin falling into that trap. As for himself, although he was close to Justin's age, Gordie had never yet experienced such lustful urges. None that he could recall, at least.

Justin's frantic overseas phone call just after midnight last night had precipitated this action, frenzied arrangements for plane tickets plus the rush packing. Roberta had pointed out that "we Whartons must stick together in time of crisis." So her task, and Alfred's, if needed, was to go to Europe and deal with it. There was no question that Justin alone wasn't going to be able to handle it, whatever it was.

Not that Gordie didn't have a role, too. He was to load one of the Wharton Valve company vans with the luggage and drive the two of them, sister and nephew, to the Providence airport. As Supervisor of Grounds, he was responsible for the plant's five maintenance vehicles and had had no trouble extracting this one from company service for a few hours.

There, mother and son would take a mid-morning flight to Kennedy. They would connect with one on Alitalia that would get them, by way of Milan, into the Venice airport by eleven thirty-six the next morning, European time. From Venice they would go to another Italian city. One he had never heard of, Padua.

Eldernapped

Good luck, Roberta, for doing whatever the hell you think you have to do, Gordie thought, as he placed each suitcase, garment bag and satchel into the van. And good luck, Justin, too.

George Freedman

Day Seven

"Held Captive"

AIUTO! AIUTO! AIUTO! AIUTO!

HELP! HELP! HELP! HELP!

I am being held prisoner against my will in the stone house inside these walls where I hope you have found this message. I am getting more desperate every minute and I can't stand much more of this.

Three American men, very awful human beings, are doing this to me and I don't know why. They are a Mr. Wharton and Sam and Vinny, whose last names I don't know. They let me walk once a day around the garden and when they aren't looking, that's when I plan to throw this note over the wall.

I beg the finder of this note to call the police and also the Senior Seminars administrator at the Casa del Santo in Padua whose name is Julie. By now she and the others must have missed me and must be frantic, wondering where I am.

This is not a joke! This is serious! This is really happening to me!

Please excuse that I am writing in English, except for the only pertinent Italian word I know—Aiuto! But surely you can find someone to translate this.

Please rescue me before it is too late!

Eldernapped

Marguerite LoPresti

This message was written on a torn-off piece of brown wrapping paper, which had been folded into a neat envelope shape and tied up in a bowknot with a strand of chive. It could be picked up along the base of the wall by anyone with searching eyes that chanced to be walking by. The wall was long and high, and its stuccoed surface was hoary with moss. Behind it, through the thick black bars of its massive iron gate, could be seen an impressive old mansion beside a quiet stream.

It's a long shot, Marguerite figured, but there's a chance it might work...

♦♦♦♦

The scene, an odd one, under the circumstances, thought Vinny, was one of domesticity. A pleasant looking woman who could be somebody's grandmother had just turned to confront him from her task of meal preparation at the miniature kitchen alcove. Marguerite was of small stature and was wearing an oversized white apron that covered her from neck to hem. She left a pile of lettuce, tomatoes, zucchini, arugala and red peppers cut up into salad-sized chunks, strips and slices. Only a bundle of chives remained to be cut, but she seemed to hesitate to subject them to her knife.

"You know what I need, Vinny?" she said. "Some string. I've looked everywhere for string but couldn't find any. Have you seen any string around here?"

"No, Mrs. LoPresti, but I'll look."

"You do that, Vinny, because I need some...you know...for cooking. Cooks always need string. In the meantime, I think I won't cut up all these chives. I'll save some of them for another time."

What foolish chatter women make as they cook, Vinny thought.

George Freedman

"What am I saying?" Marguerite's voice rising with emotion. "There isn't going to be another time. I expect to be out of here today. You hear me? Today!"

Vinny did not let himself show any visible reaction to this statement. He just stared back at her with a stony expression. This led her to give vent to a large sigh. "I don't know why I am cooking for you morons, except it's clear that none of you can cook. At least if I cook, I know I'll eat well. And it does help pass the time.

"Which reminds me, just in case we're stuck here one more day, I'd like to make out a shopping list. You did get me the ballpoint pen yesterday, but there's nothing to write on. The next time you're out, please get me a pad of writing paper.

"Yes, ma'am."

"I can finish all this later," she said, peering at the left side of his face as she washed her hands and wiped them on a clean towel. "So...all right...sit down there where the light is good. Let's see how that lacerated ear is doing,"

Vinny shuffled over to where she pointed and sat as he was bidden. It hurt to do this, because one of his legs had suffered recent damage and he used a furled umbrella as a cane.

"My goodness, you are a mess, Vinny, with that half a mustache and the raw skin next to it, added to all your other battle wounds. Don't expect me to apologize for what I did to you. With that long handlebar, it was sure easy to get a grip on it and to give a big pull. I'm actually proud of myself every time I look at it, because it proves that I'm not a person to be fooled around with. You really should shave the rest of it off and then both sides will grow back together. Otherwise the bare side will need weeks catching up.

"Which leads me to wonder, since you seem more accident prone than most people...have you ever thought of getting into another less dangerous line of business? If I were you, I would, I really would."

Eldernapped

By now Marguerite had seated herself beside him and, with gentle fingers, had removed the bandage from his ear. Careful as she was, Vinny felt a stab of pain and he couldn't keep himself from exclaiming, "Ow! Son of a bitch!"

With the bandage off, he settled back in his chair. He noted that most other nice, refined, little old women might have reacted in a negative way to his crude remark. But she had taken no notice, which was another good thing about her. Instead, as she worked on him, she kept rattling on in a calm and steady voice. "Well, I think, under the circumstances, that ear lobe is coming along quite well. No sign of infection that I can see." Her tone alternated between that of stern moral adviser and compassionate ministering angel.

"I don't know why men have taken to wearing earrings these days," she went on. Although I must admit some men do look good with an earring." Her emphasis on the word "some" led Vinny to guess that she was not including him in that category.

"One thing is sure," Marguerite continued, as she doused it with peroxide. "I'm sorry to tell you that this wound is not going to improve your looks. Although it will probably not heal badly if you see a doctor pretty soon. I am not a doctor myself, but in my days as a psychiatric social worker in some pretty tough Cinci neighborhoods, I saw a lot of bloody wounds. In my opinion, a plastic surgeon is what you really need. Anyway, it needs stitches and if I were you..."

"No doctors, no stitches," Vinny mumbled.

"Stubborn you are like most men," Marguerite responded, her deep chocolate brown eyes drilling into his, which were of a similar shade. A bit of an ethnic link there, Vinny figured with satisfaction. Even though her remark was critical of him and of men in general, for some reason it did not offend him. In fact, he found himself liking her even more, if only because she looked so nice as she said it.

"Another thing," she went on, unaware of the thoughts going through the mind of her grateful patient, "I don't believe your ridiculous story of how your earring got caught in a nail or hook as you stumbled down the stairs at the Casa hotel the other night. What hotel stairways have nails or hooks sticking out? I've been wearing pierced earrings, many of them with even bigger loops than yours, since I was a little girl and never had anything like that happen to me...or to any other woman of my acquaintance.

"In my opinion someone must have taken a dislike to you, which isn't hard to do you must admit, and pulled it out by brute force. God, how that must have hurt. And you're out the earring as well. Poor Vinny.

"But if it really happened when you stumbled on a stairway, I think your problem is that you're not much good with stairways. Next time, take the elevator."

"Well, that's what happened, lady...take it or leave it." Vinny said," his voice now full of truculence.

She next applied a neat line of Bacitracin to the earlobe in question, and tried to bring its two new forks together to a semblance of what they had once been, adding as she did so, "It's good that you got my suitcase, if only because of the first aid kit I keep in it. I never travel without my first aid kit and it never fails to come in handy, either for myself or for someone in the party."

"You wouldn't happen to have something for a cold, too, would you, Mrs. LoPresti?" Big Sam said. He had crept up behind the two and his sudden and unexpected appearance at this moment gave both of them a jolt. Indeed he must have had one, a cold, that is, because Vinny couldn't tell which was redder, his teary eyes or the moist tip of his nose, to which he kept applying his handkerchief.

"I do have some antihistamine tablets," Marguerite answered, "and some cough lozenges. And do stop wiping your nose. You're just giving the infection back to yourself every time you do that. The next time you go to the store

Eldernapped

in the village, Vinny, please pick up a couple of boxes of tissues. No, you don't have to remember...I'll just add them to the shopping list.

"Well, there you are, Vinny." She gave a final pat to the plaster that bound the small gauze pad on his earlobe. "That ought to hold, and it should keep the germs out so it can heal...one way or another."

He wanted to say thanks, but, for some reason, the words didn't come out. What's wrong with me, he wondered. Am I getting bashful in my old age?

"As for your nasty cold, Sam," Marguerite said, rummaging in the suitcase that had been open and on a chair beside her, "let me find the antihistamines. Ah, here they are." She handed the vial to Sam. "They won't cure the cold...what will? Chicken soup? Don't expect me to make you chicken soup...but at least they will relieve your symptoms."

Big Sam didn't say thanks, either, but Vinny could tell that he was feeling grateful, too.

With that, Marguerite put back into her small black bag of medical supplies the peroxide, the rolls of plastic bandage and gauze, the vial of pills and the tube of ointment. She snapped it shut and replaced it in the niche provided for it in her suitcase.

Her every movement was followed with close attention by the two men to whom she had just administered. There was an almost pleased expression in her eyes that made Vinny think that, even though the two of them had said nothing, she was aware of their gratitude. But it wasn't as though their sentiments were going to be left unexpressed, even though by someone else.

Mr. Wharton spoke up. It turned out that, along with these two, he had been present all this time, sitting off in one of the room's farther corners, "We do appreciate what you are doing to help us out like this, Mrs. LoPresti," he said, "given the awkwardness of the

George Freedman

situation we find ourselves in. Dressing wounds and cooking and all that and..."

What the hell is he doing here, Vinny wondered. The guy has his own fancy room upstairs. Why doesn't he have the decency to stay up there and let the woman have her privacy?

"Oh, for goodness sakes, call me Marguerite," she said. "And you can express your thanks a lot better by letting me out of this absurd predicament. Although I don't have any complaints about how I am being treated, I'm mad. One way or another, you terrible men are going to have to pay for what you have done, holding me prisoner."

"Look...Marguerite...and you can call me Justin...no one can be more unhappy than I am at having to keep you here. To tell the truth, I certainly wouldn't be detaining you here like this, but Roberta, my sister, insists that it has to be done this way. She knows better about things like this than I do. But our ordeal should all be over very soon. Perhaps tomorrow or the next day...as soon as Roberta gets here. I assure you, she will settle everything to your satisfaction and you will rejoin your...what is it?...
Senior Seminars group, and have a good time for the rest of the program. We will be out of your hair and you will never have to see any of us again."

"For the rest of the program? The first week is over, and that's half of the program. I've already missed the Ravenna trip and today I think they must have left by now for Vicenza to see the Palladio architecture. There were a dozen interesting lectures I've also missed...as well as a very unusual Respighi concert in one of the cathedrals. What you've really done...if you want to know what you have done...has been to ruin my Senior Seminars program, and in fact my whole trip to Europe, which it took me a whole year to save up for.

"And now my two sons are probably worried sick, They were expecting a phone call two days ago. They've

Eldernapped

probably called the Senior Seminars office by now and learned that I've been kidnapped. What kind of shock is that to inflict on your children?" At this point, Marguerite could not stifle a small sob and had to sit down and daub her eyes with a corner of her apron.

"Please, please, don't cry," said Justin, his face contorted and very near to crying himself.

"Yeh, don't cry," Vinny echoed, with Big Sam joining in the chorus, and as though at a signal, all three men gathered round her.

"Look, let me make it up to you," Justin said, his voice thick with guilt. "What can I do while we're waiting for Roberta, to...you know... to make it up to you?"

George Freedman

Day Eight

"Busy Sunday"

Cataldo's phone rang. Just as it would on any other day, even though this was Sunday. That's police work for you. Sunday is just another day. The caller was the on-duty officer at the main receptionist's desk. "There's a group of people downstairs who want to talk to you, Lieutenant," he said.

"A group? A big group? Small group? Who are they?"

"Five or six, sort of old folks...Americans, I think. From a... Senior something."

Which led Cataldo to reflect that for these elderly folk, too, Sunday is just another day. "Send them up." he said.

He knocked on his window to summon Franco. The two of them commandeered a number of chairs from here and there, setting them up in an arc facing his desk. Not a moment too soon, for the quintet of seniors, with Emily at the helm, made their appearance at the door.

"How nice to see you all again. Please sit down," Cataldo said with a bow and a sweep of the arm as gracious as though he were a headwaiter welcoming them to a choice table. By now, he knew they expected no less, for this was Italy. They took their seats as bidden. Except for the Levine woman's husband, Harry was his name,

Eldernapped

who chose to wander the walls, subjecting each hanging picture or plaque to his own idiosyncratic judgment.

Franco also chose not to sit. He took up a position just behind his boss. As though he had eyes in the back of his head, Cataldo knew that his assistant was concentrating hard, getting ready to try to understand some the discussion in English that was about to take place."

You speak, Emily." Signora Levine, the one they called Naomi, said this in a stage whisper.

That was an unnecessary instruction. Cataldo could tell that Emily was chafing at the bit and was delaying only long enough to clear her throat. "Lieutenant Luigi," she said, "we think we know how to find my son Justin."

"And with him, Marguerite," Naomi added, her voice still soft and diffident.

"Of course, Marguerite too," Emily agreed.

"It was all Pete's idea," Dorothy offered. "But of course he's a lawyer, and lawyers are good at figuring out things like that."

"A retired lawyer, my dear," Pete said, as he made a dismissive hand gesture to indicate modesty. "But the old brain still navigates down the same channels. In fact, I recall, several years ago, in a similar circumstance that came up in the case of a small oil exploration firm in Dalton, Texas..."

"The same idea occurred to me, too, even before Pete came up with it," Emily interrupted, treading without shame on Pete's lines and taking some of his credit. "Although I must admit that when he suggested I call Woonsocket, that wasn't exactly the tack I was going to take. Anyway, when I rang up Roberta."

"Roberta?" Cataldo asked.

"Yes, you remember...my daughter...Roberta... maiden name Wharton...married name Dillard. There is no doubt in my mind that she was the one who put Justin up to coming here in the first place to force me to return to the States. Then, after no one answered her phone except for her ridiculous answering machine message, and knowing that Justin wasn't there either...since he is here...I rang up Gordie. He's my other Wharton son.

"Well, Gordie told me that Roberta and Alfred were gone. They had taken a flight on Friday and by now must already be in Padua. In fact they should have arrived yesterday. 'Paduaitaly, Paduaitaly,' he kept saying as though it were one word. He had dropped them off at the Providence airport that morning.

"He wasn't exactly sure why they went on this trip except that Justin was in some kind of trouble with a woman. That's for sure, he's in trouble, with a lot of women, and Roberta and Alfred were going to get him out of it, somehow, he said. But he didn't know what hotel they were staying at."

"Then Pete suggested that Roberta would probably be at the same hotel here in town that her brother had stayed at. What's the name of that hotel, Pete?" Dorothy's voice continued to brim with admiration for the man.

"I remembered its name from our previous conversation," Pete said. "It was the Plaza. Wasn't it the Hotel Plaza, Emily? So I suggested we call the front desk at the Plaza to see if the Dillards were registered there, and if not, when they were expected, and then..."

"Of course it was pretty obvious," Emily broke in again, "that she would check in at the Plaza, since it's the classiest hotel in town. Americans think so, anyway. So just after I talked to Gordie...and well before you got around to suggesting it, Pete...I had already called the Plaza. And what do you think?"

Now she paused, while Cataldo and Franco, waited for whatever her next words would be. The woman is given to dramatic pauses, Cataldo remembered from their first meeting. "They were there all right," Emily finally resumed. "Signora Dillard and her *figlio* Signor Dillard had checked in the afternoon before, the desk clerk told me. But when I asked to be connected I was told that I

Eldernapped

was too late. They had just checked out...and that was only a couple of hours ago. The two of them were gone, flown the coop. Probably already with Justin by now, I would wager."

"Darn," Naomi said. "We just missed them. Isn't that rotten luck?"

"That's when we decided to come right over here," Harry said. He had ceased his wandering around the room and was now sitting along with the others. "Even my wife agreed that you police people were probably the right ones to trace the Dillards' movements. Have I got their name right, Emily?"

She nodded yes.

"Since the Dillards only just checked out, we realized that we had to move fast, because sure as shooting, their next move had to be to join Justin and Marguerite, wherever they are. It only took us fifteen minutes, walking fast, to get here to tell you about it. Now we can make it back to the Casa in the same time...and that's good, because we don't want to miss too much of this morning's lecture on the geology and archaeology of the Veneto."

Cataldo looked with interest at Harry. That one anyway looks as though he's got his feet on the ground, Cataldo said to himself, and maybe I'll have to turn to him during the course of this case if the others get a little too, as they would like to think, helpful. His wife in particular, who, wouldn't you know it, had once more taken the floor.

"I still think we could have handled this matter ourselves and saved you the trouble, Lieutenant Luigi," she said. "But I had to admit it might take us a little longer than the time you gentlemen would require...with all the facilities at your disposal here in the police department. That's why we didn't waste a minute in coming over here to turn it over to you, instead.

"Yet...maybe we wouldn't have been so slow in finding out where the two of them went, after all," Naomi added, on reflection. "I considered questioning the hotel doorman. Those doormen who work for the big hotels all speak English, you know...and in no time at all, maybe faster and better than detectives like you gentlemen might have managed it, I could have learned what we want to know about where they were off to. No offense, fellows, but a woman, an older woman at that, with the right approach and some well thought out questions is going to be far less intimidating than the authorities acting in their official capacities.

"I bet I would have quickly confirmed the mother/son identification from that doorman, because a pair like that would be easy for him to remember. The next thing I would have done would be to ask him which taxi company picked them up...because he probably hailed their taxi for them. I think it's a fair assumption that they took a taxi, don't you agree, Lieutenant Luigi?"

Cataldo found himself nodding his head in the affirmative, like an automaton.

"And more important, if he's a good doorman, there's a chance that he'd know the name of the taxi driver, too. Don't the same drivers go to the same hotels all the time? I would think they do. After that, it should be child's play to trace where they went. And at that point," she took a deep breath, "I would have turned it over to you."

"Thanks a lot," Cataldo muttered.

Naomi continued without acknowledging his praise. "Once you knew the names of the taxi driver and his taxi company and you got in touch with them and asked the right questions, they could surely tell you where they took the Dillards. Of course, once you knew that, the problem of finding Marguerite would be solved." Her lengthy statement concluded at last, Naomi drew another deep breath and bestowed a beaming smile on everyone.

"Let me ask you, Lieutenant," Harry inquired, "do Italian police ever swear in civilians as deputies? We do it in the States, particularly out West. All it takes is pinning

Eldernapped

a five-star badge on her chest and making sure the six-shooters in her holsters meet regulations. I think the Padua PD would greatly benefit from appointing Naomi Levine as a deputy. She is one already anyway...de facto, as you say in Italian... or is that Latin? So why not make it official?"

Cataldo did not reply. But he was sure that everyone in that room could see that he was giving deep thought to this interesting proposition.

♦♦♦♦

As an engineer, Harry valued patterns, which led him to reflect that there can be no better illustration of mankind's innate desire for order and repeatability than a Senior Seminars dining room. Thus, by the third day, as he had expected, the arrangements of who sat at which table and next to whom had been set.

This meant that an instant sociology had been created. One table of four held only retired female schoolteachers. Two others featured trios of women in business or the professions, and in these cases the fourth chair was taken by a single man. The remaining tables were occupied for the most part by couples, most married, but some not.

Through the agency of his prime informant, Naomi, Harry soon learned that certain of the unmarrieds had chosen each other as roommates when signing up months before. While a few others, not roommates at all, had formed pairs on site, of whom Dorothy and Pete seemed to be an example.

Harry and Naomi sat at a table for eight. The other six seats were occupied for each lunch and dinner by Carol and Fred Hanson, Dr. Nate and Belle Kniznick and the Misses Sarah Townes and Millicent Carter. At an adjoining table for six, their good friends from back home, Art and Irene, were combined with the O'Learys and the two maiden sisters with unpronounceable names, who never said a word to anyone except to each other, and that in a strange muttered language which he later learned was Estonian.

Tom and Kate Sayre sat at another sixer with the Dorothy/Pete duo, along with Emily and Marguerite. But in the case of the latter, her seat was empty, although reserved for her, should she ever show up.

Julie and Graziella, joined on occasion by bus driver Enrico, did not dine with their charges, but sat rather at a designated eating area next to the swinging door to the kitchen. There they could be seen combining work with eating, as, between mouthfuls, they pored over computer readouts that unfolded and folded in endless accordion strips of connecting pages.

It was a gulf breached with ease, as Harry could see. At least a half dozen times during each lunch or dinner, one or another of his fellow students would slip over between courses to request aid or information of a personal nature, which was always given with good cheer, between mouthfuls, by the two young ladies.

Being at a particular location did not mean complete isolation from the other diners. All tables were close enough to each other to encourage active cross-table banter, one stream of which was started by Dorothy. "Isn't it a shame," she asked, "how our detectives missed Emily's daughter and grandson at their hotel?"

"But only by a whisker," Pete said.

"It just goes to show," Naomi offered, her tone philosophical, "it never pays to dawdle. If the police had just run over to the Plaza the minute we told them about the Dillards being there, they might have intercepted them."

"The delay was really more on our part," Harry pointed out. "We sat through a whole first lecture this morning, as well as the coffee break, before we decided to go over to the Padua PD, and that took up the first half of the morning."

"That was probably because we only thought of it during coffee break," Emily said. "If you remember, it

Eldernapped

actually wasn't our idea in the first place to dash over to the police station. It was really my Belinda, God bless her, who made that suggestion first."

"Actually, I thought of it first, Emily dear," Naomi said. "But when I suggested it. no one listened. Except maybe Belinda...such a sweet girl. She was serving us with our cappuccinos and biscottis at that moment. The fact is, we waited only long enough to finish our coffees and pastries and in no time at all after that, there we were at Lieutenant Luigi's desk."

"And remember, he acted immediately to have Sergeant Franco call the hotel's front desk," Pete said. "Which speaks very well for him, since I can tell you from my experience most detectives don't like to take suggestions from ordinary civilians. In this case, it could only have been a matter of a minute or two before we confirmed that the Dillards had already checked out, and left no forwarding address."

"That was strange," Harry commented. "They come over here on a trans-Atlantic trip and check into a fine hotel, and then, in the early morning, after only one night, they take off. They probably didn't even unpack. What could have been their rush?"

"Roberta's always in a rush," Emily said. "She must have seen a way to grab me up right away...probably today even...and tie me up in a straitjacket and ship me back to the latest lunatic asylum of her choice. Remember this...when Roberta sees a way to get something done, she never waits, she acts. Anyway, she must surely have been on the phone with Justin. He must have told them to come stay with him, wherever he is shacking up with Marguerite."

This caused a pause in the conversation as all within earshot contemplated whether "shacking up" was the phrase Emily really meant to use, but it was quickly sundered with, "What Dillards?" a question from a previously silent voice, which turned out to be that of Sarah at Harry's and Naomi's eight-table.

"And what hotel?" Millicent asked. "Who is staying...or in this case, not staying...at a hotel?"

"And who the hell is Roberta?" was Nate's question, which followed hard on those of the two ladies.

This unleashed a torrent of additional questions from all sides, which Naomi, raising her hand, volunteered to answer. Thus, everyone, even those at the farthest reaches of the dining room, came to learn, most of them for the first time, of the conspiratorial circumstances that led to the blunder on the part of the perpetrators, which resulted in the mistaken abduction of poor unfortunate Marguerite. In the end, the entire roomful came to share a feeling of intense dislike toward Emily's malignant daughter. "If I had a daughter like that," Belle said through clenched teeth, "I'd kill myself. But I'd kill her first."

"Why couldn't those detectives trace where Emily's relatives went?" Kate said. "If we knew that, it should lead us directly to Marguerite. Surely, they went off in a taxi. Which means that the doorman at the hotel could have told the cops..."

"What taxi company that might have been?" Naomi interrupted. "Or even identified the particular taxicab company and driver, since the doorman probably would have known him? We thought of those things too, Kate." Naomi completed Kate's thought for her. "And, guess what? We've just come back from the Padua police station where we suggested that very action to Lieutenant Luigi...that he should go to the doorman on duty at the time and ask those very questions."

"There was more to our plan than just that," Harry interposed. "In fact, it was my wife's original idea to flounce up to that doorman herself and captivate him with her fluttering eyelashes, which no one can resist, as who knows better than myself? If she had been allowed to do that, she would have extracted all the required information and more from the poor guy in a matter of thirty seconds at the most. But, sad to say, the detectives

Eldernapped

managed to find out that the doorman knew very little about what they needed to know. And they did it without using her help...although it might have taken them three minutes."

Naomi chose to ignore Harry's comment, which didn't surprise him, and taking back the attention of her audience, she went on. "It turns out that the doorman...a very good looking and nice man, by the way, as most doormen are...did see the two of them, the mother and son, leave the hotel. And he remembered the incident very well because it had happened only two hours before. He loaded their luggage into the trunk of a car that came to call for them. Even though it was a big car, there was so much luggage that some of it had to go into the back seat and the rest had to be tied to its roof rack.

"What car came to call for them?" Millicent said. "You mean they didn't actually leave in a taxi?"

"No, they didn't." Pete said. "It was a private car, a big Mercedes, light blue in color, the police learned, and it had Austrian plates. Furthermore, the doorman remembered that the driver seemed to know the son, Emily's grandson...do I have the relationship right, Emily?...since they shook hands. He also remembered that they all had to jam into the front seat, the two Dillards and the man who came to call for them, because the luggage filled the back seat."

"Austrian plates...I bet they've skipped across the border," Nate offered, "and are holed up in some small Austrian village.

"Now that we and the detectives know all this," Rose spoke up, her voice plaintive, "how is that going to help us find poor Marguerite and keep Roberta's hands off Emily? And is there any way we can help those detectives? As you suggested the other day, Naomi, I'd love to think I could do something to help."

"Oh, I think we can help a lot," Naomi said with a confident smile, now operating full throttle in her "Murder She Wrote" mode, Harry thought, a veritable recreation of

George Freedman

Jessica Fletcher during one of her best episodes. "We now know much more than we knew yesterday, and I think it's enough...if we're smart...to deduce how to find them, wherever they are. I happen to have some ideas of my own on how to do this, but before I tell you what they are I'd be happy to listen to any thoughts the rest of you have, because we're all in this together, you know."

To which Harry commented from the seat beside her, for her ears only, "Careful, my love, Cataldo's the detective in charge of this case, not you. Don't get carried away..." He wondered whether she had heard him, for she took no notice.

Dorothy had a suggestion. "I know what we should do," she said. "Being Americans and all, we should get in touch with the FBI."

"Excellent thought, Dorothy," Pete said. "But as we are not within the borders of the continental United States, I would recommend the CIA instead, since they have purview over matters in foreign countries."

"How do you get in touch with the CIA?" Art said, a worried look on his face. "I don't think they would have a listing in the Padua telephone book."

"You could be wrong there, Art," was Millicent's quick rejoinder. "I would look in the yellow pages under *Espionagio*."

Millicent can be funny, Harry thought. This is a first for me. I've never come across a funny accountant before.

"I bet a helicopter could find them," Tom offered. "Back in the Korean War, I used to do helicopter surveillance, and we would find enemy positions from an altitude of about a thousand feet that we could never detect from the ground. Surely, the Padua police have a helicopter."

"Probably not," Fred countered. "I happen to know that most cities, even large ones, don't have helicopters in their police departments...unless it's Los Angeles. LAPD couldn't function without their helicopters."

Eldernapped

"Just a long shot..." Paul said. "According to those two young medical students we met, that fellow at the bottom of the staircase who got away with Marguerite's suitcase was really badly hurt. Maybe we should check the hospitals."

"I'd rather check the morgues," Emily said.

And so it went—with suggestion after helpful suggestion popping up from every table. None were any good, was Harry's judgment, especially since none came from him. Which was embarrassing. With his technical training and good imagination, he should have come up with something useful by now. No, the trouble is that all of them were merely random ideas. There was no pattern.

♦♦♦♦

The yellow Lancia pulled out of the mansion grounds and the iron gates clanked shut behind it. After pausing at the end of the driveway, the car turned left, which pointed it in a direction slightly north of west. "Look at the map, Marguerite," Justin requested. "Doesn't this road turn into S516?"

"S516...S516...I don't find any S516."

"No, no, you're looking at Sicily. Turn the map over. Look at the other side of the map."

It took a while, but then she said, "Oh yes, that's right, S516."

"Then what?"

"I thought you had studied this before we left."

"I did, but I just want to make sure."

From this interchange, it occurred to Justin that anyone would have thought they had known each other for years, rather than just days. "It won't be very far," he said. "It should be a short and comfortable drive."

"Comfortable! I've never ridden in a car before that makes me stretch out flat as though I were lying on a bed."

"Well not entirely flat. Our heads are high enough so that we can still look out the windows. These are supposed to be bucket seats, but they do seem to be more like head rests. Anyway, that's the way sports cars are. If we didn't sit like this, our heads would hit the ceiling."

"I wouldn't have figured you for a sports car type," Marguerite said with a sigh. He could tell she was forcing herself to make conversation.

"Right, Marguerite, I would never in a million years have chosen a car like this, even if Hertz had had it available for rental. But it was sitting in the garage back at the house, and Sam searched around and found a set of keys. You know, we can't use the Fiat...we'd be spotted in a minute in that one."

"Yes." Marguerite sighed again. "I know."

"So let's enjoy the scenery. Do you know, I've never been to Europe before. Still, except for all the stone buildings...I haven't seen one made of wood yet...it's not too different from what you would find in Rhody's farm country, as for example between Tiverton and Little Compton. Although, I must admit these farms are unusual. All they're growing are those rows of little bushes.

They drove on for a few miles in silence that he interrupted with a sudden exclamation. "Son of a gun!" he said. "I know what they are, this being Italy. They must be grape bushes...and these must be vineyards."

"When is your sister coming?" Marguerite interrupted. She didn't seem interested in the similarities, or differences, between farmlands in Rhode Island and Italy. "I want to settle this matter with her as soon as possible...since, obviously, I can't with you."

The disdain in her voice made him writhe with shame. "As you know," he mumbled, "I expect her tomorrow. When I talked to her a couple of days ago, she said she would get here as fast as she could, but with packing, and with no warning, and figuring out airline schedules and all, I can't imagine her arriving any sooner

Eldernapped

than tomorrow or the next day at the earliest. Still, knowing Roberta, she could even be here today. For all we know she will greet us this evening when we get home. And I'm sure you ladies will get along fine. Once you know Roberta, you might even get to like her."

"I doubt it."

"In the meantime," he continued, trying to put on a happier face, "Let us enjoy ourselves as much as we can. You, especially. I really want you to have good time today. You said you wanted to see this city we're going to, Vicenza, with all the buildings by the great architect...what's his name?"

"Palladio."

"Yes, Palladio. So let's get to Vicenza and enjoy Palladio."

After a pause during which she took a number of deep breaths, Marguerite agreed to his suggestion. What other options did she have? "All right," she said. "Just for this afternoon, let's enjoy Palladio."

Well, at least she said that much, Justin thought, which is better than her saying nothing, for he knew how unhappy she must be, a state for which he was to blame. But that didn't stop him from cautioning her. "Now remember our agreement, Marguerite. I offered to take you on this little jaunt, because I know it would give you pleasure. But you mustn't make any kind of fuss. Don't try to attract attention or reveal anything about the fact that you are..."

"Kidnapped."

"Not exactly kidnapped."

"Do you have a better word? Abducted? Snatched? Shanghaied? Hijacked? Deprived of one's liberty against one's will?"

"You know, I never meant for this to happen. It was a terrible mistake, but it should be all made right as soon as Roberta gets here. Then you can go back to your Senior Seminar and I promise you'll never see me again. This will amount to nothing more than just a few awkward days. Although you must admit, we've tried to make your stay with us as pleasant as possible.

"All right, Justin, I won't make any obvious fuss...God knows why. On the other hand, if I see an opportunity to get away from you, I'll take it."

He thought it wise to make no reply. Still, he felt confident that so long as he kept himself in a state of constant alertness, such an opportunity would not arise.

When they got to the city, Justin followed the helpful signs that appeared every few blocks pointing to its *centro citta*. As they drove down a grand avenue lined with imposing stone structures, Marguerite spotted a store front that displayed a single letter, a lower case *i*. This, she informed Justin, seasoned traveler that she was, stood for *informazione*. It was like an American chamber of commerce, where local tourist information could be obtained.

How nice the lady behind the counter was. Tall, blonde and svelte she was, Justin couldn't help noticing. She spoke to her visitors in fluent English, once she determined their nationality

The woman piled his arms high with street maps, booklets, dining guides and a detailed description, the English version, that she pulled from a rack that also offered French, German and Japanese versions, for fully thirty of Palladio's buildings, all within walking distance. "But the walking tour, most of which you can take right down our main avenue, the well- named Corso Andrea Palladio, wonderful though it is," she said as they left, "is only an introduction to Palladio. Make sure you don't miss his Teatro Olympico with its fantastic *trompe-l'oeil* stage designed by the famous seventeenth century set designer, Scamozzi. And the great Rotunda, two kilometers southeast of the city. It inspired the residence of your great president, Thomas Jefferson...Monticello."

"Yes," Justin replied over his shoulder, "we'll make sure we don't miss them."

Eldernapped

Marguerite flipped open one of the brochures. "His dates are fifteen oh eight to fifteen eighty," she said.

"Whose dates?"

"Palladio's. Whose else's?"

"Oh."

"And except for a few short intervals, he never really lived anywhere but right here in Vicenza. And by the way, it's pronounced 'Vi-chen-za.'"

"Vi-chen-za."

"Let me read you this. It says that, 'His style is characterized by columns and pilasters of composite structure on a colossal scale,' and then, here's another interesting statement..."

"Sounds fascinating," Justin said.

"Would have sounded even more fascinating if it could have been explained to us in person by the Senior Seminars guide. I remember on the first day, Julie told us that an actual architect from Vicenza would conduct the Palladio tour. Now that we've missed him, we have to be self-guided. So let's get going," Her tone of voice sounded almost school teacherish, which led Justin to expect her to emphasize that call to action with a smart clap of her hands.

Several hours later, as they were driving home, Justin said, his voice filled with awe, "No way to deny it, this Palladio fellow certainly deserves all of his great reputation. I now realize that I have been looking at buildings in the United States all my life...never realizing that they were just copies of what he did four hundred years ago. I can't get over the way he makes the windows on each upper floor smaller than the ones below so the building looks taller. And did you notice the stones that make up his buildings' walls? He gets all kinds of interesting effects because some are smooth, some have diamond shaped projections and some look like they were just rough cut."

George Freedman

"You sound like an architectural critic," Marguerite said. "Are you sure you never took a course or something?"

Justin couldn't conceal his pleasure at hearing Marguerite's favorable appraisal of his understanding of things architectural, even as he responded with modesty, "No, never took any kind of course in subjects like that. Majored in economics. The point is," he went on, "we have the same designs back home. Palladio could have designed the Bank of Rhode Island building on Stuart Street in Woonsocket. Also, the city hall in Pawtucket. And think of Providence. Except for the high rises...and even there you see Palladio's influence. Providence...at least downtown...it's Palladio's city. Son of a gun."

"I'm so glad you liked Palladio...and Vicenza," Marguerite said. Justin was sure he detected a small glimmer of satisfaction on her face that for some reason, made him feel happy.

"I owe it all to you, Marguerite," he said. "Without your guidance, I would never have known that there was a man called Palladio who did so much to make the world look the way it looks. And I certainly would never have known that there was such a place as Vicenza...Vi-chen-za, that is. Thank you, Marguerite. Thank you very much."

"You're welcome."

As Justin maneuvered the little vehicle off Rte. A6 and onto S516, he continued this pleasant train of thought. "I'm also really glad we stopped to see Palladio's Rotunda building on our way home," he said. "It did take another hour, but it was time well spent, especially since it included the extensive garden that surrounds it. You know I'm quite a gardener myself. Some day I'd like to show you around my house in Woonsocket..."

"I once saw Monticello," Marguerite interrupted. Was that a note of panic in her voice? Could she be sensing that this was almost an implicit invitation? How ridiculous, he surely had not meant it that way.

Eldernapped

"...In Charlottesville, Virginia," she went on, her voice calmer now. "My husband and I stopped in during a vacation trip. We thought it was beautiful. But now of course, after what we've seen today, I realize that it's nothing but Palladio's Rotunda done in red brick instead of gray stone. But of course the interiors of the two buildings are very different."

"Your husband?"

"Charles. He passed away seven years ago. Cardiac arrest."

A quiet period ensued as the miles were gobbled up, until Justin broke the silence. "What do you know, we're home."

Indeed they were, for they proceeded through the gates that opened in response to the Lancia's trumpet blast and then down the driveway that made a circular causeway around the house. This brought them to the front of an old stone building, once a stable and storage space for horse-drawn carriages and coaches, but now a garage large enough to hold many vehicles.

In addition to the large black Fiat, there was now a light blue Mercedes with a roof rack and Austrian plates.

"I wonder who that Mercedes belongs to," Justin said, as he closed the garage door and they started to walk back up the driveway to the front door. "We must have visitors. One thing we can be sure of," Justin said, "no one knows we're here. We've covered all our tracks, and when we checked out of the Plaza Hotel, it was as though we had fallen through a hole in the ground. We left without a trace."

"He's right, Mrs. Dillard," Sam spoke up. "Not a trace. Anyway, if anyone was gonna trace us, they would've found us by now."

This comment was seconded by his colleague, Vinny, who growled the monosyllable, "Ya."

"And what about this ridiculous excursion you...and she...have just come back from?" Roberta said, indicating Marguerite by a disdainful toss of her head.

"Do you expect me to believe that no one spotted the two of you, gallivanting, God knows where, all over Italy for the whole population to see? Pretty clever of her I must say...and sneaky...to entice you out into public places where anyone could recognize you." With this she skewered Marguerite with a baleful look of scorn and disapproval.

"Now come on, Roberta," Justin protested, "what are you blaming her for? Remember, she's the wronged one. We're the ones who kidnapped her, after all."

"Be still, Justin. Oh, I can see now what a mistake it was sending you on this errand. And don't use that word."

"What word?

"Kidnapped."

"Why not use that word?" Marguerite asked in her soft and clear voice. "It's the right word, isn't it?" This was the first time she had spoken at all, having sat in silence through all the Wharton clan's previous discussion. The disgusted look on her face, Justin noticed, was beginning to unsettle Roberta. "But maybe, in fact, kidnapping is the wrong word. Maybe there's an even worse word...or phrase...that describes what you did, like kidnapping in the first degree or kidnapping with malice aforethought."

"Oh never malice, Marguerite," Justin said. "If anything, this was kidnapping without any malice at all. And certainly without any aforethought. If it's kidnapping, it has to be kidnapping by mistake."

"Justin, you numskull, shut up," Roberta said in reaction to her brother's contribution.

However, Marguerite seemed to take no notice of this interchange. Her words flowed on as though Justin and Roberta had said nothing. "Don't worry about how to describe what you did when you abducted me," she said. "Mark will know. Mark is my older boy...a very important lawyer with the biggest law firm in Cincinnati. He expects to make partner this year. Mark will work out how to phrase it in the most damning legal terms when he brings charges against you people."

This caused a sputter by red-faced Roberta, so full of emotion as to be incomprehensible. Alfred rose from his chair to try to calm his mother.

The two made a strange, contrasting mother-son picture, Justin found himself thinking. She was tall, sallow like himself and they shared the Wharton horse face. Alfred was of moderate height and build, wore wire-rimmed glasses, and had a round, pink-cheeked, boyish face. But the eyes of the two, both pairs the identical shade of steely blue, shared the same determined look.

Marguerite was making an interesting contrasting picture of her own as she listened to Roberta's tirade, he observed. There she was, all by herself, almost lost in this hostile crowd, with her small, perhaps petite is a better word, body, sunk into in the plush of a large, oak framed chair. Yet, she was erect and dignified, her ankles primly crossed, her tasteful clothing ordered and neat, not a hair on her gray head out of place.

Justin could see that some peacemaking was in order. "But don't you see, Bobbie, that was the clever part of our little excursion today." He had reverted to his name for her from their childhood days, the endearing, diminutive version, to remind her that after all he was the older brother. "We were just strolling around like any ordinary, you might say...couple...doing ordinary sightseeing on a pleasant spring Sunday afternoon. I am pleased to tell you we did not attract any attention.

"I had to do something to amuse Marguerite," he continued, "She was going crazy stuck away downstairs in one room for days on end. And I knew that she had set her heart on seeing the wonderful Palladio buildings in Vicenza. I couldn't have us responsible for her coming all the way to Italy from Cincinnati and missing them, could I?"

"Amuse her..." bellowed Roberta. "I've known you all your life, Justin, and...take it from me...you've never amused anyone. What makes you think you can start now?"

"And we did have a good time today, didn't we, Marguerite, with that walking tour and the great lunch?" Justin said, as though he had not even heard his sister's remark. "She really knows how to order from an Italian menu, I can tell you. And then we went on to the Rotunda. Wasn't that a great garden next to the Rotunda, Marguerite?"

Marguerite did not answer. But Alfred spoke up, his voice calm, logical. "Mother may be right," he said. "This lady could have found a way to call attention to herself and given the whole thing away. Maybe she did and you, Uncle Justin, didn't know she did."

"That's what I was thinking," Sam agreed. "She's a pretty smart cookie, you know."

"Ya," Vinny said. "Ask her anything, and she knows about it."

"Don't you think I thought of that?" Justin countered. "No, rest easy, everyone. I had no fear that she would, as you fellows would say," nodding to Sam and Vinny, "blow our cover. We had a bargain, Marguerite and I. She promised that if I took her on this little trip...and the trip was my suggestion, not hers...to Vicenza...which is pronounced the way I just said it, by the way...she would do nothing that would give us away. She promised that. I trusted her, and I still trust her."

On hearing this, Marguerite shifted in her chair.

"And that is how it was," he concluded, beaming at all with self-satisfaction. But even as he did so, he knew that the disagreement between Roberta and himself, with regard to that tour, was extreme indeed, and it was enough to cause a protracted silence on the parts of everyone in that room.

Until it was at last broken by Marguerite, who said to him, "I am glad you enjoyed yourself, Justin, and I appreciate that you took me. But that does not take anything away from the fact that I have been held here

Eldernapped

against my will, and that's a crime. Furthermore, all of you in this room are guilty of this crime...and I'm sure Mark won't sit still until he makes sure all of you go to jail. "I know what I am talking about," she said, her words taking on a hard edge. "I say all of you, because the law says it doesn't matter who does the hands-on job, accessories before or after the fact are just as guilty. I learned that from my Mark. He always had such interesting things to tell me about what he was learning in law school."

"You wouldn't dare," Roberta retorted, spitting out the words. "Just you try to come up against the Dillards and the Whartons and you'll be sorry the idea ever occurred to you. Anyway, it has to be all your fault. Look what you've done to my poor brother." Roberta glared at Justin. "Suddenly, he's ready to prance around Italy with any woman he picks up in the street. And Italy! The man hasn't been a hundred miles out of Woonsocket in the last forty years. Nor has he ever so much as looked at a woman...as far as I know...in all that time."

Now it was Justin's turn to squirm in his chair.

"I can't believe how much he's changed in just one week over here," Roberta went on. "How could she..." a toss of the head in Marguerite's direction, "have made all this happen in just the few days they have known each other? The only way I can explain it is his age. I never knew that senility took this form. Which leads me to wonder whether he'll ever be any good at the company again, now that he has become unstable."

Roberta was on a roll now. It was clear to Justin that nothing was going to stop her. "I suppose the next thing you'll do, Justin, will be to become one of those silly old men who pop up in resorts wearing plaid golf pants, drinking daiquiris and taking up with any woman who wants to get into your pockets. I suppose from now on that you'll be taking more trips like this. Where are you going to next, Justin...Paris? Las Vegas? Tahiti? Club Med? I wonder, dear brother, could it be that this means

George Freedman

the time has come for you to pack it in and retire? God knows what harm you can do to Wharton Valve now that your interest in the place is being diverted so drastically. Anyway, you're old enough to retire now. What do you think, Alfred? Isn't he old enough to retire?"

Justin didn't feel he had to wait for Alfred's response. Rather, he made a sad observation of his own. "Don't be so everlasting smart, Bobbie. If I'm getting old, what about you? You're only a year younger than I am. But maybe you're right about some things," he went on, "Maybe I've stayed home too much during my life...and not seen or experienced what the world has to offer...away from Woonsocket and Wharton Valve. But it needn't be too late. Now, while I am still healthy and vigorous, I should reach out...do the things I have missed in life...even if doing so means giving up my job in the company."

Alfred still owed his mother a response to her question. But instead, he turned to Justin, "Pay no attention to her, Uncle Justin."

"Pay no attention to her!" Roberta exploded. "What kind of way is this for you to talk about your mother, Alfred? You've never..."

"Please, Mother," Alfred interrupted. "Whenever we get to the subject of Wharton Valve Incorporated and how it operates, we have to separate ourselves from the fact that you are my mother."

"I'll say I'm your mother."

Alfred turned once again to Justin. "I've always wanted to say to you, Uncle Justin, how wonderfully well you serve our company as its chief financial officer, so let me correct any misconceptions you may have on that score right now. I can't conceive of anyone who could possibly do your job better...not even a first rate, mid-career MBA with a degree from the HBS.

Justin felt unaccustomed warmth in his cheeks and brow. How embarrassing. A man of his age, blushing.

Eldernapped

"Not only that," Alfred said, "now that I've seen you operate in the last few years...as your boss...I've been thinking of a way to use your fine talents to a greater degree than in the past. You've really been under exploited...and I use that word in its best sense. To put it simply," Alfred said, "I would like to ask you to take on a number of additional, highly important responsibilities.

"No, surely you are mistaken..." Justin mumbled.

"I've been thinking of putting you in charge of consummating a merger that will drastically change the valve industry, world wide. This will occur because the party to be acquired, an Austrian firm, by the way, has developed a way to make valves without using gaskets. As you know, Uncle Justin, up to now, every valve uses no less than two gaskets." He seemed to pause to let the impact of this disclosure sink in. "If the deal goes through, it will revolutionize valve making. What do you think of that, Uncle Justin?"

Justin was finding it hard, in the midst of all this turmoil, to absorb the implications of Alfred's breathtaking announcement. But he did manage to chime in with, "Really...? No gaskets, you say? Sounds...very significant."

"You bet it is. And that's not all. I'm also planning the acquisition of a small software outfit in Natick, Massachusetts. If that works out as I think it should, we'll have the world's first general-purpose valve with a computer chip.

"Or maybe we don't have to wait. I should think you could do both at once. And if you need extra time to get these jobs done, we can hire an assistant for you who will take over the routines of your CFO responsibilities. So what do you say, Uncle Justin, are you game?"

"Well, I must say, Alfred," Justin said, "I'm very flattered to know that you think so highly of me and of the work I do. You've never mentioned it till now and I always wondered whether you were just keeping me on because I came with your inheritance."

"How can you say that, Uncle Justin? If you have a fault it's that you're too modest. Still, I always thought you realized how happy I was...and lucky...to have you in our top management team."

"Well, you never said..."

"That was a mistake on my part, Uncle Justin. I should really tell people when I think they are doing particularly well."

"You never hesitate to tell them how poorly they're doing."

"Hm..."

"But the fact is I am getting on in years," Justin continued. "Maybe your mother is right and the time has come for me to retire. "That won't be the end of the world for me. I now see that I have not lived a full enough life. And the good thing is that it is not too late."

Alfred did not seem at all put off by his uncle's words. He went on as if they had never been uttered, a characteristic, Justin noted, he shared with his mother. "Think of it, Uncle Justin, if you take up these new duties, you will have to make frequent visits to Austria. That's not far from Italy, which you seem to like. And you've already met Otto Kreutzer this evening just before he took off to return to his headquarters. He's our manager in Vienna. You'll be working with him. Nice fellow, yes?"

"Don't you think you are overstepping a little, my boy?" Roberta said, her lips drawn thin, her voice now calm and cold. "You haven't consulted me on Justin's new assignment. May I remind you," she went on, "that I am a member of the board of directors of Wharton Valve Incorporated? And no executive change at this level can go through without our approval. The board just might not want to go along with this suggestion of yours, my son."

"I think our discussion is getting a bit away from what really matters this evening," Marguerite interrupted. "Although I congratulate you, Justin, on your good job rating by your employer. Now, I want you all to know that

Eldernapped

my bag downstairs is packed. I expect to be released from here immediately. But don't call a cab. It's late, and after today's all day excursion I'm weary. However, I do expect to be out of here tomorrow morning ...early. I'm not even going to wait for breakfast. I'll have that at the Casa del Santo."

Marguerite waited. Justin figured she wanted the implications of her statements to sink in. "Yes," she went on, "you're right, Roberta. May I call you Roberta? Your brother Justin did pick me up off the street...literally. And from what I've heard tonight, you're right on another matter as well. Justin," her attention now focused on him. "I think you should prepare to get out of that company. Just as your sister said, but not for the reason she thinks. After what you've done to me, when the law comes down on you...face it...you'll be finished with that company...unless you can carry out those interesting new assignments from a jail cell.

On hearing this, Sam snarled and Vinny grimaced, Alfred's brow knitted and Roberta sat up straight in her chair and beamed cold hatred at Marguerite. As for Justin, he sighed so deeply that he felt as though his body were imploding.

"One more thing," Marguerite went on. "As you have been talking, I've been thinking about how much to sue you for. I really don't know how the number popped into my head. Two point five million dollars. One million is obviously too little for the anguish you have caused me...and five or ten million seems like too much. But two point five sort of splits the difference. You show me a judge who wouldn't award that kind of money to a nice, little elderly lady like me for the agonies you wealthy people...you are wealthy, aren't you...have caused me. Yes sir, that's it, not a dollar less. Even if Mark thinks we could get more, he'll go along when I insist.

I bet he will, too, Justin thought.

"And now," Marguerite yawned, "it's time for bed." She rose from her chair and headed for the staircase that led to the lower level. When she reached its landing, and still visible through the living room door, she turned and addressed her parting remark to Justin.

"Thank you, Justin," she said, "for a lovely day. In spite of everything, I really did enjoy it. And also, I'm so glad you gained an appreciation today for the architectural achievements of the great Palladio. If you get nothing else out of your visit to Italy, at least you'll always have that." With that, Marguerite disappeared down the stairs that led to her cell.

Eldernapped

Day Nine

"285"

"One of the surprises of the history lectures," Emily said, "was to learn that the Veneto was once part of Austria. That nice Dr. Kingsley Elgin...you know, he's the one who commutes from Verona and has an Italian wife...he went through it all for us. It was actually Napoleon and the French who took over this region in seventeen ninety-six."

Listening to her rattle on, Linda thought to herself how proud Dr. Elgin would be of her, so well had she learned her lesson.

"...And then, later on, some of his relatives, the Austrian Bonapartes, were put in charge. In fact this province was Austrian till the mid-eighteen hundreds when..."

"And that," Linda interrupted, by way of closing the subject, "is how come we are sitting this evening in this very historical Viennese coffee shop, Caffe Pedrocchi. Joey told me that the Austrians built it because they hated Italian pastries...probably not gooey enough for them...but also so they wouldn't get homesick. And now, it's still here, still serving Viennese pastry."

"Nice though he is, Dr. Elgin does drone on a bit," Emily continued. "On the other hand, he really knows his field. In just two lectures he brought us all the way from ancient Roman days in this region to Mussolini and WWII, and even to the payoff scandals in the government that were in yesterday's Herald Tribune."

George Freedman

"So..." Linda managed to squeeze in a word, at last, "I thought the Caffe Pedrocchi would be a very good place for us to meet, Grammy dear, because it's, like, interesting and famous? And it's nice and old and the Austrian coffee and pastries are wonderful, and also because..."

"I enjoy things that are interesting and nice and old. I feel I can relate to them. Although I can't claim to be famous. Also, as you point out, it is very Austrian. My third husband, Mr. Herrera...who of course you never knew, dear...and I, on our honeymoon in the fifties, spent a few days in Vienna. This place, with its Art Deco woodwork and the wall sized mirrors, looks just like a typical Viennese coffee shop. Very authentic. How strange to find it in Padua, Italy."

"It's also interesting in a literary sense," Joey added, who, in accordance with Linda's contriving, had just met his grandmother-in-law-to-be for the first time, and with his presence completed a threesome around the small green marble tabletop. "Many of the great English poets of the nineteenth century used to drop into this very building when they were doing their European Grand Tours, on their way to Venice from the Swiss Alps and Como. They would find it so pleasant that they would settle down with their coffee or wine or beer at one of these very tables...maybe even this one, who knows? And they would compose a poem.

"It was the custom to write a few lines from that poem right on the wall. Those lines were never erased or painted over. I think, if you look around, you might find some stanzas by Thackeray or Wordsworth in their own handwriting, and a lot of others, though I am not sure about Shelley or Byron."

"Really?" Emily responded, her eyebrows lifting.

This young Italian man, Linda imagined she was saying to herself, quite a handsome one by the way with those deep brown eyes and wavy brown hair and masculine Roman profile, knows something about English

Eldernapped

poets. How unusually learned he must be. Or is he just trying to impress me because I am Belinda's grandmother?

"You'll have to excuse Joey, Grammy," Linda said, beaming at Joey, with a look of utter adoration. "He grew up in this city, you see, and he knows everything about it. But enough of this talk. Can we get you anything else...another coffee perhaps?"

"Good idea, Belinda, I can always use another coffee, even this late in the day, and maybe an Austrian pastry to go with it...just for old time's sake."

She must be having a nostalgia fit, Linda thought, with fond memories of the late Mr. Herrera, just as her Grammy whipped around and hailed a passing waiter,

"Ho! Garcon, a *linzertorte* and another coffee please...*und mit shlage, bitte*. That means with whipped cream in German, you know, Belinda dear," she confided behind of the back of her hand.

"Yes, I know. But let's get down to the reason we asked you to meet us here in the first place, Grammy dear."

"To meet Joey, of course. And I've met him, and he seems to be very charming. Make sure you treat my Belinda right, young man," she added as she hammered him on his knee with her small, hard fist, "or you'll hear from me."

Linda could see that Joey was in the act of formulating a statement of assurance to the effect that his intentions toward Linda were no less than entirely honorable. Before he could get it off the pad though, she felt the time had come for her to take over the floor once more. "Yes, to meet Joey of course," she interjected. "But we had another reason for wanting to be with you here today, Grammy. We came up with an idea on how to track down Uncle Justin and the rest of his awful family so that we can rescue Marguerite. Oh, excuse me," she added, her hand going to her mouth, realizing that this was Grammy's family as well, "I didn't mean to say..."

"Say what you must, child. They are indeed awful. Except for Justin. Roberta has just swept him along. And as for Albert, probably him, too."

"I thought his name was Alfred."

"Alfred, Albert, whatever."

"The idea was that Bianca Ianella who works with me at the bar? She knows the switchboard operator at the Plaza Hotel. And this was Joey's idea..."

"No, I must insist," his hand up. "It was you in fact who came up with it. It was really her idea, Signora Adams."

"Well, all right, Joey, I came up with it. Isn't he a doll, Grammy, the way he wants to make me look good in front of you?" This called for a peck on his cheek. "Anyway, that switchboard operator was able to trace whether the Dillards made any phone calls from their hotel room before they checked out.

"And did they?"

"They did. They made one call. And guess what?"

"What?"

"Bianca's friend was able to track from phone company records the actual phone number they called, and from that we were able to get the address by calling information."

"It's in a small town on the canal between here and Venice," Joey put in. "The canal is called *Naviglio del Brento*. Naviglio means canal, so as you would say it, it is the Brento Canal. But it is also known as the *Riviera del Brento* or Brento River."

"Never mind the canal's or river's name. What actual place did they call?" Emily was getting excited, a faint blush of pink beginning to illumine her otherwise pale face.

"There are three small towns between here and Venice alongside that canal," Joey replied, revealing again his lovable tendency, Linda thought, always supplying more information than is asked for. "They're Stra, Delo and Mira. This call was made to Delo, the middle one, the

Eldernapped

one east of Stra and west of Mira, less than twenty kilometers from here. It is on a street called *Via Naviglio del Brento*," referring to a little pad he drew from his jacket pocket, "number two eighty-five."

"Bull's-eye! That must be where Justin is staying. The place we're all trying to find," Emily said with gleeful force. "Good work, you two. Roberta must have called there and got Justin or one of his two thugs to say that she and her son were in town and I bet they told them to check out of the hotel and move into their place. Then they could be with Justin...and Marguerite."

"That's what we thought," Linda agreed, pleased that her Grammy appreciated the cleverness of what she and Joey had done, which meant that Joey must now be scoring very high in Grammy's book.

Emily leaped to her feet. In a flash, she put on her coat and slung her knapsack onto her shoulders. Upon catching the eye of the waiter she called out, "Cancel that linzertorte and coffee, garcon."

She turned to her companions. "What are we waiting for? Let's go pay a visit."

♦ ♦ ♦ ♦

Two couples emerged from their taxi and stopped to study the elegant building that confronted them. It was large and coated in pink stucco. Crenellated stone projections lined the edges of its roof. "I suppose the original owners were able to station archers up there to protect the place in time of invasion," Harry offered.

"What about pots of boiling oil?" Art said. "That would be an even better way to discourage invaders."

"We're invading," Irene said. "But I would guess the people who run this place don't think of us as a threat to be beaten off."

"Isn't it grand?" Naomi said. "And look at the garden. Those lanterns against the evening sky make it look very romantic."

"We shouldn't be surprised at its grandeur," Art said, waving a small red book at them. "It's the only restaurant in Padua that Michelin lists with one star for dining and three red forks for décor and service."

"Should be good," Harry said. "Let's go in."

As they ordered, Harry thought they had been wise indeed to indulge themselves in this manner. The food in the Casa was all right, in fact better than all right, when compared with what they could expect in good Italian restaurants in the States. But it's always smart to break away during any Senior Seminars program, for one dinner at least in order to savor the cuisine and the ambience of the city.

When the wine steward appeared, they accepted his recommendation of a dry white from the region. "Vaary nice." he had said.

"I think we should have a large bottle of sparkling mineral water as well," Art said. "I notice every table in this room has a bottle in addition to their wine. It's obvious Italians never drink tap water, so why should we be different?" He signaled for their waiter to return.

"Right," Irene agreed. "When in Rome..."

Art reminded her that they were not in Rome but in Padua.

"Close enough, dear."

Like Romans, or Paduans, they each partook of some of the four available courses, *antipasto, primo piatto, secondo piatto, dolce.* But for the main course and for dessert, each couple ordered only a single serving with two plates so that they could share.

This wasn't the way we used to eat in younger days, Harry reflected, as he watched Naomi and Irene subject their main course to partition, two thirds for the husbands, one third for the wives.

The Levines and the Maglios go back a long way, forty years at least, Harry mused. How many dozens of fine meals like this have we had together in all that time? And in all of them, nowadays at least, we always seem to

Eldernapped

reach a point, as we are reaching now, when the dinner table conversation lags and then stops altogether. Why should it not, since we've already disposed of so many subjects as the years moved on.

But Harry knew this was a condition that his dear wife Naomi, if it would be anyone of the four of them, would never allow to persist. He was right. "You know," she said, "I've been thinking about Emily's Justin and Roberta. I believe Justin has rented a house or a very large apartment in the Greater Padua area. Otherwise, why should Roberta and her son find it so convenient to check out of their hotel after staying only one night? They must have moved in with Justin and are probably with him this very minute. Not only with him, but with poor Marguerite, too."

"You know, I think you're right," Irene chimed in. Which was notable, Harry thought, since she was not known for agreeing with most things Naomi says. "And how lovely it must be for Marguerite," she went on, a tone of irony combined with sadness entering her voice, an image arising in her mind of that poor woman chained to a wall in some dungeon room.

Which led Harry to ask the next logical question of Naomi, "So how do we find out where that house or large apartment is, wise guy?"

Another prolonged stretch of silence followed. They had just finished dessert and he could see that everyone, including himself, was in a condition best described as sated. It was not conducive to animated discussion.

Then Naomi, without warning, exploded. "I know!" This startled the other three out of their respective torpors.

"Please excuse me for just a few minutes," Naomi said. "This won't take me long...and if it does, pay the check and go for a walk in the garden. I'll join you shortly." With that she got up. Moving briskly with the aid of her cane, she left the dining room.

It must have been twenty minutes later when Naomi reappeared, animation in her every movement, a look of satisfaction on her face. "Well?" Harry asked with a sigh, knowing that whatever she had been up to was of a magnitude as to floor them when she chose to inform them about it, and she appeared to be in no hurry to do so.

Naomi proceeded to pick her lipstick out of her purse and to replenish what coloration had been eaten or talked off. Harry never got over being impressed with how she did this without benefit of mirror. Three deft strokes and a tissue press. The deed was done. "I know...I actually know for a certainty...where Emily's family is hiding," she said.

"You know?"

"Really?"

"No kidding?"

"I know. Really. No kidding. I know exactly where they are. And here's the address." She whipped a scrap of paper out of her purse and read off the words, "Two eighty-five Via Naviglio del Brento, in the town of Delo. The nice maitre d'...Enzo is his name by the way...tells me that's about ten miles from here on the way to Venice. In fact, we must have passed through it coming here on the bus the first day. So now that our meal is over and we're free for the rest of the evening, why don't we get a taxi and drop in for a friendly little visit?"

"Are you nuts?" Harry couldn't believe his wife. "That's not for us to do. We should call Lieutenant Cataldo. It's his job. And anyway, how did you find this out?" He couldn't restrain some grudging admiration from creeping into his voice. How indeed?

"Well," Naomi answered with a smile, her lips now glowing with the color of rose blossoms, her vial of lipstick popped back into her purse, "I figured that before he took off from the States, Justin Wharton must have used a travel agent to find this hideout and rent it for him. We can guess he knew before he left he would have to kidnap

Eldernapped

his mother...for her own good, as he would put it. And that meant he needed a fairly large room or set of rooms...all to be arranged for before he left home...to keep her for a few days so as to prepare her for the flight home. And for this he needed more space and more privacy than would be available in a hotel. I imagine that the stop he made at the Plaza a week ago was just a convenience before settling in at that hideout," she went on. "Don't you agree, Harry?"

"I guess so."

"Kidnapping Marguerite was never in his plans. That was a mistake. But having done it, why not use the same place for her, too, until they could decide what to do with her."

"Prepare Emily? What do you mean, prepare her?" Irene said.

"I don't know...fill her up with tranquilizers or drugs."

"Against her will? That's illegal." Art rendered his professional opinion.

"Which proves that they're desperate. Or stupid...or, what is more likely, both at the same time," Naomi continued. "So I asked myself, how do you arrange a hideout...a house in the country or a large apartment...from Justin's home town of Woonsocket, Rhode Island? I need not remind you that Woonsocket is four thousand miles away. Isn't that where Emily told us he and his notorious sister live? Woonsocket, Rhode Island? Easy, get a travel agent to do it."

Everyone in the group nodded in approval.

"How many travel agents could there be in Woonsocket R-I? It's not a large city, and I would guess there's probably not much travel business going on there. So I found out. Just now, while you were sitting here. All I did was call Woonsocket information. As I thought, there are only two travel agencies in Woonsocket."

"Is that so? Only two," Harry said, taking a deep breath. "How interesting."

"Anyway, with the help of that nice Enzo who let me use his phone in the restaurant office, and using our telephone credit card, I got the U.S. information operator. Rhode Island is area code four oh one by the way, if you ever have to know. I was on the line to both agents within five minutes. It's lucky, by the way, that we have the time difference in our favor because it's still business hours in Rhode Island."

This gave vent to a gasp of admiration all around.

"I told the lady at Woonsocket Travel...not the one at Ocean State Horizons Unlimited which turned out to be the wrong one...that I was a cousin by marriage to Mr. Justin Wharton. Mrs. Tiffany Fenimore Wharton is my name, though my friends call me Muffy, one of the Philadelphia Whartons...and my husband Hugh," she winked at Harry, "...and I were taking a few months of vacation in Italy and the French Riviera. This minute we were passing through Padua...what a coincidence...and wanted to be in touch with dear cousin Justin. What a shame to be in the same darling little Italian city and not get together. I told the travel agent that we had tried to call Roberta, but she must be on the same trip. There was no way for us to reach either of them until I had this brilliant idea of getting in touch with Woonsocket Travel, because who else would have arranged their trip? And huzzah!...I was right."

"Naomi, you're a pistol," said Art.

"Double-barreled," said Irene.

"You think it's so easy living with a pistol?" said Harry. "You never know when she's going to go off."

Naomi accepted this praise with modesty, acknowledging it by no more than a momentary lowering of her eyelids as she fell silent. This made Irene impatient. "Get on with it, Naomi," she said. What happened next?"

"Well, you can't imagine how honored that travel lady was to be called, live, you might say, all the way from Padua, Italy, by Muffy Wharton of the Philadelphia

Eldernapped

Whartons...who had heard of the Woonsocket Travel agency. It only took a minute for her to look up the address of the house...more of a villa actually, she said...that she herself, as part owner of Woonsocket Travel and the Wharton's personal travel agent, had arranged for them.

"Before I rang off I asked for her name...Doris, it turned out to be...and you can be sure I thanked her very sincerely for her information and that I would make sure Justin and Roberta know how graciously I had been treated by Doris of Woonsocket Travel."

"You've really outdone yourself this time, Naomi," Irene said.

These very words were echoed by Art, although Harry, having lived through other Naomi triumphs in his lifetime, chose to remain silent.

"Who wants to call the taxi to Delo?" Naomi said. Then, on consideration, "I might as well take care of it since Enzo and I are already such good friends. He'll make the call for us.

"One more thing." She turned, having already stood up, and started for the lobby. "I'm going to ask for an extra large cab. While we can crowd the four of us into an ordinary taxi, we'll need a bigger one for the return trip because, of course, Marguerite will be with us...with her suitcase."

"But the police should be called, Naomi, before we do anything," Harry was unable to hide the defeated tone in his voice.

"Oh, I don't think so, Harry. Lieutenant Luigi at this time of evening must be home with his lovely family. Why disturb him now? We'll tell him how everything turned out tomorrow morning. Also, Enzo told me the approximate cab fare. It won't be too bad." With a dazzling and seductive smile on her face, Naomi turned to face Art. "Especially if Art offers to share it."

◆ ◆ ◆ ◆

Cataldo was not at home with his lovely family. Too many things were going on at headquarters, and he had decided to work late. Franco, as well. They were standing and they looked down at sheaf of papers on his desk.

And now, there was one more paper. The secretary had just entered his office and deposited it on top of the others. Cataldo read it, then handed it to Franco. "This certainly pins down the place, doesn't it?"

"Yes, it does, right on the canal in Delo," Franco said. It was a fax from the *carabonieri* in Udine, a three-border town abutting Austria to the north and what used to be called Yugoslavia to the east, about seventy miles away. It said:

Light blue late model Mercedes with Austrian plates and roof racks attempting to cross border into Austria intercepted 1954 hours in accordance with description in all points alert. Car impounded and driver now in custody. Driver name, Otto Kreutzer. Residence, Vienna, Austria. Passport in order. Occupation: Sales Manager for European Operations of Wharton Valve, Inc., an American company. Business card confirms this. Claims to have driven to Padua to have business conference with his employer, Sr. Alfredo Dillard. In course of meeting, drove Dillard and his mother from Hotel Plaza in Padua to their lodgings in Delo, address given as Via Naviglio del Brento 285. Phone number not given but suggest you corroborate this story with Dillard. Please advise disposition of Mercedes and of Herr Kreutzer.

Although this was the only document on Cataldo's desk that provided such precise information, he determined that most of the others were consistent with it, and corroborative. For example, there was the one received the day before from the Vicenza police that had originated in the tourist information center in that city.

Eldernapped

It stated that after an elderly American couple, she, small, well dressed in white blouse, gray wool skirt, gray sweater, small gold chain necklace, no earrings, he, tall, thin, in black pinstripe suit, black tie, black felt hat, had left the center with maps and brochures for a Palladio walking tour. The person on duty at that time noticed a strange entry in the visitor book. It was so unusual that she decided to alert the Vicenza police about it. Where the signature should have been, it said instead:

AIUTO! HELP!
Marguerite K. LoPresti, Cincinnati, OH USA. Am being held prisoner against my will in town near Padua. Justin looking this way. No time to write more.

The transmitter of that message went on to advise the Vicenza police to look in the Teatro Antico because she was sure the couple was going to make that their next stop, but upon searching that famous building, they found no elderly American couple to fit her description.

"What in the world made them go to Vicenza of all places?" Franco said.

To which Cataldo replied, "Beats me." He then called Franco's attention to the next note in the sequence.

It was another fax message, written in a strange, running style, from Signorina Julie Foster, Senior Seminars Administrator, at the Casa del Santo. "We never met her, did we, Franco?" Cataldo said.

"Yes we did, at the Casa when we questioned the Adams woman and her friends, but only for a minute, because she was rushing off on a bus trip somewhere, so she turned us over to her assistant, Signorina Parziale. You know, the one who's been so helpful to us."

"Oh yes, the one called Graziella?"

"You got it, lieutenant...Graziella. That's her name, Graziella."

Cataldo turned to his perusal of Juli's fax, translating enough of it to ensure that Franco got its drift.

It began by explaining that Julie was resorting to a fax since she had been unable to get connected with Lt. Cataldo's telephone. It had been busy for the preceding two hours, which was too bad because if not for that they might have caught one of Mrs. LoPresti's kidnappers. But, it went on to say, the man has surely escaped by now which meant to her that it would be a good idea for the Padua Police Department to find some way, in the future, for her to reach him. Despairing of ever getting connected, she had no recourse but to transmit this vital information the fastest way she could, by this fax. It then went on to inform him that an Alfred Dillard, claiming to be Lucille Adams's "...or as I know her, Emily Thorndike's...grandson" had called that afternoon and asked if she could kindly connect him with his grandmother please.

The fax recounted that she told the caller that Mrs. Adams/Thorndike was not on the premises at that moment since she was on a walking expedition to the Padua Botanical Gardens with the other students, but would he like to leave his phone number so she could call him back? But Mr. Dillard then said, "No don't bother, I don't happen to have the phone number for the store where I am calling from but I'll call you back." The climax of this communication was the lady's suggestion of a clever way for the Padua police to find the man's phone number and thus the location of Marguerite's site of incarceration.

"Why don't you put a bug on my telephone?" she wrote. "It will automatically identify the phone number of the caller and then you can easily trace where he's calling from, or if that is too much trouble, maybe you can trace all this afternoon's calls received by the Casa del Santo with the phone company. Maybe they keep records for at least twenty-four hours."

"Everyone wants to be a detective," Franco said.

Eldernapped

To which Cataldo responded, "You can say that again," as he restored the missive to the pile of notes from which it had come.

Finally, there was the last message, also faxed, that had been delivered not ten minutes before from the chief of Delo's two-man police department. It used some of the same words as had been reported by the tourist office lady in Vicenza.

"AIUTO *** AIUTO *** AIUTO *** AUITO *** HELP *** HELP *** HELP *** HELP..." it said.

Like the previous day's message written in the visitor book in Vicenza, this message was signed by the kidnapped lady herself, Marguerite LoPresti. It had been picked up by a resident of that town, who just an hour before had chanced to walk past the building at Via Naviglio del Brento 285.

The finder also reported that the note was written on brown packing paper and had been tied into an envelope form in an unusual way—with a strand of chive.

"What are we waiting for?" Franco said. "Let's make our move."

"You're certainly right, Franco," Cataldo responded, pleased at the mental quickness and decisiveness demonstrated by the young man. He's had worse assistants over the years.

"Put together a convoy of three fully staffed squad cars and a paddy wagon for prisoners," Cataldo ordered. "I'll meet you downstairs in fifteen minutes. We're on our way to Delo"

♦ ♦ ♦ ♦

Julie was dissatisfied with the results of her fax message to the Padua police. It seemed like Lieutenant Cataldo might get around to reading it next Thursday, if at all.

Added to which was the uneasy feeling she got every time she pressed the SEND button of her fax machine, an action that always said to her that she has done nothing real. Did the damned fax get sent or didn't it? How could anyone be sure? At least, if she dropped a letter down the chute of a mailbox, or even got a busy signal on her telephone, she knew that something has happened. Thus, moments after sending the fax, Julie addressed Graziella, with an alternative suggestion. "Why don't we look into this ourselves," she said.

"Mmmm," was Graziella's reaction.

"Darn it...I had Alfred Dillard right there on the phone," Julie went on, her mind clicking to the crux of the problem. "If I only had my wits about me I could have led him on to tell me something about where he was calling from."

"You mean, tricked him, sort of?" Graziella said.

"Call it what you want to, my friend. I like to think of it as ordinary run-of-the mill charm. It just happens I'm very good at that sort of thing, especially with men. In fact, especially the bright ones. But I wasn't thinking fast enough. All we can hope for is that he calls back. And if he does, Graziella, make sure the phone gets turned over to me."

"Did he really sound bright?" Graziella's casual tone indicated that she was just making conversation.

"Yes, I suppose so. Wait a minute."

"What?"

"Bright enough to be in a computer store. He *did* tell me where he was, but it was just a mumble and it didn't register in my brain till just this minute when you said 'bright.' Oh, how could I have been so stupid! What he said was that he was in a computer store right around the corner from here. He said if Mrs. Lucille Adams...that's Emily Thorndike, you know..."

"I know, I know."

"...Were in, he could just walk over and be here in a minute."

Eldernapped

"Of course he could," Graziella corroborated. "He must have been calling from *Denunzio's Palazzo del Byte*. That's the only computer store near here. And, it's just around the corner. That's where we buy our floppies and printer cartridges and computer paper."

"We should go over there right now," Julie said.

"What for? Surely, he's gone by now."

"Maybe. But you never know about computer nuts."

"It's already after dinner. Isn't the store closed?"

"No, computer stores never close."

Five minutes later, the two were talking to the very computer-clerk, on her chest was a tag that indicated her specialty, SOFTWARE, who confirmed that she was the very one who had served Mr. Dillard.

The clerk was a serious and thoughtful looking young woman, with a high broad brow before which perched a pair of large-lensed, amber-framed eyeglasses. She had the cyber brain look that someone with her sort of job would have, but she also had thick coppery hair, full Italianate breasts and hips, clear pink-white skin and soft full red lips, in summary, a classic type of the region. Which caused Julie, art history specialist that she was, to comment involuntarily to herself that Titian used to catch her essence well.

Yes, Ms. SOFTWARE remembered serving a young American man earlier that afternoon. "Fairly nice looking, in his early thirties maybe, with wire eyeglasses, sports jacket, khaki pants, blondish or maybe more light brown hair, with nice blue eyes," she said. "Is that the one?"

"Yes. That is...I think so."

"And does he drive a little yellow sports car? He had it parked at the curb.

"Could be."

"Still, I wouldn't have figured him for a sports car type. More the..."

"Nerdy type?

"Yes, like most all the fellows who must come in here."

"That must be him...especially if he made a phone call. Did he?"

"As a matter of fact he did. He asked if we had a coin phone and I showed him where it was. Then, he asked me to help dial the number. Americans can never figure out how to dial our telephones. Of course I was happy to oblige."

"Was that the only call he made?" Graziella said.

"It was. He was asking the person on the other end of the line to put his grandmother on the phone. I wasn't really listening, you know. I just happened to overhear, and it was a good opportunity for me to practice my English. Anyway, she wasn't there...the old lady, that is."

Aha, we're getting someplace, Julie thought. Now's the time to bore in. "You...or someone in this store...must know Graziella Parziale," she said, embracing Graziella around her waist with affection. "She's the assistant administrator of the Senior Seminars program in the Casa del Santo just around the corner, and I'm Foster, Julie Foster, the administrator."

"My boss," Graziella piped up, just so that there wouldn't be any doubt.

"Graziella's in this store a lot," Julie continued. "Because we always need computer supplies. Senior Seminars programs always need a lot of computer supplies."

"What is this Senior Seminars?"

"You know, old people from America."

"Oh yes, I see a lot of them coming into the store. I've wondered why we've been getting so many of them lately."

"Let me tell you why we're in here. We're looking for Mr. Dillard...that's his name, Dillard," Julie said, "But before I go on, may I ask your name? I feel so silly talking to someone and not knowing their name."

Eldernapped

"I am Yolanda Santoro," the clerk said, handing Julie her business card. "How can I help you?"

"Well, Yolanda, this Mr. Dillard has come here to Italy from the United States on business, but he made a special detour from...Turin...just so he could see his grandmother who is in our Senior Seminars program. But as I told him on the telephone...his Grandmama was out. So that was the end of it...till just a few hours ago when she came back from our tour of the Botanical Gardens. She is devastated that she missed her grandson, Alfred. She's eighty-nine years old and she has fourteen grandchildren, but he is her favorite. So there she is in her room crying. And I can tell you it is pathetic to see an eighty-nine year old woman crying.

"La povera nonna!" Yolanda exclaimed. A suitable reaction, Julie figured, and one for which slipping into Italian was well justified.

"Then, just a few minutes ago, Graziella and I got this great idea," Julie went on. "Mr. Dillard had mentioned that he was calling from the computer store nearby. It could only have been Denunzio's Palazzo del Byte. So we thought we would run over here..."

"Notice, we're still out of breath," Graziella contributed.

"...In order to see if anyone in the store could tell us how we could get in touch with him before he leaves Padua. Because Nonna tells us he is on a very tight schedule and will probably have to get away almost immediately."

Yolanda's face broke into a happy smile. "Don't worry," she said. "He's not leaving Padua...not for the rest of this week anyway."

"How wonderful. What good news." Julie said. "Then maybe you could help us find him and arrange for him to see his grandmother right away."

"Signora Thorndike will be so happy when she learns this," Graziella smiled.

"Not Signora Thorndike, Graziella, Signora Adams."

George Freedman

"Oh yes, Julie, Signora Adams. We have so many old ladies, Yolanda, and they all look the same. It's hard, sometimes, to keep them straight."

"Then how can we be in touch with him?"

Yolanda was swift to react. Please hold on for just a minute while I pull his record up on the terminal." She turned to the computer at one end of her counter and addressed its keys with a soft clatter of her long fingernails. As she did, she continued to chatter. "After he made the phone call, he wandered around the store and saw our sign for our new advanced, virtual reality, computer aided design, software package...VRCAD...we software people call it for short. And the next thing I knew, he bought it."

Yolanda was beginning to try Julie's patience. "So tell us how to get in touch with him. Being an old lady, his grandmother, doesn't have much time," she said, clenching her teeth.

"Yes, here it is," Yolanda peered at her screen. "You see, I had to inform Mr. Dillard that our version of the program has only Italian instructions, but that I could get him an English version in three days. Would that be all right? And he said sure, because he was going to stay on in Padua till the end of the week, anyway."

"Oh, so that's how you learned he's staying on. Go on, please."

"So I asked could he drop in here in three days and I will have his VRCAD software package with English instructions ready for him to pick up."

"Is that what he's going to do?" Julie's patience was wearing thin. "Will he come in three days?"

But no, that is not what he is going to do."

"No?"

"No. I told him he didn't have to come in, because we deliver. We have a messenger service. And that's how I know where he's staying. He gave me the address. I have it right here on my computer. Is that what you want to know?"

Eldernapped

Julie and Graziella shook their heads with vigor, as Yolanda read off, "Via Naviglio del Brento two eighty-five, in the town of Delo."

"Thank you, thank you." Julie responded with a deep sigh of relief. "Graziella dear, whip out your pen and pad and write this down. "Would you mind repeating that address, Yolanda?"

♦♦♦♦

Linda watched with pride as Emily, world's spunkiest little old lady, drew herself up to her full four foot eleven and confronted the residents of Via Naviglia del Brento 285. They were arrayed before her in a straight line, having just emerged from their respective lairs into a chamber of grand size that looked like a combination ballroom/living room

In the center stood a tall skinny woman in a long, royal blue lounging robe, who appeared to be on the far side of middle age. Must be the terrible Roberta, Linda figured, which led her to realize with horror that she was, like, a relation? That's Aunt Roberta, no less. And next to her was a young fellow, slim, of medium height, wearing steel-frame glasses and clothed in chinos, tan sports shirt and a shapeless green sweater. He could only be her son, Alfred.

They were flanked, on Roberta's right, by a heavy-set man with a frown on his face and with a corner of his shirt hanging out of his pants, while on Alfred's left was a familiar person. He was the one who had landed at the bottom of the Casa stairwell three or four days ago. Vinny.

Well, Vinny looks a little better now than he did then, sprawled out on the floor, like a dead person. But why shouldn't he look better? My Joey, with Bruno's help, had probably saved his life. And now, for some reason, even though she had all the others available to pick on,

Emily was choosing to focus her immediate wrath on this poor slob.

"Surprised to see me here, Vinny?" she said.

He only stared back at her with lower jaw hanging.

In any case, Emily didn't seem anxious to hear his response. Before he could get a word out she posed another question. "What did you do to your ear? It doesn't look good, I'm sorry to tell you. And your mustache. Did you cut yourself shaving, poor man? I don't think that style will ever catch on. Either have a mustache or don't have one...not just half a one. Make up your mind, Vinny. Which is it?"

"Mother!" It was Roberta's stern voice that interrupted Emily's rumination about Vinny's sad appearance. "Stop this foolishness. Come over here and sit down. We haven't seen each other for quite a long time and we have lot to talk about. But first...how did you ever find this place?

"Roberta, you disgraceful young woman."

This was not meant as a compliment, Linda was sure, even though the "young woman" was in her sixties, if she was a day.

"I'm ashamed to have to admit, the way you have treated me, that I am your mother. I'm not sitting down to talk to you because I'm simply not talking to you...ever again. If you try to say anything to me I just won't answer."

Having concluded this interchange with her daughter, Emily turned her attention to the three men who remained, in the shadow of their leader, stoic but shifty eyed "One of you, please answer this question, where is Marguerite LoPresti? That's why I'm here...to free her from you kidnappers. Just unchain her and tell her that Emily is here to take her home."

"Emily? Are you Emily now?" Roberta snorted. "What more proof can anyone need," she asked the ceiling, "that my poor mother has lost her marbles?" Receiving no reply, either from the ceiling or from any of those

Eldernapped

assembled, she went on. "Your name is not Emily, Mother dear. It is Lucille...Lu-cille." Roberta separated the two syllables so as to make the name more clear, "Whar-ton, do try to remember that."

"I haven't been a Wharton for the last forty-five years...or is it fifty-five?" Emily said, thus breaking her vow of silence, it hadn't lasted long, Linda noted. "And I've enjoyed every minute of it. Anyway the legal name is Adams now, even though I am not using it right now. I can use any darn name I choose...and I choose Emily. Em-i-ly Thorn-dike, Roberta dear," mimicking her daughter's sarcastic phrasing. "Do try to remember that. Which reminds me," she continued, "this is Belinda Adams," thrusting her forward, "my granddaughter out of Mr. Adams, my fourth husband. Cedric, he was. You must remember him. We did invite you to the wedding, and I think you actually came. So that makes Belinda, God save her from undeserved burdens, and you some sort of blood relatives...by which I mean, through my blood, not Cedric's"

Roberta threw a stony glance at Linda. Their eyes met.

Linda felt her flesh creep.

"Isn't that a blast?" Emily went on, "What does that make you two, some sort of step aunt and niece-in-law twice removed? But you don't have anything to worry about, Belinda dear. You are perfectly normal...and so will your children be...because if you think about it, none of your forebears can possibly be related to the Wharton side."

Thank goodness for that, Linda thought, as she examined the person in question and found her, on further inspection, even less attractive than on first impression.

"And these two fine young men," Emily said, turning now to point to each in turn, "are special friends of Belinda's. This is Joey and this is Bruno. Both are big and strong...so don't try any more monkey business with me. I'm not by myself any more."

Her face took on a crafty look as she pursued the point further. "So, at last," she taunted, "here I am. You've got me just where you want me." Why don't you just go ahead and grab me, like you did Marguerite, and tie me up in a straitjacket and ship me back to the U.S.A. by airfreight to some nuthouse? I dare you!" Emily uttered that statement with such force it left her breathless, but after a short pause during which her audience remained transfixed, she said, "I'd like to see you just try. It's obvious," she laughed, "you wouldn't dare. Because, with these two young men beside me... both doctors by the way...I now have protection. Although I must confess, we don't have guns, so if you want to shoot us, Vinny or Sam...I know at least one of you must have a gun in your hip pocket or under your armpit...I suppose we can't stop you."

Linda made sure her face remained unmoving and expressionless. But she was pleased to see Joey and Bruno, European gentlemen that they were, step forward one pace in perfect synchronization, and make a small bow each from the waist.

"Fabiano," Joey said.

"Parelli," Bruno said.

After which, they resumed their previous positions in the four-person row that made up he group supporting Emily.

"I suppose you're Albert," Emily said.

"Alfred, mother, not Albert," Roberta said. "She never got the boy's name right from the day we christened him," Roberta addressed this to no one in particular as she gazed again at the ceiling.

"Why should I get it right? I've only seen him two or three times in my whole life."

"Well, he is your grandson."

"I have many grandsons, and I never mix up their names. The trouble is you never invited me to visit while

Eldernapped

he was growing up. Only now, you pretend to be a good daughter so that you can put me away and take charge of my money."

"You know we invited you many times, Mother, but you were always too busy with your other families all over the country."

"A person can always sense when she's really wanted and when the invitation is insincere."

Linda could see, from the way he was shuffling his feet, that Alfred realized the time had come for him to say something. "I am so pleased to see you at last, Grandmother," he said. All eyes turned to him. "And you are right. I can't remember the last time we saw each other. I must have been just a kid. But let me assure you, no one wants to force you to do anything you don't want to do. What Mother has had in mind all along has been your best interests and your health. And I must say, Mother dear, from what I see, you...and Uncle Justin...might have been just a little mistaken about how much help Grandmother really needs. She looks perfectly able to take care of herself."

"Oh, Alfred dear, you can't possibly know the terrible things she is capable of from just seeing her here."

"Not in any way as terrible as the things you are capable of, daughter dear," Emily said. "But, poor thing, maybe you're not entirely to blame. You probably did get some of your headstrong tendencies from me. Still, I'll only take a small amount of the blame because, as I look at you, I see your father, God rest his soul, more than anyone.

"Darn right, I take after Dad. And I'm proud of it," Roberta said, her eyes flashing, her mouth making a severe straight line across her face. "If you had appreciated him more, maybe you and he would never have..." Her voice trailed off.

"I appreciated him all he deserved to be appreciated, my dear," Emily said, the line across her face matching that of her daughter's. "As for you, Alfred, I'll reserve judgment for now. "Enough of this," she cried. "Now that you have mentioned Justin...and goodness knows where he gets his character, certainly not from Robert or from me...where is he? I know how you can twist him around your little finger, Roberta. And Marguerite, too. Produce them so that we can get out of here. If we leave now, we'll get back to the Casa before bedtime.

"That's right," Linda said, at last summoning up the courage to offer a few words of her own. "We have a nice big car parked outside. It's Bruno's father's, and there will be plenty of room for all of us, Marguerite included."

Before anyone could make a response to Emily's request, there was a clang.

The gate." Roberta said. "Someone is at the gate. Vinny, go see who it is."

♦♦♦♦

"Emily, Linda, you found this place, too. Shoot! I thought we would be the first ones," Naomi said. "Well, anyway, we located these scoundrels before Lieutenant Luigi and Sergeant Franco could. Won't they be pleased when we call and tell them to come over to lock up this crowd?"

"I wouldn't be so sure of that, Naomi," Harry said. But as he did so he knew that she didn't hear him, since her attention now focused on the Dillard/Wharton side of the room.

"I don't think I've had the pleasure," Naomi said to Roberta. "I suppose you are the infamous Roberta. Hmpf!" This single cryptic monosyllable contained all the eloquence it needed to express her considerable disdain.

"Enough, Naomi," Harry interjected, with more force this time, feeling that for once he had to make clear who was the true head of his household. "We're not here to have any discussions or express any opinions, Mrs.

Eldernapped

Dillard. We're here for one reason only, to take Marguerite LoPresti back home with us."

"I'm not so sure I agree with that, Harry," Irene spoke with some heat. "I have a lot of opinions I would like to express. And by the way, aren't those two," she said, pointing, "the same hoodlums who invaded our bus the day we got here?"

"And the next day, at the Scrovegni Chapel," Art added.

"You're both correct," Naomi said. "That one, the little shrimp with the bandaged ear, he was the one who fell down the stairs at the Casa the other night, and then escaped."

"Of course he fell down the stairs," Irene said. "He had no choice. You tripped him up."

"With my cane," Naomi added.

"Good girl, Naomi."

"But we should listen to Harry, Irene dear," Art offered, his legal brain not diverted by the interchange on the subject of Roberta's hired hands. "This is none of our business."

"Way to go, Art," Harry agreed, thankful to find support from this quarter.

"Let Emily and her daughter settle their family disagreement separately," Art went on. "We're just here for Marguerite. Would you kindly get her?" He addressed Roberta now, "And please don't delay. We don't want to spend any more time here than we have to."

"He's right," Harry echoed. "We have a taxi waiting outside."

"And the meter is running," Art concluded, always one to watch a buck.

"You want her...you find her," was Roberta's terse response.

A battle-ax if I ever saw one, Harry thought.

"I give you the run of the house."

"Mother..." Alfred looked embarrassed. "Let me explain." Alfred turned his attention to the visitors.

George Freedman

"Let me handle this, Mr. Dillard," Sam said. "I'm Sam Peterson, and me and my associate, Mr. Anzaldi here, work for these people. The point is..." He addressed each of the two visiting foursomes in turn. "None of us know who this Marguerite person is who you're all talking about. Isn't that true, Vinny?"

"That's right. Oh sure. Me, too. I never heard of no Marguerite neither." Vinny was thinking faster than Harry would have thought him capable of doing.

"It's true that we've been on assignment to find Mrs. Dillard's mother for the last four months or so," Sam went on. "We're not denying that...and you sure are one hard-to-find customer, Mrs. Adams. But now we've found her. Here she is, Mrs. Dillard," pointing to Emily. "She's found. So our job is done. Case closed."

"You didn't find me, you overweight piece of scum," Emily said. Remember that, Roberta," her attention now addressed to her daughter, "when you pay him. And if you had worked up any sort of bonus deal for his finding me, forget it. He didn't earn it."

"Thank you, Mother, for your valuable advice." Roberta's voice dripped with sarcasm.

"If you people don't believe me," Sam continued unfazed, as though the previous interchange had never occurred, "go look for your Marguerite...did I get her name right?...anywhere...be our guest...upstairs, downstairs, in the garage...anyplace. You won't find her, because she ain't here. She was never here. Except it's a little messy downstairs. Hey, Vinny, why don't you go downstairs and...you know...neaten up."

"Don't let him go!" Naomi reacted. "Couldn't you hire smarter detectives, Roberta? Who do they think they're fooling? It's obvious that if Vinny gets downstairs before we do, he'll manage to hide Marguerite before we get there. And you, whatever your name is..."

"Peterson, is my name, ma'am, like I told you, Sam Peterson of Meadowlands Detective Agency in Secaucus, En Jay, ma'am. What can I do to be of service, ma'am?"

Eldernapped

"Catch him, somebody, that little man." Linda shouted, her right arm extended, her forefinger pointing. "He's trying to sneak downstairs. He's going to get rid of Marguerite."

Vinny no longer stood alongside Roberta, Alfred and Sam Peterson. "See, there he is," she continued, her voice now at high pitch. "He's trying to sneak out of here. Stop him, Joey!"

Following her pointing finger, Harry saw that the little creep had in fact crept behind the backs of his three comrades and was already out of the room, though still visible through the doorway.

Linda's words were all Joey and Bruno needed to hear. The two medical students leapt across the room in Vinny's direction.

The sight of those two strong young male bodies catapulting in his direction must have upset Vinny. As he scrambled away from them, he lost his footing. What followed was the crashing sound of a human body falling, out of control, down a long flight of stairs. It was accompanied by a scream that faded as it made its way downward.

"The man does seem to have difficulty with stairways," Harry said, this observation being addressed to no one in particular, but he noticed that at least half of the people in the room were nodding their heads in agreement.

Now was heard a prolonged groan, as though from a wounded animal. Joey and Bruno exchanged a glance which expressed, "Here we go again." With which they, too, rushed down the staircase.

At the same time, there was a violent clanging of the gate bell, followed by an insistent, violent thumping on the gate so loud that it echoed throughout the house. Those sounds were accompanied by loud male voices yelling in Italian. Harry didn't have to know the language to make out, *"Polizia! Polizia!...."* Nor did one have to be Italian to recognize the sounds of dogs barking. From their different tones there must have been at least three. He could even guess at their function, if not their breed. They had to be police dogs.

Most chilling of all was the screaming of police sirens. Next came the sound of the mansion's front door bursting open. At the same moment some three or four of the full-length windows on two opposite sides of the large room burst open. In an instant, the place was full of cops. Harry surmised that not since an eighteenth century ball or a nineteenth century wedding had the house held so many guests.

Two of the new arrivals, neither one in uniform, stepped forward to take center stage. Harry turned to Naomi. "You won this one, my love." he said. "You did beat Lieutenant Luigi here...but just barely."

"All right, everyone," Cataldo said in his quite understandable English, "stay right where you are. Nobody move."

The man by his side, Harry recognized Franco, followed this with a statement in Italian of similar length and, one would guess, of identical content.

"Now...which one of you is Justin Wharton?" Cataldo continued. His narrowed eyes swept the faces of the culprits arrayed in various locations around the room.

"None of us actually," Naomi spoke up. "But if you ask me, Lieutenant Luigi, Justin must be downstairs...and Marguerite too."

At that instant Cataldo seemed to be a thunderstruck man. He stood in silence, staring with pop-eyes at Naomi, whose unexpected presence at this place and at this time could not have been particularly welcome to him.

"Wha...wha...what...what...?" Cataldo managed at last to sputter.

"Am I doing here?" Naomi filled in. "Just doing my part to help you out, Lieutenant Luigi. And not just me. The others with me have been a big help, as well. So you owe them some thanks, too. Surely you remember my

Eldernapped

husband, Harry," she said. Harry felt her clutching his jacket lapel as she pulled him out of the crowd to be better seen. "He's always been hanging around whenever we've talked, haven't you, Harry dear?"

"Hi, there, Lieutenant," Harry said with a wave of his hand.

"And these are the Maglios, Irene and Art, two more of us Senior Seminarians, who I don't think you've met, yet." The Maglios nodded. "And there's more where they came from...ha-ha...but of course they're not here right now, being back at the Casa."

There must have been something comforting in her rippling laugh. Or perhaps Cataldo realized that this woman was an inexorable force that it is useless to oppose. Harry could have told him that. He sighed and would have gone on with his investigatory duties, but his intentions were once again thwarted, this time by the appearance of the press.

A half dozen reporters pushed into the room. From the letterings on their cameras, Harry recognized that they represented one of Padua's major television stations. He had seen those call letters numerous times in the last week on the television set in the Casa's lounge.

Cataldo, however, did not seem to enjoy having them there. As he sighted them, he exploded into impassioned vituperation in Italian, indicating that he had no intention of allowing them into the room to observe and record his actions.

As Franco and a couple of his policemen started to herd them out, a handsome woman, Harry observed, in a smashing purple outfit, separated herself from the others. She was holding a microphone in her left hand, a reporter or some sort of news anchor. She launched into a heated reply of her own.

In the end, the television people did as they were told. They picked up their respective gear, which they had just put down, and left the crowded room, to set up in the foyer outside.

George Freedman

As they were leaving, Harry noticed that the lady reporter was scanning all the faces in the room, only to find that most of the people were averting their eyes from hers. Was she not was going to be able to get a statement of value from any of them for tonight's eleven o'clock news? But wait, her face lit up. There was a ray of hope. Harry knew at once what must have caused it. Oh no, he thought, she's spotted Naomi.

One face, cheerful and intelligent, stood out from the nondescript and sulky others. As the reporter walked out, Naomi made an almost imperceptible affirmative nod to her.

Naomi wouldn't look bad on TV, with her lovely silver hair and her tasteful, light pink outfit. In addition, she walks with a cane, which, Harry guessed, the reporter must have thought would certainly evoke a bit of additional *simpatia* on the part of her regular TV audience.

Without warning, Joey and Bruno appeared, followed by Vinny, his arms around the shoulders of two of the policemen, and hopping on one foot.

"He'll be all right," Joey announced, "just some new bruises and a bad ankle sprain."

"Also, a pull of the left groin," Bruno added, to complete the diagnosis.

"Did you thoroughly search the place down there? Did you find the woman? LoPresti? Did you come across the man who is with her, Justin Wharton?" Cataldo's questions were directed to his underlings.

"He's asking whether they found anyone downstairs," Linda translated.

There were more questions. But when the four policemen, two of them still holding Vinny in an erect position and the other two guarding Joey and Bruno, kept answering, "No, no, no, no," it became clear that they had found no other persons in the basement regions. So where the hell could they be, Harry wondered.

Now, he could see that the young man standing next to Roberta was once again giving evidence of a desire

Eldernapped

to speak. Must be her son Alfred. "May I speak, officer?" he said. "I have information about where my Uncle Justin and the lady you are looking for...Mrs. LoPresti...might be right now. And I think you and our visitors would like to have me tell you."

The room fell quiet. He had succeeded in gaining everyone's attention. Furthermore, it was obvious that he knew how to deliver an important statement with ease. And why should he not, Harry asked himself. Is he not the president of an industry-leading American firm with God knows how many thousands of employees and with plants all over the country?

"The truth is," Alfred went on, his words measured and slow, "Uncle Justin and Mrs. LoPresti are...this minute...probably in Ravenna, a city which I understand is about eighty miles from here. This morning they appeared at breakfast all dressed for a jaunt. If you want to try to pick them up, Officer, I think I can describe what they're wearing.

Cataldo nodded.

"She was in an nice looking pants-suit, sort of a green color I would say, and carrying a straw picnic basket, God knows where she got it. Uncle Justin had on a white polo shirt, plaid sports jacket...sort of yellow...and light brown trousers. Which is remarkable, because in all my life I can never remember Uncle Justin in a sports jacket. Or for that matter without a necktie."

"The two of them went shopping late yesterday afternoon," Roberta added, her voice all but inaudible.

Harry felt an unexpected but familiar jab directed to his left rib cage. "Hi...I'm back," Naomi announced.

"I didn't know you were gone."

"Had to go to the john."

"I'm not surprised." And he wasn't, considering how long it had taken for the taxi ride, coupled with the excitement of the occasion.

"Have I missed anything?

"You sure have. Alfred just told us that Marguerite and Justin aren't here. They've have taken off for Ravenna."

"To see the mosaics?"

"What else?"

"Well, I have some news too. That TV lady... Filomena Tarantino is her name...is the leading TV anchorperson in all Padua.. In fact, I'm sure we've seen her on late television. I happened to run into her on my way to the bathroom."

"I'm not surprised at that either."

"She's going to interview me right after she talks to Marguerite, and then I'll be on the eleven o'clock news tonight. But now it seems she won't be able to talk to Marguerite because you're telling me Marguerite is gone."

"Which means she'll have to settle for just you. But I'm sure you'll manage," Harry said.

"I'm not so sure," Naomi countered. "She said she was very anxious to ask me about the Vicenza connection. Do you know what's the Vicenza connection, Harry?"

"Never heard of it. But pipe down...let's listen to what Alfred is saying."

"...They announced to us," Alfred said, that they would take the small car, the Lancia, not the large Fiat. They seemed to like the Lancia better for some reason. They informed us that they intended to spend the day visiting the various mosaic sites that I understand are quite famous in Ravenna.

"As Uncle Justin explained to us, Marguerite...Mrs. LoPresti, that is...had expressed such distress at missing the Senior Seminars trip to Ravenna due to our holding her captive here that he wanted to, in his words, make it up to her, by taking her on this excursion. I suggested that he had already made it up to her yesterday when he took her to Vicenza, but it was his position that he had more making up to do.

"Oh, so that's the Vicenza connection," Naomi whispered to Harry, as she administered another body jab.

Eldernapped

"I would say he had," Emily spoke up. She had been quiet through all this. "But that's one thing about my oldest boy. He's always had a strong feeling for doing his duty as he saw it and then going overboard, so in the end he does even more than is required."

"Maybe even a little more than just duty in this case," Naomi added, her voice now louder than a whisper so all in the room could hear.

"Uncle Justin said they would be back by evening," Alfred went on, acknowledging his grandmother's comment with a smile in her direction. "But if it got too late...and I think," looking at his watch, "it is already getting to be too late, they might put in at a hotel or motel along the way. In that event, they won't show up until after breakfast tomorrow morning." "Can I answer any questions for anyone?"

There was one, or perhaps it was less a question than a crucial piece of new information bearing on this case. It came from Franco. Harry had noticed a few minutes earlier that Franco had left the room, having been beckoned out by one of the policemen. Now he was back. He was brusque as he made his way through the crowd to come up alongside Cataldo. What he had to say was for Cataldo's ear only. As he delivered his private message, it was getting to be rather a long one, he kept gesticulating with both arms, pointing in the direction of the entrance to the mansion.

Cataldo's face took on an expression of stunned blankness. He seemed to collapse into utter defeat as he clapped his hand to his forehead and sank into a nearby padded chair.

"Poor guy," Harry muttered to himself. "Whatever Franco told him must be pretty bad."

Now, the discussion between the two officers became audible to all, and even though in Italian, it contained enough recognizable words to impart a certain drift to what they were saying. The words included Graziella," "Autobus," *"Vecchi studenti"* and

George Freedman

"*Amminstratora* Julie Foster." Their interchange came to an end with a limp wave of Cataldo's hand, which Franco interpreted to convey some sort of assent, for he nodded in the affirmative and left the room.

In almost no time he was back, trailing behind an array of folk familiar to many of those present. Harry couldn't keep himself from crying out, "My God, look who's here!"

He recognized Graziella, who was keeping close to her good friend Franco. Behind them, Julie. She was followed by two young men in business suits, one of whom was carrying an attaché case. This quintet managed to force its way into the center of the room already crowded with Dillards, private investigators from New Jersey, the Emily/(Be)Linda combo with their two-man entourage of soon-to-be medical men, the couples Levine and Maglio, detectives Cataldo and Franco and eleven or twelve assorted uniformed representatives of Padua's finest. Most of the latter were lined up against the walls, except for the two who continued to hold Vinny in an upright position.

At the doorway stood yet others from the Casa del Santo. Their number merged with the bodies already in the adjacent foyer, consisting of Ms. Tarantino and her accompanying, newsgathering staff.

Harry could identify Tom and Kate Sayre, Enrico the bus driver, and. beside him the Kniznicks, Nate and Belle. Harry could just make out the Estonian sisters behind Tom's wartime buddies.

Where were Pete and Dorothy, Harry wondered, and the rest of their classmates? Was there any reason to think they weren't all present, too?

"We've come to get Marguerite LoPresti," Julie said with cool determination as soon as she found herself in front of Lieutenant Cataldo. "I had the bus available, and Enrico was hanging around, so I figured, what the hell, why not use it? If I get into trouble with the Senior Seminars executive office, so be it. Then I thought it would be a good idea to bring along support, because who knew what kind of mad people we were going to meet up with here. And everyone wanted to come. Anyway, it's certainly good to see you here, Lieutenant."

Harry noticed that, as she proceeded, her voice sank into virtual inaudibility, a consequence of the fact that she seemed more and more stunned and intimidated as she came to realize the size of the crowd confronting her. Her words, fainter and fainter, were now spoken with a quaver, yet she summoned up the courage to go on. "We know Marguerite's in this building, someplace," she managed to say. "So let's quit stalling. Where is she? We can get her right back to the Casa where she belongs...."

Cataldo interrupted her. "Take her," he said. "If you can find her. No one is going to stop you. But on the other hand, don't bother. She's not here. As far as I can tell, she's walked out of here of her own free will."

Cataldo's acquiescence to her request was lost on Julie. "Do you know who these men are?" she went on. "They're Marguerite LoPresti's two sons who just flew in from Cincinnati to rescue their mother. This one," indicating the shorter blonder one, the one with the attache case, "is Mr. Mark LoPresti, who incidentally is an attorney, and the other one...excuse me, I forget your first name..."

"Ron," he volunteered.

"Is, of course, also Mr. LoPresti. Mr. Ron LoPresti."

With which the young man designated as Attorney Mark LoPresti stepped forward and took center stage from Julie. Harry could see that he had understood the significance of the information Cataldo had just imparted, even if Julie had not, for a look of relief had come over his face. It was matched by a similar expression on that of his brother who also worked his way forward so that the two LoPrestis stood together, shoulder to shoulder, as they faced the crowd.

Any mother would be proud, Harry thought, to have two such loving sons. They had, without hesitation or a moment's warning, flown to her side from half a world away.

"Where is she?" Mark said.

"And how is she?" Ron said.

"I'm sure she is in very good health," Cataldo said. "In fact I have the impression that she's having a wonderful time even as we speak. Even though I have never met her, I already know that she must be one of those wonderful American ladies who has fallen in love with our beautiful Italia."

"The fact of the matter is," Alfred spoke up, "we don't know exactly where she is. She's certainly not here in this building. She's someplace between here and the city of Ravenna, I would guess."

"Who are you?" Lawyer LoPresti asked.

Before Alfred could answer, his mother spoke up. "I am Roberta Dillard, Lucille Wharton's daughter, and this is my son, Alfred." She turned to her son and murmured, "Alfred dear, I think you shouldn't say anything more to Lawyer LoPresti till we decide on our position on this matter."

Harry could only conjecture that Alfred had not heard his mother's request, for Alfred answered the question with a quiet voice, in his own words. "I'm Alfred Dillard, grandson of Lucille Adams, the person we mistook your mother for. Here's my card." He extracted several from a little plastic envelope in a side pocket of his sweater, giving one each to the brothers LoPresti, and one to Julie. He made sure Cataldo got yet another.

After pocketing the card with a momentary glance at it, Mark LoPresti extracted from his breast pocket a similar small packet from which he took his business card and handed it to Alfred. "I am Mark LoPresti, Esquire, attorney at law, and something tells me that it is you, Mr. Dillard, and certain members of your family," throwing a significant look at Roberta, "against whom I will file legal action with regard to the abduction of my mother, Mrs.

Eldernapped

Marguerite LoPresti of fifty-three Walnut Ave. Cincinnati, Ohio."

Julie chimed in, not waiting for Alfred to respond,. "You're the one who called me and asked to speak to Emily."

"That's right," Alfred responded. "If by Emily, you mean my grandmother, Mrs. Adams, I suppose it was you I talked to. But as you recall, she wasn't there. You told me she was at the Botanical Gardens at the time."

"You said you were calling from the computer store around the corner."

"Yes, I was. That's where I was...in the computer store just around the corner."

Harry found this discussion of a computer store less than interesting. Instead, he wondered whether Cataldo, even in the midst of this turmoil, could keep from being impressed in high degree by the fact that all these many good people had gone to so much trouble to seek out this particular building in this little town this evening.

Harry further guessed that Cataldo's mind might then have swerved into another line of thinking, which was that, at last, this charade must be over. Everyone who could possibly have shown up here did. And most important of all, the woman must be safe. In fact Harry wouldn't be surprised if she was kicking up her heels that minute on the dance floor of some trendy nightclub in Ravenna.

Indeed, Harry had been right on. He read Cataldo's mind, for the man rose from his chair and signaled his troops to gather their things and depart. But there was sudden evidence that the stream of visitors had not run dry.

It was a single person, a woman, who had just added herself to the crowd in the foyer and was standing framed in its the doorway. "Halloo, Mr. Dillard. Yolanda Santoro here, from the software department of Denunzio's Palazzo del Byte," she shouted from the door, her intelligent brown eyes experiencing no difficulty in picking her customer out of the multitude and fixing on his.

Harry couldn't help noticing that she was quite attractive, her thick red hair cascading over a loop of lustrous, green scarf that topped off her stylish, tan trench coat. "Excuse me for not knocking," she went on. "But the gate was open, and there was no one there to greet me, so I just walked in. By the way, what's going on here? Some sort of party? Anyway, Mr. Dillard, I have your Microsoft virtual reality VRCAD software here on three CD-ROM disks, along with the English language instructions. It came into the store sooner than I expected."

Her words shut off all others. Every mouth was open. Every eye was on her.

"I happen to be staying the night with my Aunt Serafina who, lives near here in the town of Stra," Yolanda continued. "I figured you for a man who would still be up at this time of the evening, so I said to myself, why wait for a messenger to deliver it to you, I could be the messenger myself.

"In fact, if you can break away from your guests for a few minutes, Mr. Dillard, we could boot it onto the hard disk of your notebook computer right now and I would be happy to go over it with you, which I assure you will make it easier for you than grinding through all the instructions in the manual, English or not."

Eldernapped

Day Ten

"Beneath the Bridge of Sighs"

The first nine days of "The Veneto: Its Art, Music and History," were themselves now history and it was hard to believe that so many events had been crammed into such a short period. Hard to believe, also, as Harry pointed out to those at his table on the morning of the tenth, in only three more days the program would be over. And in four days, all of them would be gone.

We can all be thankful, the other breakfasters reminded him, that at least the crisis through which they had been living had passed. Yes, there was still an open and shut case of elder harassment, should Emily choose to pursue it in the courts. There were several who felt that she should be unrelenting in this matter, for is this not an offense that ranks with child molestation and wife beating?

Pete commented that he was not sure that elder harassment had hit the law books yet as a valid felony, defined in legal terms. To which, Art added the proviso that if and when it did, he doubted it would constitute more than a misdemeanor.

None of this mattered in any case, because Emily then said that she wasn't sure what she would do, "Probably nothing," she shrugged.

There was an even more serious matter to be resolved, the criminal act itself, the cruel abduction of one of their own, Marguerite LoPresti. What will Marguerite do about that, especially since she now had at her disposal the considerable legal expertise and wisdom of her son Mark.

Also, probably nothing, in view of the rumor that Marguerite, too, might not attempt to seek compensation for the distress she had undergone. But rumor was all it was, for she had not been on the bus ride home last night to confirm or deny. Nor was she with them now, as Harry felt he had to remind them, thus putting a damper on the good spirits of all within earshot.

"Let me remind you," he said. "Here we are, having breakfast at the Casa together, as we do every morning, but Marguerite isn't. Where in fact is she? Did she really go to Ravenna?"

"And with that rotten, conniving Justin Wharton?" Irene added.

"Conniving, yes...but maybe...just maybe..." Millicent equivocated, "not all that rotten."

More questions and comments followed, the most interesting of which, Harry thought, was the one by Fred Hanson who asked whether this continuing non-presence of Marguerite's was no less than another cruel abduction, an abduction within an abduction, so to speak.

But several, Kate and Sarah among them, joining with Millicent, took the opposite view, which was that in the best case, Marguerite might actually have gone with Justin Wharton of her own free will.

So it went till, used up by these indeterminate conclusions, they all fell silent. Which was just as well, since, as on all other mornings, there came from the corridor the familiar clump, flop of the wooden heels and soft soles of Julie's and Graziella's sandals. They must have shopped for them together, as women do, Harry figured, probably at Padua's famed Saturday flea market at the *della Prato Valle* fair grounds. Naomi had dragged him there a few days ago and he'd noted that sandal craftsmen abounded.

Eldernapped

It required no more than an additional few seconds for Julie and Graziella to enter the room and to take up their regular announcement station in front of the refills table. Such admirable examples of contemporary young womanhood they are, was Harry's reaction. He was sure he was joined in this opinion by most of his male comrades in the room, as he contemplated their intelligent and energetic demeanors, their fresh faces, their clear eyes, their crisp and colorful blouses, their tight pants.

"Good morning, all," Julie said, her voice chirpy. "This is your lucky day. Today is Venice day. The sun's out and it's warm but it won't get too hot and it will be beautiful there. The bus leaves in twenty minutes. So chop chop. Finish up. We'll all meet just outside the Casa where Enrico and the bus are waiting. Any questions?

"Yes," Millicent said. "Where the hell is Marguerite?"

"Well," Julie replied with a big smile, "you'll all be pleased to hear that she is very well and free to do anything she wants to do and to go anywhere she wants to go. She telephoned last night and Graziella and I both talked to her. But she was in a hurry, something about having a lot of important business to go over with her sons. That meant we won't be seeing her today. But tomorrow or the next day for sure. Anyway, she wants to get back together with us all real bad."

"See, Mr. Calamity," Naomi said to Harry, "Marguerite is okay. With all your joking, deep down you're always looking at the dark side."

"Happy to be proved wrong," Harry replied.

"But where is she staying?" Carol said. "She has her nice room, all paid up, right here at the Casa. Why isn't she staying here?"

"Well, we didn't get around to asking her that, did we, Graziella? But I'm sure we'll find out very soon when we will see her. Now, getting back to our schedule, let me remind you that tomorrow is our free day. I hope you

George Freedman

have some fun plans for trips or shopping or just hanging around. The day after that, Thursday, after our regular morning and afternoon program, we will attend Wendy Gross's evening concert at the Santo in a beautiful small concert room one floor above the vestry where it will take place.

"And, oh...I almost forgot to tell you this. I did remember to tell Marguerite about the concert, and she said, one way or another, come hell or high water, she was going to be there, which means that in any case we'll surely see her there."

This happy announcement evoked expressions of pleasure all around.

"Wendy's giving us that concert," Julie continued, "because she likes you guys. She doesn't do it for every group. She does it out of the goodness of her heart, without pay, because Senior Seminars doesn't pay her to do it, and believe me, when Wendy gives a cello concert, it's great, it's as good as any pay-at-the door concert you can see all year in Padua. We'll gather around eight-thirty Thursday evening in the hotel lobby after you've all had a chance to rest. We'll walk over. Any questions?"

"Yes," Kate spoke up. "How do we dress for the concert?"

"As always, it's up to you. But you might want to dress up for this one. I'm going to wear an outfit that will knock your eyes out."

"Then I'm certainly coming," Harry spoke up. "I hadn't thought I would at first, but now that I know that...ouch!" This last syllable followed a swift poke to his ribs by one of Naomi's elbows, after which he found it prudent to finish, "...it will be a cello concert, wild horses couldn't hold me back. I love the cello."

Julie chose to ignore Harry's remark. "Let's get back to the business at hand," she said. "As I told you today's all-day trip is to Venice...or as we say in Italy, *Venezia*. The bus will take us to the Venice train station where there's a vaporetto dock. On the bus, I'll hand out

Eldernapped

your vaporetto tickets so no one has to stand in line to buy them. "When you get there, everyone is on his or her own. Do whatever you want to do. On the bus, Graziella will be giving out city maps, and she and I will circulate around to answer any questions about things to see and places to eat. All I ask that you do is to gather in front of St. Mark's church at five, so we can all get back on the vaporetto and then to the bus. Be on time, because we won't wait for you. Any questions?"

"Yes, Julie. I have a question," said Fred, his brow furrowed as he perused his Venice guidebook. "Why do they call it the Palace of the Doges. What's a Doge?"

"I can tell you what it's not, Fred dear," said Carol. "It's not the same as an Arizona doggie, as in whoopee ti yi yo, git along little doggie.".

"She's right, Mr. Hanson," Julie said, struggling to keep a straight face. "A Doge of Venice is the big boss...like the governor of the whole province of Venezia. Any more questions?

"No? Okay. Getting back to our gathering at the end of the day, some of you don't even have to do that. If any of you want to stay on into the evening, there is public transportation so you can get back to Padua on your own. You can even stay overnight in a hotel if you want to. I see several of you have brought suitcases. As I told you, tomorrow is our free day, and in that way you can get a second day in Venice. But the real message I want to leave with you is that I trust you to behave as mature adults."

"We certainly are that," Nate volunteered.

"So don't do anything immature that will get me into trouble with my bosses," Julie concluded. "Any more questions?"

♦♦♦♦

A number of loose groups had constituted themselves. Several, for no better reason than that their members had found themselves standing next to each other at the dock for Stop, *Approdo*, #9 on the Grand Canal, *Canale Grande*, where they had debarked from their vaparetto at Julie's signal. Others, because certain individuals, over the preceding week, had found themselves gravitating toward each other. One such group consisted of tablemates Harry and Naomi, Nate and Belle, Pete and Dorothy, and Millicent and Sarah. Their first communal action was to follow a suggestion by Naomi, who had spotted a restaurant with outdoor tables fifty yards away.

"But it's too early for lunch," Dorothy said.

"But not too early for our regular morning cappuccino with biscotti," Naomi reminded her.

"Oh, do you think they'll serve us just coffee? They look like a complete meal restaurant and its not lunch time yet," Dorothy persisted.

"If they're not, I'm sure I can persuade them," Naomi replied. Several heads nodded in the affirmative, indicating others in the group thought so, too.

"I think it's fine that we're starting out here, which is sort of at the rear of the great tourist attractions like St. Mark's Square and the Palace of the Doges and *Caffe Florian*," Nate said, as he sipped his espresso. "The best of Venice is in the small back streets where the people live." By way of confirmation, he looked up and waved at a lady of advanced years on the fourth floor of an adjacent fourteenth century building. She was hanging her morning's wash on a clothesline that spanned the *canalleto* at a right angle from the Grand Canal. She waved back.

"I certainly agree," Harry added. "Naomi and I always try to avoid tourist congestion, especially in Venice. Still, if you haven't been to St. Mark's church you should see it. It is a tourist attraction for good reason. It was built... or started at least, I think...in the ninth century and is one of the most remarkable buildings in the world. And you had better not miss the other places Nate mentioned, either."

Eldernapped

"But what is wrong with where we're sitting this very moment?" Sarah spoke up. "Isn't that the *Rialto* Bridge just up the canal a piece? I've seen pictures of that bridge ever since I was a little girl."

Everyone turned to gaze at it. There it was indeed, a hundred yards upstream, its two sides lined with little stores. They had just come under its magnificent arch before docking at #9.

"You know, I think I recognize this very dock where our vaporetto dropped us off," Belle said. "Did anyone see the movie *Death in Venice* that was based on Thomas Mann's book?" Dirk Bogarde...you know, the British actor who plays the hero, is a composer who falls in love with a beautiful boy. He comes off his vaporetto with his luggage right here, just as we came off ours today...I'm sure of it.

"I always went for that Dirk type," Belle said. "Tall, debonair..."

"Which is why you married me," Nate added. "I happen to fit that description to a T...especially the debonair part."

"And that British accent," Millicent said. "I love men with British accents. But what do you expect? He's British."

"You could be right about this dock, I seem to remember it from the movie, too," Dorothy said. "What a great book that is. I must have read it four or five times. If you want to know, that's probably why I picked this Senior Seminars program, because of the way that book described Venice.

"In fact, I originally signed up for the Venice program that's going on at the same time," she went on. "But it was full, with a waiting list of something like seventy-two, so I got my second choice, Padua, instead. I knew Padua was close to Venice and that it would have at least one Venice day. And I'm so happy and thrilled to be here, even if it's just for one day."

"As a matter of fact, two days," Pete reminded her as he leaned over to tap the two small suitcases at their feet. "We'll be here tomorrow, too, because that's how we're going to spend our free day.

"I'm so happy that you're so happy, my dear," Pete went on, reaching across the table to pat her hand. "I was worried that you were disappointed with your Padua selection."

"Disappointed? No, Pete, I'm far from disappointed.".

"As for me," he continued, "I'm delighted, Dorothy, that you got your second choice, I mean."

"I'm so glad you're delighted, Pete."

Harry, noting that this dialogue was getting mushier by the minute, decided it would be a good time to steer the conversation away from these expressions of mutual delight. "What a coincidence," he said. "I have a similar reason for picking Padua, Dorothy. But first let me say that like my chum, Pete, I too am happy that you are happy, and I am sure all of us at this table are equally happy for you."

Everyone nodded in agreement.

"But let's get back to the first subject. Would it surprise you to know that my reason for signing up for the Padua program comes from literature, too?"

"Is that so?" Naomi said. "So how come this is the first time I ever heard of it?"

"You did hear of it...you did. Remember how when we were first discussing this trip? And I busted into song?"

"No."

"I admit that Cole Porter is not quite the great literary giant that Thomas Mann is," Harry went on. "But I consider him a major literary figure too. Some of his song lyrics are real works of art. Let me repeat something from one of his songs that I sang you at the time, Naomi. Then maybe you'll remember, because that decided us. That very day we sent in our application with Padua as the first choice...and, would you believe, Dorothy...we also had this day in Venice in mind."

Eldernapped

Then, quite without tune, but with fervor, Harry sang:

We open in Venice
Then on to Verona,
And next to Cremona,
Lots of girls in Cremona.
And then on to Parma,
Da da da, da da Parma.
And Mantua and Padua.
And back again...
To Venice...

"As it happens," Harry said, "Naomi and I had been to every one of those cities that Cole Porter lists in his song... except one. Padua. The others, Venice, Verona, Cremona, Parma, Mantua, we've been to all of them. So this was our chance to rectify that omission...to complete that list"

"My sister's been to Verona," Millicent said. "Loved it. She saw Juliet's balcony."

"I've seen that balcony," Sarah said. "You can imagine young Romeo standing in the street below, right where I was, mooning up at her."

"Nate and I were in Cremona about forty years ago," Belle added. We saw Stradivarius's workshop."

Harry could see that it was up to him to get this conversation back on track. "Remember, Naomi dear," he said, "the wonderful slab of parmesan cheese we got in Parma. How we made a picnic lunch in Parma's central park with some prosciutto and a great loaf of Italian bread and a bottle of wine? Everyone who walked by kept saying *buon appetito*? It's one of my fondest memories of our travels."

"That happened in Perugia."

"You're mistaken, poor Naomi. We're all afflicted with memory problems at our age, aren't we? If you think hard you'll recall that it was in fact in Parma. "So, as I was saying, that's how come we chose Padua." With this, Harry beamed a happy smile at the others.

Except that Millicent had something to add. "I know that song. It's from Cole Porter's *Kiss Me Kate*, and it takes place in Venice."

Harry nodded in the affirmative, "That only proves my point, doesn't it?"

With the cappuccinos and espressos consumed, Nate, who had appointed himself tour director, pulled a folded piece of paper from his shirt pocket. "Before I read you my choices of places Belle and I want to visit, please keep in mind, no one has to do these things," he said. "If anyone wants to join us, you're more than welcome. In fact we'd be delighted if you came with us. But remember, it's all walking, because there are no vehicles in Venice. Imagine that, a whole big city with no cars or trucks or taxis."

"Unless you count the vaporetti and the garbage barges and the water taxis," Naomi said, always ready to set right any incorrect impressions.

"I'm coming with you. In fact you won't be able to shake me," Millicent said.

"Me, too," Sarah agreed.

"Us, too," Naomi added, thus making up Harry's mind for him, but he was used to that. "But read us your list, Nate," Naomi added with a sparkling smile

Before Nate could begin, Pete spoke up. "Dorothy and I won't join you, I'm sorry to say. We've decided to take a gondola ride next, and then we've learned of a very nice little private restaurant that may not be comfortable for a large group like this."

"And we won't be coming back with you to the Casa this evening either," Dorothy added.

"Oh, yes," Belle said, all innocence, "I am sure all of us envy you the great art and architecture you will see tonight and during the free day tomorrow, which the rest of us will miss."

♦ ♦ ♦ ♦

Eldernapped

It was a quarter to five and the Senior Seminars entourage, already two thirds reconstituted, had begun to gather at the carved bronze doors that make up the entrance to St. Mark's venerable church. Harry could see a sizable, faraway batch of the missing ones working their way St. Marksward, across the great square and through the hoards of pigeons and tots tormenting them. He guessed that the missing ones had been basking till now in the shade of the colorful umbrellas deployed in front of Florian's historic cafe, listening to its musicians delivering schmaltzy operetta tunes fresh from the nineteenth century. He could also tell that they were coming at a slow pace, as though reluctant to depart the scene.

"Okay, group, did everyone have a good time?" Julie said.

"Yes."

"Sure did."

"Magnificent."

"What an unbelievable place."

"My feet hurt."

"I can't wait for a hot shower."

"I should have brought my collapsible cart for lugging all these packages."

"Is everyone here?" was Julie's next question.

To which Graziella, after a few moments of peering into faces and consulting the chart on her clip board replied, "Yes, everyone but Signor Crawford and Signora Hinckel."

"Oh, they're not coming back with us, didn't you know?" Belle spoke up.

"They've got better things to do than join us old folks," Millicent added.

"Of course," Julie said. "I forgot to tell you, Graziella. They're staying the night in Venice, which means we're all set. We'll just walk over to the other end of the cathedral where it faces the water at vaporetto Approdo number fifteen. You can see it from here."

She was interrupted by a loud call from one of her charges who yelled, "No, they're coming too...see?"

And in fact they were, as fast as their legs could take them, Pete swinging their two small suitcases, one in each hand.

"Must have had a fight," Harry overheard Nate commenting to Belle.

"Not necessarily," Belle said. "You're always such a cynic."

"We'll see," Nate said.

Harry was pleased to learn that it was Belle who made the correct guess for, as the pair drew up before their classmates, Dorothy exploded with, "Wait till we tell you who we saw!"

"You'll never believe this," Pete added.

"We thought we could catch you before you got on the boat so we could tell you...and whew, We made it," Dorothy said.

"So, who did you see? I bet I can guess." Naomi ventured.

"Right!" Dorothy said. "Marguerite. Marguerite herself. Our Marguerite."

"Where? Where did you see her?"

"They were in a gondola we passed in one of the small canals, the one with the Bridge of Sighs. They waved to us, but we went by too fast for us to say anything except, 'Hi there.'"

"They?"

"What they?

"Someone was with her?"

"Who was with her?"

"We don't know who that man was next to her," Dorothy said..

"But we can guess," Pete said. "The two of them sat there in that boat side by side...sort of stretched out, and leaning back on a big red cushion. She had a parasol and looked very happy and very nice."

Eldernapped

"In a blue dress with fine white trim...spring weight linen, it looked like."

"He was a tall, thin guy in green pants and a yellow sports shirt and a loud sports jacket," Pete picked up on Dorothy's words without pause, "...brown and yellow plaid...and his whole getup was topped off with a Red Sox baseball cap. Where do you get a Red Sox cap in Venice?"

"I saw a T-shirt store on one of the canals that sold things like that," an anonymous voice offered from deep in the crowd, "and I almost picked up a Green Bay Packers shirt, but my wife wouldn't let me."

"Bridge of Sighs...they call it that because it connects a prison with a palace," Harriet Aptheker observed, who almost never spoke up.

"You want to know who I think it must be?" Art offered. Harry could tell that his friend's keen attorney's mind was churning as in the old days. "It must have been that Wharton guy who kidnapped Marguerite...what's his name?"

"Justin. It must be my boy Justin. He would never kidnap anybody," Emily wailed.

Day Eleven

"A Quiet Day"

In a subterranean stone chamber that could have once been a dungeon, but was now the Casa's *Centro di Salute*, Health and Fitness Center, Harry trod the mill. He was raising a sweat, but getting nowhere. Enough of this, he thought. Why use up energy walking on an endless belt when I can do it under far more interesting conditions, just strolling the streets of Padua? So he gathered his things, and left.

In their room Naomi sat, still in her robe and with her hair tucked under a large turban contrived of many windings of towel. "Oh, it's good to have had a chance to wash my hair," she remarked by way of greeting. "When it dries I am going to sit in the garden and write letters to the girls, and then I'll read."

"Why write letters? We'll be back home before the letters get there."

"Doesn't matter. I'll write them anyway."

"As for me, I'm going for a walk till lunch."

"Go already."

This was all according to plan. After the turbulent events of the last week and a half, they decided that the time had come to sit back and do nothing. Their free day would be a quiet one.

George Freedman

Day Twelve

"To Life"

Just after sundown, but with twilight still lingering and with Julie in the lead, some thirty ladies and gentlemen emerged from the lobby of the Casa del Santo and held up traffic as they crossed the street. They were on their way to the Santo, the great Basilica of Saint Anthony of Padua that loomed before them two blocks away.

But for their venerability they could have been a field trip of grammar school kids in the charge of their teacher. There was much jocularity, more on the part of the males than the females. Testosterone never really runs dry, Harry noted, as they arranged themselves into a lengthening line of pairs. As they moved forward, Naomi thumping along with her cane, and Harry percolated to the rear to take up their accustomed position as the last pair.

What a good-looking group they made, Harry observed. Enough to cause several passersby to pause to watch them, for where else would one see so many well-scrubbed and alert elderly folk in a single, well defined assemblage. Most of them were well dressed, too, some, in fact, resplendent.

"I always adore dressing up for concerts," Sarah said, lovely in an off-the-shoulder deep blue number of some shiny fabric. Her remark was echoed by Rose, who for her part, at last, not in a unisex costume matching Paul's, looked gorgeous in a suit of off-white. It featured a

Eldernapped

deep frontal V, the better to emphasize her attractive décolletage. It gives you hope, Harry reflected as he looked them over. We ain't dead yet.

The men, too, were elegant. Pete, forever loyal to his navy blue admiral's jacket with its gold buttons topped by an ascot of dazzling white, never looked spiffier. Tom, in a gray blazer with black flannel trousers, the sharpness of the creases of which were hard to explain considering he was living out of a suitcase, was a paragon of erect posture and dignity. Nate had on a dark brown three-piecer such as he might have worn to a pediatric conference, but with a zany necktie. It served to remind everyone that he was not practicing pediatrics any more. Even Harry himself was wearing a tweed jacket, very British, with white shirt and tie.

"You look nice for a change," Naomi said.

"Why do you think none of the women can keep their eyes off me?" Harry said.

But no one gave such a riveting impression as did Julie. In her floating gown of beige chiffon, the gossamer hem of which failed by a few inches of making it to her knees, she could that moment have stepped from the pages of *Elle*. Her luminous eyes and her upswept coiffure revealed for the first time that she had a long, slim, swan neck. She could have been a reincarnation of the young Audrey Hepburn.

Is that beauty really our teacher, Harry wondered, watching her as she moved on her way with little steps, no clumpy sandals on her feet now, but high heeled slippers instead. Bejeweled and Cinderella-small they were. This is going to be a great concert, he thought.

Once inside the vast church, Julie led them down the central nave, past three or four deep and dark chapels, thence, through a small door. It opened onto a sweeping marble staircase at the top of which was a grand marble passageway. It was barely lit by rows of low wattage bulbs confined in wrought iron cages.

George Freedman

At last they emerged into the concert room, a large rectangular chamber, windowless and fitted with hanging drapes of black velvet alternating with baronial flags and religious paintings. It was set up for an intimate audience of eighty or so. There were a half dozen rows of heavy, hand-carved chairs facing a raised platform that held a piano, a music stand and two chairs.

"This is not usually a concert room," Julie explained, "That happens only when Wendy asks for it. Otherwise, it's some sort of official church meeting room, which is used only when the cardinal is in town and drops in."

"Like a board of directors' room in a big company," Millicent suggested.

"I suppose," Julie said.

Some tens or twenties of other concertgoers were already there, indicating that the concert was not just for the scholars of the Senior Seminars program, but was extended to a small and select local audience as well.

It being too early for the performance, some wandered about, gazing at the walls and enjoying the medieval grandeur. Others simply stood around in conversational clusters. One of these was made up of young people, among whom Harry could see were Linda and Joey.

"We should say hi to Linda and her boyfriend," he told Naomi as he pushed her in their direction, which she allowed him to do without resisting. "And if we don't catch her attention right off, at least we can overhear what they're saying," he added. They found that while overhearing is one thing, understanding is another. Still, they did get a pleasant impression of good fellowship, expressed in at least four European languages.

Linda welcomed them with her characteristic, sweet smile. "We're mostly all cello students of Wendy. And you would be surprised at how many of us come from so far away. Because it's such an honor just to have her as our teacher. Some are from Holland and some from

Eldernapped

Spain and Germany and one from Greece. But I'm from the farthest away, because I'm all the way from the good old U.S. of A." Her remark must have been appreciated by Joey, since he acknowledged it with an affectionate squeeze around her waist.

"Wait till you hear Wendy play." Linda concluded. "You're really in for a treat. Maybe she isn't, like, Yo-Yo. But who is?"

There was also a good representation of middle-aged folk in the crowd. One of them, herding his family before him, headed for the Casa cluster. Addressing one particular person from the group, he bowed. "Signora Thorndike...Emily," he said, "let me introduce my family. This is Costanza, my wife, and Paolo, who is in his first year at the University of Padua and Evalina, who is entering next year, and little Rico."

"Oh, Lieutenant Luigi, it's so nice to see you here. I'm so pleased to meet your family," Emily responded with a wide smile. "I have my family here, too...some of them, anyway. I believe you met both of them a couple of nights ago when we had that big brou-ha-ha in Delo.

"Indeed I did, Emily. But in the confusion I didn't have a chance to get to know them. It's so nice to meet them here under so much more pleasant circumstances."

"This is my grandson, Alfred Dillard, my escort for the evening." Emily pushed him forward, prompting nods of recognition and a perfunctory handshake between the two men. "And my granddaughter Belinda is here too, someplace in this hall. Oh, there she is. Belinda, Belinda my dear..." Emily's penetrating voice resounded from the ancient walls. "Come over here and say hello to Lieutenant Luigi and his lovely family. And bring Joey."

"I figured you for a music lover, Lieutenant Luigi," Naomi declared, as she and Harry were in turn introduced to the Cataldo family. "But where is Sergeant Franco? Doesn't he like music?"

"He does, but not this kind," Cataldo replied. "In fact he's at a rock concert tonight in the soccer stadium.

I'm told that Padua is considered one Italy's leading centers for that sort of music. But that's what makes the world go around...we all have different tastes. Isn't that so, Evalina?"

Evalina made no reply to her father other than a deep sigh, giving the distinct impression that had she a choice she would rather be at the soccer stadium with Franco than at the Santo with Mom and Dad.

This prompted Belle to say, "I know who went with him. Our own Graziella. She told me she's a great rock music fan."

"But more of a Franco fan, if you ask me," Nate added.

"It's so nice to see you here and to meet with you and Costanza and your handsome children," Naomi went on, not to be diverted by matters such as the relative merits of rock and classical. "But if you'll forgive me for bringing up matters of business," her eyes now boring into Cataldo's. "It's also lovely to be seeing you under these happy circumstances, now that the abduction of Marguerite LoPresti is solved...or is it?"

"Yes, it is official...and with your help," he admitted, almost too graciously, Harry thought. "So the case is closed. But I do confess that I would feel better if I were to see Signora LoPresti...in the flesh...as you say. I've never actually laid eyes on her and sometimes I wonder if she even exists."

"The mythical Marguerite." Harry said.

"Oh, she's very real, Mr. Levine, not mythical at all," Alfred interjected. "I've met her, and was with her for a fair amount of time yesterday...and a very nice lady she is."

"Well," Julie, who was standing at the outer edge of this little group, spoke up. "If she's so real, where the devil is she? She told me on the phone she would be here tonight. What a climax that will be to Wendy's concert! But I don't see her."

Eldernapped

"If she told you she'd be here tonight, she'll be here tonight all right," Alfred assured her. "I've now had enough contact with Mrs. LoPresti to know that if she says she'll do something, it's as good as done." But the assurance in his voice lost force in his last half dozen words. Stunned by Julie's beauty is what he is, Harry could see.

At the same time, Harry could tell that he must be coming to the realization that this gorgeous creature is the very same person who had burst into Uncle Justin's villa with her entourage of a busload of over-sixties a couple of evenings ago, and who had contributed her share to the chaos of the occasion. She looked pretty darn good then, too, even in a casual getup of jeans and T-shirt.

Tearing his eyes away from Julie, Alfred regained sufficient composure to make yet another statement for the benefit of the assemblage. "Uncle Justin is coming, too. Mrs. LoPresti's bringing him...to this concert, I mean. "But not Mother. I know for sure that Mother's not coming, because just this morning at the Venice airport I put her on a plane back to Woonsocket...along with her two detectives, Sam and Vinny."

"A clean getaway," Harry whispered to Naomi.

Naomi nodded in the affirmative, as she whispered back, "Nice to know that that bitch is on another continent by now." Then, going on aloud, "I suspect it's just possible she wasn't invited, anyway."

"No, she wasn't, which come to think of it, I guess, is just as well." Alfred added with a reluctant smile.

At this moment, there was a stir at the entrance to the room. Everyone turned. There, framed dramatically at the doorway was a trio of late arrivals. A woman and two men. The woman was Marguerite LoPresti, no longer mythical.

She was in a dress that seemed to Harry to be fashioned of pure silver. Its gleam radiated the full length of the ancient chamber. How many other silver clad, grand dames had it hosted over the previous half-dozen centuries? More than a few, no doubt. Could they have rivaled the impression this lady now made, he wondered. Hardly. And while Julie reigned as the unrivaled beauty queen in this hall, this was only in terms of her own youthful and evanescent age group. Moving up the years scale to the category served by the Padua Senior Seminars program, Marguerite took over.

As Marguerite made her way into the room, she assumed no self-conscious or artificial airs. Instead, her joyous smile transmitted itself in all directions.

As always happens in such circumstances the two men who had come in with her were thrust into the background by virtue of the radiance she emitted, but further probing revealed that one of them was none other than one of Marguerite's sons, the one who was not a lawyer.

"What a handsome hunk," Irene commented.

Which elicited from Kate, next to her, "Must be into body building."

He flanked Marguerite on one side while the gentleman who took up a position on her other was tall, thin, almost cadaverous, in his middle sixties, wearing a dignified black suit.

As the new arrivals continued toward the front of the hall to join their friends, the lights flashed on and off. The concert was about to start. Any Marguerite reunion would have to be postponed for now. It was time for the concertgoers to find their seats.

The room went dark but for a circle of illumination on the concert platform. A rear door opened. Wendy strode forth, her cello in one hand, her bow in the other, a gracious smile on her face. Following her, a respectful six paces behind, came a diffident young fellow of about thirty, in a tuxedo, her accompanist. If Julie gave off a hazy golden incandescence in her chiffon and if Marguerite was a shaft of silver light, Wendy glowed darkly in a wide-skirted expanse of black velvet. Warm applause greeted her.

Eldernapped

As the two musicians took their seats, it became evident that Wendy's skirt was wide for a good reason, for how else was she to nestle her instrument between her legs and against her groin, her knees filling the indentations at its middle while its neck snuggled between her breasts. Soon, she would stroke it with her bow. Is any other musical instrument so sexy, Harry wondered.

What followed was a heavenly concert indeed. She started with Bach, Tartini and Vivaldi, the latter two probably having performed these very pieces themselves in this very room some centuries before. Then the program went forward in time to Brahms and Prokofiev. One after the other, the great melodies and harmonies spilled forth. Thus it was apparent to Harry that he and all the others in attendance were lucky and privileged to hear her. The applause resounded.

"Why isn't she better known?" was the question someone raised after the lights came up.

"Well, you know, we've already learned she's a home body, doesn't like to leave her nine year old son and travel for more than a few concerts a year," someone else explained.

But even this remarkable concert experience turned into little more than prelude, if not anti-climax, for in that hall there was a greater attraction than even Wendy Gross, marvelous cellist. It was Marguerite, with Justin Wharton by her side. There he is, Harry said to himself. The bastard! And everyone, including Wendy herself, gathered around them.

Emily and Marguerite embraced each other with tight hugs and affection. As their companions watched, reflecting on what both had been through, there was hardly a dry eye. This set off a riot of hugging all around, as each fellow Senior Seminarian flung his or her arms around Marguerite in turn. Happy words were exchanged.

"How great you look!"
"Did you ever lose hope?
"Introduce us to Justin."

"Where did you get that gorgeous dress?

"How was your gondola ride?

There was one more sobering question. Someone said, "Did you suffer much?"

Paul took the liberty of answering for her. "She couldn't have suffered too much, the way she looks," This was his considered medical opinion, Harry surmised.

"But I did, you know. I suffered terribly," Marguerite replied. "Although I must admit there was no physical abuse."

"You hear what she says, Paul? That proves you don't know anything about what she went through." Rose's quick reaction followed his insensitive statement. "How do you think any woman would feel when confined as a prisoner against her will by a bunch of men? Men automatically seem to assume that it's okay for them to dominate women any way they want to, no matter what."

Paul raised his hand as though to protest that nothing could have been farther from his thoughts. Harry's heart went out to him. How often he, too, had been accused of mean, anti-female thoughts when making a similar, innocent statement.

"Yes, it was hell," Marguerite said. "I hated every minute of it. They had me confined in a basement room, and it ended up that I did all the cooking for everybody because if I didn't, who would have? And I couldn't be in touch with my family and I was missing the Senior Seminars program and all of you nice people..." At this point, her voice started to tremble. There was little question that she was about to break into tears.

Harry felt like going over to comfort her, and in fact started to do so, but the tall, bony man who had come in with her beat him to it. He took her into his arms and patted her back in a comforting way as he made awkward sounds such as, "Come now...come now...don't upset yourself." He next focused his soothing words into a straightforward question. "But it wasn't all so terrible, was it, Marguerite?"

Eldernapped

"It was, it was terrible...but it had some compensations, Justin dear."

"Also, we finally did manage to convince Roberta that trying to exert her will over Mother was a bad idea," Justin went on, addressing those who surrounded them. "Because Roberta's really not such a bad sort, after you get to know her. She just wanted to do right by her mother, but she made a few mistakes in what to do and how to do it."

He was pressing his luck with this one, for a small frown appeared on Marguerite's brow as she said, "I'm not as sure about your sister as you are, Justin dear. If you want my opinion, it was my son Mark who finally made her come around...if she really has come around."

Dear. Harry's body tensed at the sound of that word. Marguerite had said dear to the man. Twice.

"Whatever happened, that's water over the dam," Marguerite said, her arm now extending around Justin's waist. "We're putting all that unpleasantness behind us." And when asked what she intended to do about a monetary settlement for the distress she had suffered, she responded, "What settlement? I don't need a settlement."

"But why did your son, the lawyer, meet with the Wharton family, if not to make a settlement?" one of the seniors asked.

"He flew to Padua just to make sure his mother was all right," Marguerite answered. "And now that he knows I'm all right...Mark is such a good boy...he's flown home. A young man like him has loads of responsibilities with his job in the law firm and his wife and two beautiful children."

"That's true," Alfred affirmed. "He was on the same plane as Mother. I saw him at the gate at the Venice airport this morning."

"But Ronnie is still here, although he leaves tomorrow," Marguerite said, standing on tiptoe to give her other son a peck on his cheek.

George Freedman

"I'm not sure about tomorrow, Mom," Ronnie said. "I might stay around a few more days, or even a week, because there actually is some business I think I can do in Padua," As he spoke, he seemed to fix his eyes on Julie.

"What business?" Marguerite said. Harry could tell this was a surprise to her,

Before Ronnie could answer, Emily interrupted to say, "He did one more thing, Marguerite dear, that Mark of yours. He also made sure that I am all right. "Mark LoPresti is now my lawyer, and if anyone wants to get my opinion on anything...anything legal, that is...you have to go to him, not me. He set up...what is it, Alfred...'power' or something...so no one can take charge of what happens to me from here on, except him."

"Power of attorney, Grandmother," Alfred said.

"That's right, power of attorney. I don't have to run around the world any more to get away from my hateful kids. And that means I can even give up going to Senior Seminars, one after the other as I've been doing. Although you can be sure I'll never give them up entirely."

How nice, Harry reflected.

"Please, Mother," Justin said in plaintive voice. "I know I did something wrong, but please, don't think of me as hateful. I love you, Mother, and never want anything but the best for you. Please forgive me."

Who can resist such heartfelt pleading on the part of a spurned child? Not Emily, Harry observed, as she bade her tall, gaunt boy to bend far down, which he did creakily, so she could implant a mother's kiss on his brow. "I forgive you, but it was still an awful thing you did."

"You can be sure I will never do anything like that again, Mother. In fact, I'm a changed man. And it's all due to Marguerite. I came to Padua, thinking I was only going to act as a sort of ambassador to you from the family. But I ended up realizing that this trip, just being here in beautiful Italy...and meeting this wonderful lady here..." pointing to Marguerite, "were, instead,

Eldernapped

ambassadors to me. Envoys, sort of, into my mind...and into my heart."

Harry heard a stifled sob. It was Millicent. "That's so beautiful," she whispered. Her face was red. Tears flowed down her cheeks. But a smile broke through the tears.

"I realize that up to now in my life I have retreated from every kind of good, personal relationship which might have made my existence happier," Justin went on. "That's strange, you know, because I always had you as an example of the better way to live. So I wonder, why didn't I follow your example, Mother? You never turned away from anything...or anyone...exciting and fulfilling. Sadly, I...I did. Until now. Now, I know that I should live all I can. It's a mistake not to."

There was a sudden silence. Who could do anything but applaud Justin's heartfelt apology. Maybe he's not such a bad guy after all, in spite of what he did to Marguerite.

It seemed to Harry as though everything had been said. Sure enough, as though someone gave a signal, everyone moved to the door and left, for the concert was now, in its several aspects, over.

They group of seniors journeyed through the marble hall with its long row of dim lights, down the long marble stairs and past the candlelit chapels, each with its few shadowy worshipers. At last, they emerged into the street to once again form into pairs as they headed back down the block and across Via Cesarotti toward the Casa del Santo. As before, Naomi and Harry brought up the rear.

◆ ◆ ◆ ◆

It turned out that the final couple in the procession, lagging even behind Naomi and Harry, was Julie, and not altogether to Harry's surprise, Alfred. It wasn't difficult for Harry to overhear their conversation.

"I want to thank you, Julie. May I call you Julie? You have treated Grandmother so well in this difficult time for her. She can't tell me enough about how considerate you and your assistant, Gr...Gra..."

"Graziella. Graziella Parziale."

"Yes...have been to her. Without your help and support, God knows what might have happened to her."

"I can't agree, Mr. Dillard."

"Please, call me Alfred. Or Al."

"Alfred. I can't agree," Julie repeated. "Your grandmother is one feisty lady. I think she can handle anything without much help."

"Well, maybe. But I still think I have a lot to thank you for. You run this enterprise so smoothly and you make all your customers happy and content. It's extraordinary, really...with all those people being at least double or triple your age. It's clear to me that you have a lot of managerial talent. Have you ever thought of taking on a management role in a business? You would be darned good at it."

"So you are in some sort of business?"

"Yes, I am. The family business. Wharton Valve, Incorporated in Woonsocket, Rhode Island."

"What a coincidence. I'm from Connecticut. New London."

"New London's not far from Woonsocket."

"Can't be more than an hour's drive. Do you have a good job with Wharton Valve, Incorporated?"

"Not bad. I'm the president."

"So, aren't you sort of young to have a job like that?"

"Oh, that's because it's a family business and I'm...excuse me for saying this, it sounds so sexist...I am the only male heir. They had no choice but to put me in charge."

"How modest you are."

Eldernapped

"Which brings me to something I wanted to talk to you about. Here I am, all alone in this Italian city, and I don't speak the language. Except for my grandmother and Belinda, both of whom I hardly know...I am rather on my own. I'm not so sure I can handle it well, because, I don't know if you've noticed, I am a rather introverted and shy person. Shy is a better word to describe me than modest. What I want to say is, I would appreciate it if you would give me a few pointers on how to go about things here. It occurred to me that a convenient way to do that would be if you would have dinner with me, say, tomorrow evening?"

In for the kill, thought Harry, didn't take him long.

"If you feel so strange here in Padua, and with Mrs. Thorndike not being threatened any more, why don't you just go home?"

"Oh I would. I really mustn't be away from the plant for too long, because..."

"Things would fall apart?"

"Right. But it happens I have business here for at least a week, because we...Wharton Valve, that is...have just opened a Vienna office, and from there we expect to consummate at least one important business arrangement very soon."

"Then why stay in Padua? Shouldn't you be in Vienna?"

"Padua is near enough to Vienna, driving distance, in fact. But I don't have to be there in person, since I can function well enough from here with my notebook computer. It has both e-mail and fax capabilities as well as a miniature printer attachment."

"Uh huh," Julie responded.

Harry couldn't tell from her tone whether she was impressed with modern notebook technology or not. Guys have new ways to impress young women these days. He remembered how fascinated the young Naomi was when he described the magnificent blast furnaces he had seen in Pittsburgh. "Roses are red/Violets are blue/Blast furnaces are gorgeous/And so are you," he had written her. But Pittsburgh doesn't even have blast furnaces any more.

"But as for dinner tomorrow night," Julie went on, "I'm afraid I have to say no. Tomorrow night's the last night of this session. It's the night of the going-away party...and of course I have to be there. In fact, I want very much to be there, because I feel closer to this group than I have to any other."

"I agree. It would be a terrible party if you weren't there. "How about the next day, Saturday?"

"Okay. I'd love to go to dinner with you on Saturday." Julie said. "What time? How about eight? We can meet in the Casa lobby."

"Couldn't be better. Or more convenient, either. I am staying in the Casa now, myself. Grandmother got me a room there. Besides, I didn't want to stay on at the villa in Delo anyway...felt I was in Uncle Justin's and Marguerite's way.

"I can imagine."

As they arrived back at the entrance to the Casa, Harry and Naomi waved good night to Alfred and Julie and joined Irene and Art Maglio who were sitting at one of the tables of the adjoining ice cream shop.

"Those two," Naomi said. "I think something may be brewing between them, even though they only met less than three hours ago."

"No, that's not so," Art pointed out. "The first time they met was during the fiasco in the big house in Delo."

"That doesn't count. They hardly talked to each other that night."

"I knew you were going to say that, my love," Harry remarked, "about something brewing, I mean.

"You could be right, Naomi," Irene chimed in. "I'm not a betting woman, but I would bet he just asked her out."

"I'll take that bet. How about a quarter?"

"Cheapskate. Make it fifty cents."

Eldernapped

"You're on. But wait a minute. How can we bet? You're on the same side I'm on."

Harry and Art said nothing, but continued to spoon their Italian ice cream. Harry was happy in the knowledge that it would be his last act of the evening before he and Naomi made their ways up to the third floor to sleep.

◆ ◆ ◆ ◆

The evening did not quite end there for Julie after Alfred bade her a pleasant good night. Poor fellow, she reflected, he had had a busy day, what with delivering people to the airport and engaging, no doubt, in long business calls and e-mailings and faxes, back and forth, to Woonsocket and Vienna. For her part, Julie knew she still had administrative, or maybe a better term to describe them might be management, duties to perform. She greeted the desk clerk with a smiling but brisk *buona sera*. She was checking on her messages when she became aware of the stalwart presence of Ronnie LoPresti by her side.

"Ms. Foster," he said, "Or, do you mind if I call you Julie?"

"I don't mind. Julie is my name."

"Well, I've wanted to tell you how much I appreciate what you did done for Mom these last few weeks, especially, a few nights ago. You commandeered that bus and herded all of us into it so that we could go to rescue her from those terrible people. That took two things, Julie, imagination and spunk. And it's obvious you've got both of those."

"But we didn't rescue her. By then, she'd already rescued herself. Anyway, the bus was just sitting here, back of the Casa, and Enrico...he's the bus driver...he happened to be here, too. And everyone wanted to go."

"I also want to thank you for suggesting that Mark and I take over Mom's room here at the hotel. That's really been convenient for us during these last few days. It was very thoughtful of you."

"Why not? The room was already paid for. And it has two beds."

"I'm going to need it for another few days, it turns out. Is that okay?"

"No problem for tonight and tomorrow night, but after that you'll have to vacate it, because this session ends that day and a new group is coming in."

"Well, can you tell me where I can get another room after that because I expect to spend five or six more days, maybe even a week, here in Padua."

"No problem, Mr. LoPresti. You can still stay right here in the hotel. I know it has empty rooms because an acquaintance of mine just informed me that he was able to book a room today without any problem. That's because the *festa* that celebrated St. Anthony's seven hundred and ninety-ninth birthday has just ended. The pilgrims have all gone home."

"Please, call me Ron, or Ronnie."

"Ronnie. So what keeps you here, Ronnie?" Julie continued to shuffle through the mail and make a few bookkeeping entries in a ledger. "Now that your mother's kidnapping is solved?"

"Well, she doesn't need me to take care of her, since someone else seems to be doing that very well now."

"I guess."

"But I do have business. I'm looking into record companies and distributors here. Did you know that Padua is a leading center for tapes and CD's for all of Italy?"

"Really? So you work for a record company?

"Yes, I run a small chain of record stores. Have you ever heard of Cantaloupes?

"No. That's the name of a record store? Seems a strange name."

"Sorry you think so. But I'm the one who thought up the name...and everyone seems to like it. Of course,

Eldernapped

we don't stock Tartini and Vivaldi, and I don't think we'll ever post a picture over any of the record racks of Wendy Gross playing her cello. The fact is, the Cantaloupes stores are mostly for the..."

"Hip crowd?"

"You got it. And as you must already know, Padua is quite a hip town. I might even want to start a Cantaloupes right here some day. Well, not right here. I was thinking of someplace near the university.

"You say it's a small chain?"

Yes, only ninety-four stores, mostly in Ohio, but a few over the lines in Kentucky and Indiana, too."

"And you say you're running them?" For some reason Julie's interest was now piqued.

"Well, yes, I'm running them. I'm the president."

"Good for you. I suppose it's some kind of a family business that you stepped into?"

"Are you kidding? Our family never had any business. No, I started there eight years ago as a sales guy in the rock department. Worked my way up through punk and rap. And talking about working my way up..."

Julie could sense that Ronnie was now getting impatient. "How about coming to dinner with me tomorrow night?

"Can't. That's the last night of this Senior Seminars class and I have to be at the going-away party."

"Oh yes, I can see that. Won't be much of a party without you there. How about the next night, Saturday?"

"Sorry I'm busy Saturday night, too."

"Then, what about Sunday for lunch?"

"Well, I can make that," Julie replied. "I'd love to have lunch with you on Sunday. But we'll have to watch the clock. That afternoon Graziella and Enrico and I have to take the bus to the airport to gather in the next class of Senior Seminars students.

"Just as the world keeps making new little kids at one end," she observed, her words slow-paced, her manner thoughtful, "it also keeps producing these older folks at the other end...and sending a new batch of two or three dozen or so of them to Padua every two weeks.

"But we should be able to work in lunch before they get here, Ronnie. How about noon? We'll meet in the hotel lobby?" she concluded, her face illuminated with an expression of pleasure that she made no effort to restrain, for this had been an evening well spent.

Eldernapped

Day Thirteen

"I bet you will"

While most of Harry's classmates were mildly stimulated by walking through the ancient corridors of the University of Padua, three of the Senior Seminarians were thrilled and overwhelmed by it. These were the two physicians, Doctors Nate and Paul, and Harry himself.

What excited the former two was the famous *Teatro Anatomico*, the Anatomy Theater, a high wooden staircase of many spirals around which medical students since the sixteenth century used to position themselves to watch the latest cutting and stitching techniques as they were practiced in the round landing below, their heads hanging over the long curving banister. "Everyone agrees," their guide, a fourth year medical student, pointed out, "this is where modern surgery began."

"There's no better way to learn medicine than just looking at the real thing," Nate said, as he peered down onto the empty operating table.

To which Paul added, "That's still the way we do it, although nowadays a lot of schools use closed circuit TV."

"And this is one of the original operating tables," the guide continued. "It used to hold the patients or the cadavers, whichever they were working on that day."

"Wow," Nate said.

"As far as I'm concerned, this makes the whole trip worth while," Paul added, his voice filled with awe.

Unmoved by all this, Emily inquired whether the guide knew Guiseppe Fabiano and Bruno Parelli, who were also fourth year medical students.

"Oh yes," he replied, "Fabiano, Neurosurgery. Parelli, proctology."

"Well, Guiseppe...but we call him Joey...is going to marry my granddaughter, Belinda."

"Guiseppi Fabiano...very fine fellow. You are lucky to have such a grandson, and he is lucky that you will be his grandmother." He responded with the gallantry everyone had come to expect from Italian men.

"Grandson-in-law. And, yes. I think so, too."

As for Harry, the historic spiral staircase of the Anatomy Theatre, though interesting, was no match, thrill-wise, for the U's other major attraction, Galileo's Chair. Harry had not known till now that the great Galileo, the man who had almost single-handedly invented the very idea of technological innovation and had pursued it single-mindedly against all odds, had been a professor at this university for eighteen years.

"It occurred to his students," the guide said, "that their beloved professor needed a podium of some sort to lecture from. So one night, some dozens of them, all unskilled in the craft of woodworking, gathered a lot of wooden planks and hammered them together into a creation of the most awkward and amateurish design conceivable. But at the same time it was of a design most endearing, a highly personal monument to their eminent mentor.

"...And Galileo used it for every lecture he gave was for the next decade or so that he remained in Padua, each time mounting those shaky nine steps and putting his lecture notes on that splintery lectern you see over there."

As Harry gazed at it, he felt his body begin to tremble. His face must have gone pale, since Naomi grabbed his arm. She must have known at once what he was up to. "No, Harry, don't!" she shot at him. "Don't you see that red rope around it that keeps people from

Eldernapped

touching it and the sign that says, *entrata prohibito*. That means crazy Americans get put in jail and then get deported if they *entrare?*"

"Don't care if I do get put in jail," Harry shot back. Like a bolt of lightning, he was over the rope, up the nine steps and standing on the same wooden planks that his hero, Galileo, had stood on so long ago. The student guide made a futile effort to stop him, but Harry was too fast for him.

Now Harry made a movement with his hands as though he were putting his lecture notes on the lectern. Then he opened his mouth, about to say, "Today's lecture will deal with the physical basis of..." At that instant, he was in heaven.

◆◆◆◆

It was the first time in the entire two weeks that the breakfast room was being used for an event other than breakfast. It was eight P.M., well past the Senior Seminar's final dinner. The room looked the same as always, except that it was festooned with a pair of twisted red and white paper ribbons that ran from its farthest corners, intersecting each other in midair.

Harriet Aptheker, hardly heard from during the preceding two weeks, came to the fore at last and had strung up the ribbons which she bought with her own money. Concerning which, Harry commented to Naomi, "Better late than never."

As he scanned the room, Harry noted that every classmate was present, except for Marguerite. But she had not been with them for most of the program anyway, so her absence made no perceptible impact. Julie and Graziella were on hand, too, as was Enrico.

Somehow, a number of very American-looking strawberry shortcakes with generous whipped cream topping had been obtained. Rumor had it the shortcakes had been concocted from local ingredients by Julie's and

Graziella's very own hands. They served them along with coffee, decaf only at this late hour.

With the cake and coffee now finished Nate rose from his chair and made his way to the front of the room. "As the senior member of the seniors in this room," he proclaimed, "I have decided to designate myself as your spokesman. Any objection?" There being none, he went on. "So everybody settle down and I'll make the ceremony short and sweet.

"Belle and I have been to sixteen Senior Seminars in the States and around the world, making this the seventeenth," he said. "And I guess that makes us the record holders here."

"Don't be so sure about that, Nate, my boy," Emily spoke up. "If I count up all the ones I've been to...if I can remember them all...I bet I've been to over twenty. Furthermore, I can probably challenge you on who in this room is the most senior, but for now, I'll let it go."

"There's always a smart aleck in every crowd," Nate said. "But while she's counting, I'll proceed. "I am sure it will surprise no one here if I say that this one has been the most unusual and exciting Senior Seminars that any of us has ever been to. There was much vigorous head nodding, which Nate took as expressions of assent.

"But, thank God, it has turned out all right. The very fact that Marguerite LoPresti is not here with us this evening confirms that. Why should she waste time with us when she now has her Justin?"

Nate continued, "To bear this out, I have a note from her which she sent to Julie by way of Justin's nephew Alfred. It says..." Nate pulled a page of paper from his shirt pocket and smoothed its folds and read:

Sorry I can't be with you all for the farewell party, but Justin and I have booked ourselves for the Hotel Sacher in Vienna where he has to be for business.

Eldernapped

By the time you get this note, we will probably be there. And thank goodness we are going in a regular sized car instead of that little monster sports car we had to use up to now.

I just want to thank all of you for how you stood by me in my distress of the last week and a half. And then, when you all showed up en masse to rescue me at the big house in Delo, even though Justin and I happened to be out at the time, sorry about that. That was just grand of you and I love every one of you for it.

Of course, we know that your being there was Julie's doing and I love her especially.

"What I'm really sad about is that I can't be with you in person tonight to say goodbye to you wonderful people one by one, but who knows, maybe we'll meet again. I have your addresses, so don't be surprised if some day you get a note from me.

"And it's signed," Nate said, as he refolded the page and reinserted it in his pocket, *With heartfelt affection and appreciation, Marguerite.* Also, there is a P.S. that says, *Justin sends his appreciation, too.*

"Isn't that nice," Dorothy observed. "What a lovely person she is."

"It's more than nice," Naomi added. "Don't you see what she's hinting at...you guys...with that statement about getting a note from her? She's going to invite us to the wedding."

"All of us?" someone said.

"Why not? Didn't all of us, in a manner of speaking, bring her and Justin together?" Naomi continued. "Anyway, with his money, they can afford a big wedding."

"That's ridiculous," Emily spoke up, her sharp, penetrating voice injecting a modicum of reality into the discourse. "Justin will never marry anyone without getting my approval first...and he's never even mentioned it to me. Not to say I won't approve...after I look into it."

"I hope it's in the summer," Dorothy said. "Living in Oklahoma, I don't have many dressy winter clothes."

"No sweat, for us," Irene interjected, a smug look on her face. "Living in Boston, we have all the winter clothes we need."

To which husband Art added, the look on his face no less smug, "And it'll be convenient for us. Woonsocket's not much of a drive from Boston."

"But what if it's in Cincinnati?" Millicent said. "Don't weddings usually take place wherever the bride lives? Then, I can drive there easily from Muncie."

"I think that happens only if the bride's parents make the wedding," Art said, but in this case..."

"Twenty-six!" Emily's voice, once more cut like a knife through those of her fellow students. "Twenty-six at least." She caused a moment of stunned silence. "And I know I must have forgotten one or two, so the real number must be around twenty-eight."

"You mean you've been to twenty-eight Senior Seminars, Emily? Wow! Good for you," Nate said. "You certainly beat Belle and me. I now pronounce you the Champion Senior Seminarian in this room. A round of applause, please, for the little lady."

Applause.

"Make it twenty-nine," Emily wasn't through yet. "Tomorrow morning I'm off at six for the airport, before the rest of you are up, to get a connecting flight for Madrid. I'm signed up for a one-week Senior Seminar that sounds wonderful...in the mountains around Segovia. It starts the day after tomorrow. "We'll be bird watching. Everyone has to rent a four-wheel drive, all-terrain vehicle, because we'll be miles from any roads.

There was another stunned silence.

Sarah said, "But where will you sleep and how will you eat?"

"Oh, I've got my back pack with my one-man tent in it. The Senior Seminars people will provide the food, and we'll eat around a campfire. I'm certainly looking forward to it, but as Nate just said, it will never match this one for excitement. What I need right now is a little peace

Eldernapped

and quiet. How can you get more peace and quiet than bird watching?

"You know," she went on, "this will probably be the last time I schedule Senior Seminars one week after another, which is a bit of a strain, don't you think? I don't have to do that anymore, now that Roberta has been stopped from trying to kidnap me. In fact, there's no reason I shouldn't even go back to being Lucille Adams, again."

"How nice for you," Nate said with a deep breath. "Marguerite's note isn't the only item Julie got from Alfred. She also handed me this box of business cards that I am supposed to hand out to everyone here. I bet none of you will ever guess who sent them. Anyone?"

He had no takers. Without further ado, he handed out the cards. MEADOWLANDS DETECTIVE AGENCY was printed on each card. There was a Secaucus, New Jersey address and numbers for phone, fax and e-mail in finer print, and, in a font that leaned sharply to the right for each letter, were the names and titles of Samuel Peterson, President and Vincent Anzaldi, Vice President. There was also a legend or motto in italic script, *Private Investigators for Private Problems.*

"Was there any message, Julie, that came with these cards? Yes? No?"

She shook her head in the negative.

Then, perusing his card with care, Nate said, "Well, the next time my mother runs off to God knows where with God knows who, I'll know just whom to call on to help me find her and bring her home alive. I can't think of any other detectives in the world who could do it better. I'm so glad they left us their cards. Don't you all agree?"

A wave of laughter rippled across the group. Except for Art, "I'm not so sure about those two," he said. "From what I've seen, I doubt they are really the best ones to get for a job like that, which..."He was stopped in mid-sentence by Irene. "That's a joke, Artie dear, Nate was just making a joke."

"Oh."

"Now to go on," Nate said, "let me also comment on another unusual aspect of this program. We were actually able to meet some of the families of some of our fellow students. For example, there are the two fine young men, Mark and Ron LoPresti, who flew the ocean on virtually no notice to come over here to do what they could to help their mother. It's wonderful to have sons like that, and I know Marguerite must be very proud."

"By the way, isn't one of them still around?" Tom said. "I think I saw him in the lobby this evening."

"Yes, he's around," Julie spoke up. "Ronnie will probably stay four or five days. Mark is the one who went home."

"Wonder what's keeping him in Padua," Naomi asked, which caused Harry to give her an elbow jab in her ribs. Why haven't I thought of giving her a few pokes of my own until now, he wondered.

"Can't say," Julie said.

"And then we have Emily's family." Nate continued. "What a pleasure it has been to meet so many of them. First, there was Emily's lovely daughter, Roberta..."

"Boo!" erupted from most of those in the room.

"And her son, Justin..."

Dorothy shouted, "Hooray!" causing everyone to look at her.

"Oh, Dorothy, you're such a romantic person," Sarah observed.

"And why shouldn't she be?" Millicent said, with a significant look at Pete, who beamed a serene smile back.

None of this broke Nate's pace, for he had now came to Alfred, whom he described as an exemplary representative of his generation, barely into his thirties and already the president of his own company. "You must be very proud of your grandson, Emily."

"Of course, he's president," she replied. "The family put him in that job. But in spite of that, as far as I

Eldernapped

can tell from the stock statements I get every quarter, he's doing all right. In fact, in the few conversations I had with him, I rather like him...reminds me a little of Robert."

Noting a look of puzzlement on the faces of some of her classmates, she explained further, "His grandfather, the founder of the firm, my husband *numero uno*. And yes, Nate, I am proud of him."

"He's still around, too," Tom said. "He came through the lobby this morning."

"You'd think he'd have gone home with his mother," a voice from the crowd said, "Why is he still hanging around? Do you know, Julie?"

"I haven't a clue."

"Probably business," Tom speculated. "When I saw him he was carrying one of those laptop computers and he was rushing off as though he had a meeting to go to.

If that was a frown on Julie's face, it came and went so fast as to be imperceptible to all but Harry, who wondered about it. Could Alfred have been on his way to that computer store around the corner from the Casa to seek expert help on some pesky computer program?

"Let us not forget your granddaughter, Emily, Belinda, or Linda, as she seems to be called sometimes. Speaking as one who has granddaughters of his own and therefore as an authority on the subject, I want you to know, as if you didn't know already, that she is a real sweetie...in addition to being a raving beauty."

"Don't forget, she plays the cello, too," Emily made clear. "She's very talented, but not as good as Wendy of course...not yet anyway."

"But more than all those qualities," Nate continued, "she is one of the luckiest of women...because she is going to marry a doctor. Isn't that right, Belle?"

"More or less," Belle responded. "But as I always remind you, lover, I married you in spite of your being in medical school. It was my mother who wanted a doctor in the family, and I certainly wasn't going to do what she wanted me to do. Yet I did it. So you're the lucky one."

"We also have another pair of lovely people who seem to have found each other in this charming city," Nate went on. "Dorothy and Pete."

Cheers resounded in the room.

Dorothy's face turned red, even as Pete patted her hand, but it went redder yet as Nate remarked, "Should the two of you ever need the services of a good pediatrician a few years from now, I'd be willing to come out of retirement, just for you."

Laughter abounded.

"Tell me, Julie," he went on. "Does Senior Seminars ever charge a finder's fee?

There was more laughter.

"No," Julie replied. "That's just another great Senior Seminars service. It's on the house."

"Graziella seems to have found a friend, too," Nate went on. "Support your local police, I always say."

Graziella didn't respond, but Harry thought her wide smile was sufficient reaction.

"Not only did Sergeant Franco get support from us, and from Graziella in particular," Nate continued, "so did Lieutenant Luigi. I have a feeling we've made a lasting impression on him. Which leads me next to mention our classmate, Naomi.

"Naomi, my dear, would you be surprised to know that the whole group has banded together to give you an award. And this is unusual, because in all my sixteen previous Senior Seminars I can't remember anyone getting an award before. Will you please come up here."

"With her eyes wide in surprise, Naomi turned to Harry. "What in the world..." she said.

But Harry, who knew this was coming, gave her a kiss full on her mouth. "I'm sure you deserve it," he said. "Whatever it is."

Eldernapped

She stood and, moving with as much grace as any human could with a cane and made her way up to Nate's side.

There were calls of, "Good for you, Naomi," and "Bravo," and the like, as well as a piercing whistle from one of the airline pilots that vibrated the walls, showing that advanced age had not caused him to lose the knack.

Nate handed her a package, festively wrapped with a large pink bow, and shook her hand. Then, he leaned over and bestowed a fatherly kiss on her cheek.

There were cries of, "Open it, open it," which, after having leaned her cane against one of the tables, Naomi proceeded to do. What she pulled from it were three items, a tweed cap with matching visors back and front, a gargantuan pipe in the shape of a hook, and a magnifying glass with a long metal handle.

"If you haven't already deduced, Naomi...and you must have, because you are certainly the best deducer in this room...this is your Sherlock Holmes detective kit. It wasn't that easy to put together here in Padua, I assure you. And here's a certificate that comes with it. It says, 'To Naomi Levine, Best Detective in Senior Seminar...' And we all signed it."

Naomi was speechless. Then she managed to say, "I've never won an award before..."

"Yes, you did, Naomi," Harry yelled through cupped hands, "Don't forget your spelling medal from the seventh grade."

"So I want to tell you how thrilled I am to get this one and how honored I am that you gave it to me."

Good old Naomi, thought Harry. Nothing rattles her. Not for long, anyway.

"Although I really have no use for the magnifier or the pipe, I know I'll wear that hat a lot. I've got a plaid jacket and skirt it'll go with beautifully and make an outfit that all my friends will envy."

"You're wrong, Naomi," Nate said. "A life of brilliant crime-fighting stretches before you and I'm sure

George Freedman

you will make good use of all this stuff when you take on your next case. As for the one you have just finished, we all agree, without the guidance you gave to Lieutenant Cataldo, the great LoPresti kidnapping case would never have been solved so elegantly. So this expresses our appreciation and admiration of your skills."

"More of an eldernapping than a kidnapping," Harry said from his seat. "Is there such a word...eldernapping?" Then he turned to Naomi and said, "If you are Sherlock Holmes, dear, does that make me, Dr. Watson?"

"Of course, honey. I've always thought of you as my Dr. Watson."

"We did offer Lieutenant Cataldo the opportunity to sign this card for Naomi," Nate said. "But he declined the honor. However, he did say to tell you, Naomi, that he certainly was grateful that he had a chance to work with you, because he learned a lot from you about the detective business. Now that your work in Padua is over, he is sure America will be just as grateful to get you back, so that you can solve more mysteries over there. And he wishes you Godspeed. In fact he says the sooner you go home to your own country, the better. "

"Of course he wants her out of here," Belle said. "He can't stand the competition."

"Right on," Millicent said.

"One more thing," Nate continued. Lieutenant Cataldo wanted me to tell you that he'll never forget you. The next time he's on a particularly difficult case, he knows the image of your face will rise up before him to inspire him to greater efforts."

"Hmm..." Naomi said, as she gathered up her award and its box and its pink ribbon and started back to her seat.

"Don't go yet, Naomi, we have one more thing for you," Nate said. It's a video cassette. "We got it from the TV station that did your interview with their anchorwoman after our mass invasion in Delo. In fact, she autographed

Eldernapped

it for you. See," squinting to make out the words, Nate read, *'a mi cara Naomi Levina,'* and it's signed, *'Filomena Tarantino.'* Isn't that nice?

"We've all seen it already. Everyone who didn't catch the news show that evening or the morning news the next day had a chance to see the video on Julie's VCR. Somehow Naomi missed it, but now that she has this cassette, she can relive the experience any time she wants."

"In regard to Naomi's pursuing that new crime-fighting career, " Harry spoke up, feeling that all this discussion about Naomi was lacking in one regard, namely some input from himself, "...you people probably don't know this yet..." He stood now, the better to address the crowd, "...but this detective kit is going to come in more handy than you think. Would you believe my bride here has just got an offer from a real detective agency? It's from..." There was silence as he dug out the business card he had just been handed and read it, 'Meadowlands Detective Agency,' MDA for short.

"Mr. Samuel Peterson...he said I should call him Sam...called this morning from a coin phone at the airport, as he waited for his plane. Since Naomi wasn't around at the time, I took the message. Anyway, Sam said that having observed how brilliantly my wife tracked down Marguerite, his firm would like to offer her not just a job...they want her to be a partner. They want her to run the new Boston office they plan to set up. But Naomi doesn't know yet whether she'll accept their offer."

"Take it, take it..." the group began to chant.

"I'll think it over," was Naomi's modest reply. "Except that you all know there never was a phone call from Sam Peterson. Harry...my inventor...just invented it. And thanks for this wonderful award. I'll cherish it forever." With that, she returned to her seat.

"We can always depend on Harry for the light touch, can't we," Nate mused. "I have a feeling he deserves some sort of award, too...for Leading Senior

George Freedman

Seminars Wit. But we figured one award per family is enough."

"That's the way it's always been," Harry said with a sigh, as he resumed his seat. "Whenever the Levine family does anything good, Naomi always gets all the credit."

"On a more serious note," Nate went on, speeding up his words, since some in his audience were nodding and one or two had already fallen asleep, "I want to mention Wendy, who couldn't be here tonight. Wasn't that a brilliant concert she gave? The woman is a great artist.

"By the way, we all know she's divorced, and now I think I can guess why. Her husband must have named Vivaldi as correspondent for alienation of affections.

"And, finally, in behalf of all of us, I want to invite Julie to come up here."

As she stood beside him, he said, "Julie, we all love you. It's been a delight to have you as our administrator and teacher because you did everything so well and with so much warmth and flair. It's been a real pleasure to be associated with you. In fact, you are a credit to your age group and your sex...and I don't see why some smart young fellow hasn't snapped you up by now."

"Nate, stop that," Belle called out. "Keep to the subject."

"Also Graziella and Enrico," Nate nodded at each in turn. "You've got a great crew, as well. So we all pitched in and we want you to have these little expressions of our appreciation." He handed Julie three small envelopes."

"Oh, Dr. Kniznick, you know we're not supposed to accept gifts." But by this time he had left her side and taken his chair beside Belle. Which left a glowing Julie all by herself, facing the crowd. "Thank you, thank you. I love you, too," she declared. "And I know that, like you, I will remember this Senior Seminar longer than all the others, because of what we've gone through together. And

Eldernapped

we were successful, weren't we? We did get Marguerite back...one way or another.

"Now, let's get back to business, campers," her face suddenly changed back to its strict administrator expression. "Tomorrow morning you are all leaving. Back you go on the same bus you came on to the Venice airport. Except for Emily who will have left already."

Of course she would have left before us, Harry reflected on hearing this. Emily's one of those special little old ladies. They're always doing things ahead of us ordinary people. I sure had her spotted correctly when I noticed her flitting among the posts outside the airport.

"Be there at eight fifteen promptly." Julie was still giving out useful instructions. "Because, as you know, Enrico waits for no man or woman. Any questions?"

There were none. She always makes everything so clear, Harry thought. Quite a girl.

Then, suddenly, Julie's face softened. "Gosh," she said with a sigh. "In a day or two you'll be scattered all over the world. We'll probably never see each other again, but it was sure nice knowing you. Still," she went on, recovering now and back to her normal tone, "the day after you're gone, this coming Sunday in fact, Graziella and Enrico and I go back to the same airport to pick up another thirty or so of you...and the whole process repeats...although I don't ever expect to have another kidnapping...or eldernapping ...again.

"I know those new students will be wonderful, just as you have been. And you know what? Meeting folks like you with all your energy and interest in the world makes me not afraid of getting older. In fact, I look forward to it..."

"Maybe you do," an unidentified voice spoke up. "But we don't." That caused a moment of reflective silence.

Nate must have felt he had to break the somber mood that invaded the room. "That's why we move so fast," he said. "People always think old people slow down...but that's wrong. Being on a shorter time scale than the young, we sometimes pack a lot more into the time we have. For example, for me this two-week Senior Seminar has been equivalent to a whole college course."

"See, that's what's so great about you guys, always upbeat," Julie declared. "I will stick by my original statement...because of you, I look forward to getting older...not right away, but some day."

"Me, too," Graziella chimed in. "And don't worry. Dr. Kniznick...you don't have to be concerned about Julie not being as you say, snapped up." For this, Julie gave her a sharp, sisterly slap on the arm, which led Harry to wonder, what Graziella knew that the others did not?

Harry's reflections were interrupted by that familiar poke to his ribs followed, as always, by an interesting Naomi observation. "Before we get on that bus tomorrow, I'll find out what Graziella is referring to," she said.

To which Harry responded, "I bet you will."

George Freedman's goal in life is to create things. It doesn't matter to him whether these are inventions (he's a professional inventor with several dozen patented products which have reached the public in a wide range of markets) or books and articles. He gets the same kick from doing either. In addition to three books in technical fields including one on "The Pursuit of Innovation", he has published children's' stories and is now engaged in producing the Harry and Naomi mystery series of which "Eldernapped" is the first. Other career milestones include heading new product development for a Fortune 500 company, presidency of a high tech company, college teaching, chairman of an international scientific society and serving as editor of two technical/scientific journals. He and his wife live in suburban Boston where he has been a member of town government. In addition to writing and inventing, he enjoys his family, reads, takes courses, listens to music, gardens, and travels.

9 780970 430434